Vengeance in the Vines

Vengeance in the Vines

Rylie Sunderland Mysteries Book 2

Rachele Baker

Fleur de Soleil Books

ISBN (paperback) 978-1-962167-04-8

ISBN (e-book) 978-1-962167-05-5

Cover illustration by Alan Ayers
Cover design by Dawn Adams

Vengeance in the Vines

Chapter 1

The air was heavy with the smell of wine grapes as Rylie drove through the Napa Valley on her way to St. Helena. Rows of grapevines spread out on either side of the highway for miles. Excitement tingled through her body. Bella, her five-year-old golden retriever, panted happily as she looked out the windows of the SUV from her seat in the back.

Rylie followed the GPS directions a few miles out of town to the house where she would be staying with Bella for the next month. The little one-bedroom house was perched on a hillside across the road from a vineyard. She let Bella out of the SUV, and they went inside to check out their new home. The house was decorated in a contemporary style that felt warm and homey with hardwood floors, a sliding barn door to the bedroom, and large windows framing gorgeous views in every room. After getting unpacked and going to the store for groceries, she called her best friend Sophie.

"Hi, Sophie. Bella and I are here, and we're all settled in. Do you want to meet up somewhere?"

"Sure. How about we meet for lunch in St. Helena at the Goose and Gander? We can sit outside in their garden under the trees," Sophie said.

"That sounds great. I'll meet you there."

Rylie put the Goose and Gander restaurant address into her SUV's GPS and followed the directions to get there.

"Rylie! It's so wonderful to see you!" Sophie threw her arms around Rylie in a warm hug. "I can't believe how long it's been since I've seen you! I haven't seen you since I visited you up at Lake Tahoe this past summer."

"I know. I'm so glad that I got a locum veterinarian job here in St. Helena so we can hang out. I have at least a month of work here while the veterinary hospital owner recuperates from surgery. Where's Lucien?"

"He went to the Napa farmers' market to get some things for the restaurant. He likes the Saturday Napa farmers' market because it has a lot more vendors than the one that we have in St. Helena on Fridays. I texted him to let him know we're having lunch at the Goose and Gander in case he gets back in time to join us," Sophie said.

The hostess seated them outside in the garden under some trees.

"This is really nice," Rylie said. "I love eating outside."

She looked up as she saw someone approaching their table.

"Lucien!" Rylie stood up to hug Lucien. "I'm so glad you were able to join us."

Lucien grinned. "I'm always up for a good meal. The food here is great."

He sat down at their table. The hostess appeared almost instantly with another menu.

"Did you find lots of great produce for the restaurant at the Napa farmers' market?" Rylie asked.

"Oh, yes. I love to go to the farmers' markets and then create new recipes based on whatever is in season," Lucien replied. "Customers love our seasonal specials."

"You know, I've never actually eaten at Vinterre," Rylie said. "I'll have to make it a point to eat there while I'm here."

"The St. Helena Chamber of Commerce annual Celebrate St. Helena awards dinner is this Monday night at Vinterre. The restaurant is closed to the public on that night. I have a very nice menu planned. Why don't you come? You can be Sophie's Plus One since I'll be in the kitchen all night."

"That's a great idea. Do you want to come, Rylie?" Sophie asked.

"Sure. I'd love to."

The three of them chatted over lunch. Then Lucien left to do some errands.

Sophie's face fell as she watched Lucien walk away. Something wasn't right.

"What's wrong, Sophie? You've told me that you think something is going on with Lucien, but you've never given me any details."

"Oh, Rylie. He's been working late for months now. Sometimes he doesn't come home until I'm already in bed asleep. I feel like I hardly see him anymore. When he is around, he's distant and seems distracted. Every time I try to talk to him about it, he tells me everything's fine and I should stop worrying."

"Oh, Sophie! I'm so sorry! Do you think he's having an affair?"

"I've wondered about that. But this is a small town. Somehow I think that if he were having an affair, I would know about it."

"Do you think he might be having problems at the restaurant?"

"I don't know. When we had the big wildfire just north of here a couple of months ago, the electric company shut off the power to everyone in this area for four days as a precautionary measure. The restaurants and shops around here lost a lot of business during that time. But it seems like Vinterre has been doing fine since then. I drive by it from time to time, and there are always lots of cars there," Sophie said.

"Wow, Sophie. I don't know what to say. I wish there was something I could do to help you. I just don't know what I can do."

"It helps just to have someone to talk about it," Sophie said. "I'm glad you're staying in St. Helena for a while. We can do things together on your days off when I'm not working."

"How's your interior design business doing?"

"I'm always busy. If you're looking for something to do on one of your days off, I can show you one of the houses that I'm working on." Sophie smiled, but her smile didn't reach her eyes. "So what days are you going to be working?"

"I'll be working Monday through Wednesday every week," Rylie replied. "I start work on Monday. So I have the rest of today and tomorrow to explore the area and have some fun."

"I wish I could join you tomorrow, but I'm on a deadline to complete a project design for my contractor by Monday. If I don't get it to him by Monday, he's going to take on another project. And if that happens, he won't be able to get to my project for six to eight weeks."

"I understand. I'm fine with exploring the area by myself. I've been researching places to see in the Napa Valley online for the past couple weeks. But if you have anything special that you really think I should see, I'd love to hear your suggestions."

"I think you should have Sunday brunch at Auberge du Soleil. It's a luxury hotel and restaurant in Rutherford. It's only about ten minutes from here. You can have brunch outside on their deck. They have spectacular views of the Napa Valley from their deck. And their food is amazing. If you want to go, you should call for a reservation this afternoon. You can't get in without a reservation."

"That sounds really nice. I'll give them a call when I get home. I've got to get going now. I don't like leaving Bella alone in a strange place for too long, especially since we just got here. See you later, Sophie."

Rylie went home to her excited golden retriever.

"Hi, Bella! Were you a good girl while I was gone?"

Rylie ruffled Bella's golden fur and scratched gently around her ears. She called Auberge du Soleil and made a reservation for Sunday brunch the next day.

She was worried about Sophie. What was going on with Lucien? Sophie was her best friend, but she had never been especially close to Lucien. He had been one year ahead of them in college, so the only time she ever saw him was when he was with Sophie. Still, she wondered if she should try to talk to him and discreetly try to find out what was going on.

When she woke up the next morning, sunlight was streaming through the French doors leading out to the deck off her bedroom. She got some coffee brewing and then took Bella outside to do her business. After Bella had thoroughly sniffed and explored everything in the yard, they went back inside, and Rylie got Bella her breakfast. Then she got her e-reader and went out on the deck to enjoy the view with her coffee and a good book.

Around 11:00, she showered and got ready to go to brunch at Auberge du Soleil. She chose an indigo blue A-line dress with double shadow stripes around the hem. She checked out her look in the mirror. The dark blue dress accentuated her natural blond hair and blue eyes. Happy with her choice, she drove to Auberge du Soleil. They seated her outside on the deck as she had requested. She gazed appreciatively at the wonderful views over the vineyards and valley below.

She looked around at the couples seated around the deck. Most of the women were wearing dresses. The men were also well dressed. Everyone looked relaxed and happy. She felt a brief stab of loneliness but quickly squelched the feeling.

It was a three course, prix fixe brunch. It was an expensive splurge, but she had already decided that she could afford it this one time just for the experience. She ordered a Mimosa to start. She chose the potato gnocchi with wild mushrooms and pea shoots for her starter and duck confit hash with bordelaise sauce for her entrée. She planned to have the chocolate crémeux with brownie sponge cake and espresso gelato for dessert. It sounded heavenly. After she placed her order, she took a sip of her Mimosa and sat back to enjoy the view. The freshly squeezed orange juice in the Mimosa was a perfect blend of tart and sweet.

Each course was as much a work of art as it was delicious. Rylie was thoroughly enjoying her meal when the peaceful atmosphere was disrupted by a man speaking loudly on the other side of the deck. She looked up and saw a heavyset older man with gray hair and dark bushy eyebrows angrily gesturing and talking to the man seated across from him. The old man suddenly got up from the table and strode quickly across the deck toward the door. He almost knocked over a waitress on the way.

"Put it on my tab!" he yelled at the shocked waitress.

"Of course, Mr. Marchetti," the waitress replied. She almost got knocked over again as the man who had been seated with Mr. Marchetti rushed after him.

Rylie almost choked as she recognized the man. It was Lucien.

Her first instinct was to call Sophie and tell her what she had just witnessed. Then she wondered if she should bother Sophie right now when she was working under a strict deadline. She decided to wait until late afternoon to call Sophie. She wasn't sure if she was making the right decision, but she hoped she was.

She finished her meal and decided to walk around downtown St. Helena and check out the shops. She parked on the main street and walked from one end of the small town to the other. She smiled when she saw the bone-shaped pet supply store sign with the cute name of Fideaux.

She turned off the main street onto the street where Vinterre was located. She tried to discreetly check out Vinterre as she walked past. It looked like they were very busy. She kept walking for a block or so and then walked back on the other side of the street.

Almost directly across the street from Vinterre, she saw a restaurant called The Grapevine. It looked like it had been converted from an old Craftsman style house. But whereas Vinterre was bustling with customers, The Grapevine looked empty and abandoned. She stepped up onto the front porch and peered in the windows. Other than a few derelict pieces of broken furniture, it was empty inside.

"Can I help you?" A man's voice laced with anger and sarcasm startled her. She quickly turned around to see a thin man with dark hair and a dark stubble beard standing on the sidewalk watching her.

"I was just walking by and saw this restaurant. It looks like it was a nice place, but it seems to have been abandoned," Rylie said. "Do you know anything about it?"

"I should. I'm the owner. And you're trespassing. Get off my property."

Rylie stared at the hostile man for a minute while she collected her thoughts. There didn't seem to be anything she could say that was going to go well.

"No problem. I was just about to leave anyway."

She strode past the man and headed back toward the main street of town where she had parked. She got in her SUV and drove home.

She waited until late afternoon to call Sophie. She told Sophie about her encounter with the owner of The Grapevine restaurant.

"Oh, that's Oliver Davison. He isn't the friendliest guy, is he? His restaurant went out of business about six months ago. I think it was probably at least partly due to his less than charming personality. One of my friends has a daughter who worked for him as a waitress one summer. She said he was horrible to work for. I guess they had a really high turnover of employees because of it."

"Oliver used to have a very good chef," Sophie continued, "but that chef left about a year and a half ago. I think that's when The Grapevine started to have problems. The new chef's food wasn't up to the same standard. I had dinner there with a client one night after Oliver had hired the new chef. We were very disappointed with our meals. The service was poor, too. I've never gone back there again. There are plenty of excellent restaurants to choose from around here. Quite a few of my friends told me that they stopped going to The Grapevine, too. You can't stay in business if you don't have any customers. I think Oliver is very bitter about losing his business."

"Yes, he seemed really angry when he talked to me. I didn't feel like just peeking in the windows was that big of a deal," Rylie replied.

"Don't let him upset you, Rylie. He has issues, and they have nothing to do with you. Just ignore his rude behavior."

"Thanks, Sophie. At least I know now why he was so antagonistic."

Rylie took a deep breath and told Sophie about seeing Lucien at Auberge du Soleil with the older man named Mr. Marchetti.

"Do you know Mr. Marchetti?" Rylie asked.

"I don't know him personally, but I know he owns Il Capriccio Bar on Main Street," Sophie replied. "I'll ask Lucien about it when he comes home tonight."

Rylie was happy to see Bella waiting to greet her when she got home after a busy first day at her locum veterinarian job. Her first day had been a bit stressful. She had to learn the veterinary hospital's protocols, find out what medical equipment they had for her to work with, and see what medications and supplements they had available in their in-house pharmacy. She liked everyone that she worked with, but she needed to learn the strengths and weaknesses of each of the support staff so she knew who to go to when she needed something.

Bella was looking up at her with a huge golden grin wagging her tail so hard that her whole back end was swaying back and forth.

Rylie smiled. "Hi, Bella! Were you a good girl for me today?"

She reached down to ruffle Bella's golden fur. She got Bella a bacon, egg, and cheese dog biscuit which Bella rapidly consumed.

"Let's go outside to go potty, Bella!"

Rylie walked outside with Bella. She filled her lungs with a deep breath of the air deliciously infused with the scent of grapes. After Bella did her business, they went back inside. She got Bella her dinner and got herself a mineral water with lime. Then she showered and got dressed for the Chamber of Commerce awards dinner at Vinterre.

The entrance to Vinterre was charming with a beautifully landscaped front lawn and patio surrounded by an olive-colored picket fence. Tiny white fairy lights sparkled in the grapevine arbor over the cobblestone path leading to the front door.

Rylie stepped inside. The chandeliers suspended from the tall ceilings and exposed brick walls gave the restaurant a feeling of rustic elegance. Each round dining table was set with a white linen tablecloth with a centerpiece of white flowers with dark green leaves. Tall white taper candles glowed in the middle of each centerpiece. The dark wood floors and rustic antique furniture pieces along the walls added to the ambience. Sophie had done an amazing job with the interior design.

The room was packed for the Chamber of Commerce awards dinner. She told the hostess that she was with Sophie Marchand. The hostess guided her to a small table along one wall where Sophie was seated and handed her a menu.

"Hi, Sophie!" Rylie smiled.

"Hi, Rylie! You look so pretty tonight." Sophie said. "This is Patricia Davenport and her husband Jonathan."

"Nice to meet you," Rylie said.

"Nice to meet you too, Rylie," Patricia said. Jonathan smiled at her and laid his cloth napkin on his lap.

Rylie took an instant liking to Patricia. Patricia's short bob of blond hair with long bangs suited her bubbly personality. Her husband, Jonathan, seemed more reserved.

"Even though Sophie is my best friend, I live pretty far away in the East Bay, so I haven't eaten at Vinterre yet. I'm looking forward to it," Rylie said.

The menu offered a choice of three course dinners featuring either ribeye steak with demi-glace, salmon with truffle cream sauce, or risotto as the entrée. She decided on the ribeye steak with potato rosti, cream of baby spinach, and grilled local porcini mushrooms. When the waitress came to get her dinner order, she ordered a glass of a Napa Valley cabernet sauvignon to go with her meal.

Rylie looked around the room to see if she recognized anyone. Oliver Davison was seated at a table in the corner looking down at his plate with a dark scowl on his face. Lorenzo Marchetti was on the opposite side of the room regaling the people at his table with a story liberally punctuated by broad gestures. A true Italian.

Patricia followed her gaze. "Lorenzo Marchetti has a big personality."

"Very big." Jonathan said.

"Now Jonathan," Patricia said.

Rylie exchanged a glance with Sophie.

"This is a small town, so I imagine that everyone knows everyone around here," Rylie said.

"Pretty much," Jonathan said. "Lorenzo owns the bar down the street, Il Capriccio. He probably knows more about the people in this town than anyone else after tending bar all these years."

A waiter with a dark sweep of long hair nearly covering his eyes was serving Mr. Marchetti's table. He accidentally knocked over a glass of water as he set one of the plates down. He apologized and hurriedly gave everyone their meals before making a hasty exit. She saw a flash of irritation cross Mr. Marchetti's face. Then he resumed his story telling.

Rylie enjoyed every bite of the delicious meal. The steak was so tender she could cut it with a butter knife. She had never had porcini mushrooms, but they were excellent.

After dessert and coffee had been served, the Chamber of Commerce awards were presented for Lifetime Achievement, Business of the Year, Citizen of the Year, and Employee of the Year. Rylie noticed Lucien standing near the kitchen in his chef's coat watching the awards ceremony.

"And last but not least, we would like to thank Lucien Marchand for hosting our awards ceremony this year and for a fabulous meal!" Everyone started clapping. Some people got up from their tables and kept clapping. Soon the whole room was standing and clapping to show their appreciation for the amazing meal.

Lucien stepped out into the room. "Thank you. I'm happy that everyone enjoyed their meals. I hope to see you all here again soon."

Rylie sat back down with the rest of the people at her table.

"That was awesome. I'm so glad everyone recognized Lucien for preparing such wonderful meals. I've got to get going now. I have to get up early for work tomorrow. Thanks for having me, Sophie," Rylie said.

"Thanks for coming, Rylie. Talk to you later," Sophie said.

"Nice to meet you both," Rylie said to the couple. "I'm sure I'll see you around."

She stepped outside and enjoyed the magical feeling of walking under the grapevine arbor sparkling with tiny white fairy lights as she headed to her SUV.

The next two days at work went well as Rylie settled into the flow of the veterinary hospital. On her first day off on Thursday, she spent some time exploring downtown St. Helena and then took Bella hiking around Lake Hennessey.

The next day she decided to check out Wappo Dog Park with Bella. The dog park had a large grassy area surrounded by trees. There were some benches and lawn chairs set up for people to relax on while their dogs played. The park was mostly empty. Rylie saw an older couple sitting on a bench while their goldendoodle sniffed around the park. As she got closer, she recognized Patricia and Jonathan Davenport from the Chamber of Commerce awards dinner.

Bella ran straight up to the goldendoodle. The goldendoodle looked startled at Bella's sudden appearance. Bella and the goldendoodle sniffed noses from a safe distance. Then Bella did a play bow to show the goldendoodle that she wanted to play.

"Hi Patricia and Jonathan. I'm Rylie. We met on Monday night at the awards dinner. This is my golden retriever, Bella. Is that your goldendoodle?"

"Yes, that's Charlotte. I think she's happy to have some company now that your dog is here. Please join us."

"Thanks." Rylie sat down on the bench next to the couple. "Does Charlotte like to play frisbee? I brought Bella's frisbee to play with her. It's a soft rubber frisbee so it doesn't hurt her mouth when she catches it."

"I think Charlotte may have chased a frisbee or two that someone else brought to play with their dog. I'm sure she would enjoy it," Patricia said.

Rylie got out Bella's frisbee and called the dogs over.

"I'll throw the frisbee for them," Jonathan said.

"Sure," Rylie said. "I always throw it so it goes just above Bella's head. I don't want Bella leaping up into the air to catch the frisbee and then injuring herself when she lands."

"No problem," Jonathan said. He took the dogs out into the middle of the park before throwing the frisbee for them. Rylie and Patricia chatted comfortably for a while.

"I belong to a small group of women that meets once a week to do fun things in the area," Patricia said. "We usually get together on Thursdays. I think it would be a great way for you to get to meet some of the local women. We have women of all ages in our group. Would you like to join us this coming Thursday? We're going to go on the Napa Valley Wine Train for their gourmet lunch trip. I'm sure there's still time to add you to our group reservation, if you'd like to join us."

"That sounds like fun! I'd love to join you. I've always wanted to go on the Napa Valley Wine Train."

"Great! Why don't we exchange phone numbers? I'll call or text you with all the specifics after I call them to add you to our group reservation," Patricia said.

"Thanks, Patricia."

Jonathan came back with Bella and Charlotte looking happy and tired. Bella was grinning with her tongue lolling out one side of her mouth. Jonathan handed Rylie Bella's frisbee.

"They had a great time," Jonathan said.

Rylie smiled. "I can tell! We're going to call it a day now. Talk to you soon, Patricia. Bye!"

When they got home, Rylie got a mineral water with lime and went out on the deck to call Sophie. She made plans to go to Beringer Vineyards with Sophie and Lucien on Sunday.

Saturday passed uneventfully. On Sunday, she drove over to Sophie's house to meet up with Sophie and Lucien for their trip to Beringer Vineyards. They headed to Beringer

Vineyards in Lucien's SUV and signed up for the next tour. After touring the wine caves and tasting three of the Beringer wines, they walked over to explore the historic Rhine House that was built as the home of the original owner in 1884. They admired all the unique architectural details including the stained glass windows in the massive wood doors leading into the house and the beautifully carved fireplace mantel and woodwork. Then they wandered outside to the lawn in back of the house where a band was playing. Chairs and tables had been set up in front of the band. They found some chairs and sat down to enjoy the music.

"This is such a wonderful place to hang out," Rylie said. "The property is so beautiful. Do you come here often?"

"You know how it is when you live somewhere," Sophie replied. "You never appreciate what you have as much as the people that come to visit."

Lucien was looking around at the other people listening to the band.

"Oh hi, Ashton! How are you?" Lucien said to the guy sitting next to him.

"Hi Lucien," Ashton replied. "I've been better, man. We responded to a 911 call yesterday afternoon and found Lorenzo Marchetti dead on the floor in his house. He didn't show up for work yesterday. His staff were concerned because he's never not shown up for work on a day that he's scheduled. They called him on his cell phone a bunch of times, but the phone kept going straight to voice mail. Finally, one of them went to his house to find out what was going on and found him dead."

"What?" Lucien replied. "What happened? Did he have a heart attack or something?"

"We don't know yet. We won't know anything until after the autopsy," Ashton replied.

Lucien's mouth hung open in shock. Sophie touched his arm.

"Are you going to introduce us, Lucien?" she asked.

Lucien turned to look at his wife. "Oh sorry, honey. This is Ashton Devereux. He's one of our local EMTs. I met him at Il Capriccio when I was having a drink there after work one night some time ago. Maybe a year ago now?"

Ashton clapped Lucien on the back. "Yeah, we see each other at the bar from time to time. I still haven't made it to Vinterre yet. But it's on my bucket list."

"Hi Ashton. I'm Rylie Sunderland. I'm staying here in St. Helena for a month or so while I work at a local veterinary hospital filling in for the veterinarian who owns the place. He needed some time off to recuperate from a surgery."

"Hi Rylie. Nice to meet you."

"Did you see anything to suggest that someone might have broken into Lorenzo Marchetti's house when you were there yesterday, Ashton? Like maybe it was a robbery gone bad or something?" Rylie asked.

"No, I didn't see anything like that. But the police detective and his team went through every inch of that place."

"St. Helena has always been a very safe place. We rarely hear about any kind of crime occurring here," Sophie said. "And I've never heard of a murder being committed in St. Helena."

"I haven't either," Lucien said. He looked at Ashton.

"Me either," Ashton said. "And I grew up here. Hey, I've got to get going. I didn't get much sleep last night, and I'm wiped out. I'll see you around, Lucien. Nice to meet you, Sophie. And you too, Rylie."

They sat in silence for a few minutes after Ashton left. The band went on a break and people started getting up out of their chairs.

"Are you two ready to head home?" Lucien asked.

"Sure," Sophie replied.

Each of them was wrapped up in their own thoughts as they walked to Lucien's SUV. Rylie felt a knot in the pit of her stomach.

Chapter 2

L ucien pulled into their driveway and parked.

"Do you want to come in for something to drink, Rylie?" Sophie asked.

"Sure."

As they were heading to the front door, a car pulled up in the driveway in back of them and parked. A handsome man who looked to be in his mid-thirties with dark brown hair and a lean body got out of the car. Rylie noticed the badge clipped on his belt. She swallowed hard.

"Hi. I'm Police Detective Aaron Michelson," he said as he approached.

"Aaron! What a surprise!" Sophie said.

"Oh, hi Sophie. How are you? I'm here to talk to your husband. Is this Lucien?"

"Yes, this is my husband Lucien and my best friend Rylie," Sophie replied.

"Is this the Aaron Michelson that you did interior design work for last summer, Sophie?" Lucien asked.

"Yes," Sophie replied. "That was one of my favorite projects."

"I'm sorry I'm not here for a social call," Detective Michelson said. "Lorenzo Marchetti was found dead in his house yesterday afternoon. We won't know the exact cause of his death for a while, but the medical examiner has told us that his death does not appear to be from natural causes. We are now treating it as a homicide."

Rylie felt the blood drain from her face. Lucien and Sophie weren't looking that good either.

"I'd like to ask you a few questions, Lucien," Detective Michelson said. "Is there someplace we can talk privately?"

"Anything you have to say to me, you can say in front of my wife and Rylie," Lucien said. "I have nothing to hide."

"Okay, then. Do you want to talk out here in the driveway, or would you like to go inside?" Detective Michelson asked.

"Oh please, come inside, Aaron. Can I get you something to drink?" Sophie said.

They went inside and sat around Sophie's dining table while she got drinks for everyone.

"I'll get right to the point," Detective Michelson said. "Lorenzo Marchetti's staff told us that he didn't come in to work at Il Capriccio on Tuesday because he thought he had a touch of the stomach flu. He was at work on Wednesday and Thursday, but on Friday he called in sick again. On Saturday, he didn't show up for work at all and he didn't call in. His staff tried calling him all day, but he never answered the phone. Finally, one of them went to his house to check on him and found him dead on the floor."

"I know. We were just at Beringer Vineyards, and I saw my friend Ashton Devereux there. He's one of the EMTs that responded to the call," Lucien said.

"We know that Lorenzo Marchetti ate at Vinterre on Monday night before he called in sick with the stomach flu,"

Detective Michelson said. "It could just be coincidental. Or maybe he ate something bad at Vinterre."

"A lot of people ate at Vinterre on Monday night, " Lucien replied. "We had the Chamber of Commerce awards dinner there. I haven't heard of anyone else getting sick. If I had served something bad that night, you'd think that a lot of people would have gotten sick. And I don't serve bad food at my restaurant. We only use fresh produce and high-quality meats. We have an excellent reputation in this community."

"I know the reputation of your restaurant," Detective Michelson said. "But we have to explore all possible angles. We'll know more as the autopsy proceeds. Do you know anyone who might have had a problem with Lorenzo Marchetti?"

"No," Lucien said. "But I'll think about it and let you know if anyone comes to mind."

"Okay. Thank you," Detective Michelson said. He turned to Sophie and Rylie. "Do either of you know Lorenzo Marchetti?"

"Not really," Sophie said. "I just know that he owned the bar on Main Street. I never hung out there."

"I'm new in town. I just got here on Saturday. So I didn't know him at all," Rylie said. Detective Michelson held her gaze for a moment, then turned away. Rylie's breath caught in her throat.

"Thank you all for your help," Detective Michelson said. "Lucien, please don't plan on leaving town anytime soon without talking to me first. I might have more questions for you."

"No problem, Detective," Lucien replied.

Early the next morning, Rylie walked into Valley View Veterinary Hospital and smiled at the receptionists on her way to the doctors' office. She put her purse, lunch, and bags down on her desk, put on her white lab coat, and draped her stethoscope around her neck.

"Hi Cassandra. Hi Addison," she said to the veterinarians sitting at the other desks.

She sat down at her desk and looked at the computer to see what she had on her appointment calendar for the day. A girl in turquoise scrubs with waist-length light brown hair walked into the doctors' office.

"Hi Miley. What have you got for me?" Rylie asked the girl.

"I have your first appointment for you. It's a dog with itchy skin and a rash on his belly. And the owner says his ears have been bothering him, too. You're in Room 2."

She handed Rylie a clipboard with a check-in sheet on it and led the way down the hallway to the second exam room.

Rylie saw appointments every thirty minutes until lunchtime. The highlight of her morning was a cute yellow lab puppy that came in for his first puppy shots. She didn't have time to type all of her medical records into the computer by lunchtime. She got a yogurt out of her lunch bag and worked on typing up her medical records from the morning's appointments over her lunch break. She finished just in time for her first afternoon appointment.

Rylie checked the name on the check-in sheet that Miley handed her for the 2:00 appointment: Oliver Davison and his cat Oreo. She wondered if it was the same Oliver Davison that owned The Grapevine restaurant that had been so rude to her when she saw him last Sunday. She took a deep breath and opened the door into the exam room with a smile on her face.

"Hi, I'm Dr. Sunderland."

She locked eyes with Oliver Davison. She could tell that he recognized her. She decided to act as if nothing had happened and carry on in a professional manner.

"I understand that Oreo hasn't been eating well for the past two weeks and that she's been losing weight," she said.

She put her clipboard down and went over to pet the black and white cat sitting quietly on the exam room table.

"Yes. She's always been a picky eater. But the past couple of weeks, she's hardly touched her food. I've bought her all different flavors of cat food, but I haven't been able to find anything she'll eat. Sometimes she'll take a couple of bites of one of the foods, but then she just walks away from her bowl."

"Has she been vomiting?" Rylie asked.

"Yes, for a while now. Just small amounts. But I keep finding it all over my house," Oliver replied.

Rylie saw the stress that Oliver was feeling over his cat's lack of appetite. She could tell that his cat was very important to him.

"I'm going to do a physical exam on Oreo and check her out. Then we'll talk about what might be going on with her."

Rylie listened to Oreo's heart and lungs, felt her lymph nodes, palpated her abdomen, did a skin tent test to check her hydration status, and looked in her ears, eyes, and mouth.

"She's very dehydrated," she said finally. "See what happens when I pick up the skin between her shoulder blades and then let it go? The skin goes back down very slowly. It should snap right back into place when I let it go. Like this." Rylie demonstrated using the skin on her forearm. "She's about 10-12% dehydrated."

Rylie discussed her differentials for Oreo's lack of appetite, vomiting, and dehydration with Oliver. Her primary differential was kidney disease.

"We need to do some bloodwork and a urinalysis to find out what's going on with Oreo. I can run the bloodwork in-house so we'll get some answers right away," Rylie said.

"Oh good. I definitely want to do that," Oliver said. The tightness in his facial features eased a little.

Rylie had her nurse provide Oliver with an estimate for the cost of the treatment plan that she was recommending. After Oliver agreed to the estimate, Miley sent Oliver up front to wait in the reception area.

Rylie brought Oreo out back to the treatment room so that the veterinary nurses could collect blood and urine samples and run the bloodwork and urinalysis on the in-house lab machines. She went to see her next patient while Oreo's bloodwork was running.

The bloodwork and urinalysis confirmed her suspicion that Oreo had kidney disease. Rylie discussed the bloodwork and urinalysis results with Oliver. She recommended that Oreo be hospitalized with an IV catheter and IV fluids to rehydrate her and flush the toxins out of her system. She explained that they didn't have staff at their veterinary hospital overnight to monitor sick patients and that she felt that Oreo needed to be taken to a 24-hour facility. She recommended a nearby 24-hour veterinary hospital.

"Thank you for your help, Dr. Sunderland," Oliver said. "Oreo means everything to me. I'll do whatever I have to do to help her get better."

"You're welcome, Oliver," Rylie replied. "The 24-hour veterinary hospital will send me daily reports and updates on Oreo so that I can monitor her progress. I hope she does well."

As she watched Oliver leave with Oreo resting comfortably in her crate, she reflected on how he was so different today than he was the last time she saw him. She could see that he really loved his cat. She hoped that if she ever saw him around town again that he would at least be civil to her.

On Thursday, Rylie drove to Napa to meet Patricia Davenport and her friends at the train station for their Gourmet Express lunch trip on the Napa Valley Wine Train. She spotted Patricia standing outside the station with a group of women and walked over to join them. Patricia introduced her to the other four women: Liza Cresswell, an older woman with shoulder-length white hair and a large smile, Maggie Sheldon, Kinsley Logan, and Carolyn Beaumont, who appeared to be in her early 40s. Carolyn seemed quieter and more reserved than the other women. Maggie and Kinsley looked like they might be close to her in age. Kinsley greeted her with an infectious grin. Rylie liked her instantly.

"Come on, ladies." Patricia smiled. "Let's find a couple of tables across from each other in the large dining car. We're scheduled for the first seating, so we'll eat our lunch in the dining car on the trip to St. Helena and then have our dessert in one of the lounge cars on the way back."

They walked along the antique rail cars to where a woman was standing to guide them onto the train. The dining car had rows of tables for four lined up under the windows on each side of the burgundy-carpeted aisle. Heavy gold drapes framed the views from each window. The tables were set with crisp white linen tablecloths, artfully folded white cloth napkins, and wine glasses. Antique dark wood chairs upholstered with gold, green, and brown fabric were placed at each table. Above the windows, antique wall sconces lit the space and accentuated the architectural details of the curved ceiling.

It was an opulent atmosphere. Rylie had read online that the restoration of the antique rail cars had been designed to make passengers feel as though they were being transported back in time to the early 1900s when the rail cars were originally constructed.

Patricia guided her to a table with herself and Liza Cresswell. The other three women sat at the table across the aisle. A waitress brought them their menus and took their drink orders. Rylie chose the salad to start with goat cheese, roasted grapes, toasted almonds, and champagne-Dijon vinaigrette. For her entrée, she chose the sliced beef tenderloin with forest mushrooms and a ruby port glaze, blue cheese-potato purée, and asparagus.

"I've certainly been eating well since I got here," Rylie said. "The food at Vinterre at the Chamber of Commerce awards dinner on Monday night was fabulous. This looks like it will be wonderful, too."

"Is this your first time on the Wine Train?" Patricia asked.

"Yes. I've wanted to go on the Wine Train for years. I just never got around to it. You're fortunate to live in such a gorgeous area with so many fun things to do," Rylie said.

"I know. I'm very appreciative of that," Patricia said.

"My husband, Harding, and I decided a long time ago that we didn't want to get to the end of our lives and regret that we never took time to enjoy ourselves," Liza said. "We made a life change many years ago when we were in our thirties. We were both working full-time jobs that we hated. We were so busy we rarely even saw each other. We were fortunate to find a small family winery in St. Helena that we were able to purchase for a fair price. It was a steep learning curve for us, but we love our life now. It was the best decision we ever made."

"Did you learn how to make wine yourselves, or do you have a winemaker?" Rylie asked.

"Oh, no. We have an incredibly talented winemaker. We also have a vineyard manager and other people who work for us. The only thing we have to do in the winemaking process is to help our winemaker taste test the wine when it's time." Liza smiled.

"That sounds like a great job," Rylie said.

She gazed out the window. The view was idyllic. They were passing through miles of beautiful vineyards and wineries.

"Liza has a Shih Tzu named Sammie that she brings to the dog park on occasion," Patricia said.

"Oh, great!" Rylie said. "I'm sure that I'll be taking Bella to the dog park from time to time. Maybe we'll meet up there sometime."

They chatted amicably about their dogs and other things over a delicious lunch.

Liza's face lit up when she spotted a young couple making their way through the dining car. "Derek! Stefanie! How are you?"

The couple stopped at their table. "Hi Liza! What a surprise to see you here!" Derek said.

"Patricia, Rylie, I'd like you to meet Derek Firth and his beautiful wife Stefanie. Derek works in the tech industry in San Francisco, but they come for wine tasting and to buy wine from us several times a year," Liza said.

"Sorry we haven't been to your winery in a while," Derek said to Liza. "The last time we were in St. Helena about five months ago, Stefanie had a bad fall in the ladies' room at Il Capriccio. There was a puddle of water on the floor, and she slipped in it. She ended up having a miscarriage. It was quite a blow to us. We were so excited to have our first baby."

"Oh no! How horrible!" Liza said. "I'm so sorry."

Liza took Stefanie's hand in hers. Stefanie's eyes were moist.

"Do you think you'll try again eventually?" Liza asked.

Derek's jaw clenched. "We've been trying. We haven't been able to get pregnant again."

"Did you see a doctor?" Liza asked.

"Yes," Stefanie said. "She said everything is fine and I should be able to get pregnant again. But it hasn't happened. The first time we tried, it happened right away. I'm scared that something is wrong with me even though the doctor said I'm fine."

Derek put his arm around his wife. "We've got to get back to our lunch. It was nice meeting you Patricia and Rylie. I'm sure we'll see you and Harding at your winery soon, Liza."

The couple left to go to their dining car.

"That's so sad," Rylie said. "They seem like such a nice couple."

"I know. I feel horrible for them," Liza said.

On the trip back from St. Helena, the women went into one of the lounge cars for dessert. The lounge car had rows of overstuffed chairs upholstered in gold colored fabric lined up in front of the windows on each side of the center aisle. The chairs swiveled 360 degrees to allow for conversations with fellow passengers. Dessert and coffee were served on the ledge in front of the large arched windows framed with gold fabric drapes.

Rylie was interested in getting to know the younger women in the group, so she sat down between Maggie and Kinsley in the lounge car. She discovered that Maggie owned a women's clothing and accessories boutique in downtown St. Helena called Casual Chic. Kinsley was a traditionally published mystery author. They enjoyed an animated conversation over dessert and exchanged cell phone numbers before they got off the train back in Napa.

As they were leaving the train station, Maggie said, "I'd love to have you come and see my boutique, Rylie. Come in anytime on the days that I work, and I'll give you a special "Welcome to St. Helena" discount. I work Monday, Tuesday, Wednesday, and Friday."

"Thanks, Maggie." Rylie smiled. "I'll definitely stop by sometime. I need some new dresses and nice clothes to wear when I go out."

When she got home, Rylie took a mineral water with lime and her cell phone outside and sat on a chair on the backyard patio. Bella followed her outside and curled up nearby.

She called and chatted with Sophie for a while about her lunch trip on the wine train with the women's group. Then she asked Sophie if tomorrow would be a good time to visit her at one of the houses that she was working on.

"I'm working on a big renovation right now," Sophie said. "The owners wanted the house to have an open concept, so my contractor removed some walls and reconfigured the rooms. We basically gutted the entire house and started over. The new kitchen is in and we're very close to the time that I can have the new furniture and furnishings delivered. I'd love to have you come over and see our progress. I have lots of "before" photos that I can show you so you can see what we started with."

"That sounds great. I'm excited to see what you've done with the place. How about I meet you at the house at about 10:00 tomorrow morning?"

"That sounds perfect. See you then," Sophie replied.

Chapter 3

Rylie drove up to the house that Sophie was renovating the next morning around 10:00. The front door was open, so she walked in.

"Sophie?" she called out.

Sophie walked quickly toward her from the other side of the house.

"Hi, Rylie, come on in." Sophie smiled warmly. "Let me take you on a tour of the place."

Sophie led Rylie on a tour of the old farmhouse that she had beautifully remodeled. She showed Rylie photos of the interior and exterior of the home before the extensive renovation. The house was now open concept with a large kitchen flowing into a spacious living room. On one side of the living room, glass doors folded back completely for access to the patio and lushly landscaped backyard.

Comfortable lounge chairs were scattered around the outdoor pool and spa. The house had an airy feeling with exposed beam vaulted ceilings and white oak floors. The chef's kitchen showcased modern appliances and decor while retaining a homey country feel.

"You've done an amazing job here, Sophie," Rylie said. "This is gorgeous!"

"Thanks, Rylie. I'm almost done with this project, and then it's on to the next."

"I don't want to bother you when you're working, Sophie," Rylie said. "But did you ever find out from Lucien why he was arguing with Lorenzo Marchetti at Auberge du Soleil? If Detective Michelson hasn't heard about that yet, I'm sure he will eventually."

"Yes, I did talk to him about it. He said that Lorenzo wanted him to host his niece's wedding reception dinner for 200 people at Vinterre. He told Lorenzo that he doesn't do that type of thing at Vinterre. He's not set up for it. He told me that Lorenzo got really angry and stormed out of the restaurant."

"I saw Lorenzo storm out of the restaurant. He was steaming mad. He almost knocked over a waitress on his way out. Doesn't that seem like a kind of over the top reaction to Lucien not wanting to host his niece's wedding reception dinner?" Rylie asked. "I wonder if there is more to it than that."

"I got the feeling that Lucien wasn't telling me everything," Sophie said. "He seemed very tense and uncomfortable when I tried to talk to him about it. Maybe the way he's been acting so distant and distracted lately has something to do with Lorenzo Marchetti. But I can't imagine what that might be."

"Hmmm," Rylie said. "Maybe all three of us - you, me and Lucien - could do something fun together on Sunday. Maybe if Lucien spent more time relaxing and having fun, he would loosen up a little and feel more comfortable talking about things."

"That sounds like a plan," Sophie said. "What do you have in mind?"

"There's no shortage of things to do around here. I'd be happy to do any of them. We could go on some winery tours and tastings, we could go to Robert Louis Stevenson State Park and hike to the top of Mount St. Helena, we could go sit in the hot spring mineral pools and get mud baths in Calistoga. Whatever you and Lucien would like to do would be fine with me."

"Let me think about it and get back to you. I'll talk to Lucien tonight and see what he says. We haven't spent a whole day together having fun in a long time. I'm sure I can convince him to go unless he has something really pressing that he needs to do."

"Great! I'll talk to you later then."

Rylie drove back home and went inside. "Hi Bella! My sweet girl. I feel like I need some fresh air and exercise. I'm sure you'd like that, too. Let me see what I can find for us to do around here."

She checked the AllTrails app on her cell phone. She found a dog-friendly hiking trail along Lake Hennessey about twenty minutes away.

"Would you like to go for a nice walk, Bella?"

Bella bounced up and down on her front legs in reply and started panting excitedly. Rylie put Bella in the back seat of her SUV and buckled her into her seatbelt. As they drove up to Lake Hennessey, she was happy to see that it was a pretty little lake surrounded by rolling hills.

They walked along the shoreline trail with Bella taking the lead. Bella's nose was to the ground sniffing everything in sight. Rylie inhaled deeply of the fresh air. The quiet and peacefulness of the lake was just what she needed so she could try to sort out her troubled thoughts about Lucien and Lorenzo Marchetti. She wondered who could have hated Lorenzo so much that they wanted him dead.

She thought back to the young couple she had met on the Napa Valley Wine Train. Did they blame Lorenzo Marchetti for Stefanie's miscarriage since her accident happened in his bar? If they blamed him for that, they would probably also blame him for the fact that she hadn't been able to get pregnant again since her miscarriage. But they seemed like such a nice couple. She couldn't imagine them doing something so heinous as committing murder.

Bella spotted some Canada geese in the water and started to chase them. She didn't get far since Rylie had her on a short leash. She bounced up and down on her front legs and barked once or twice. The geese ignored her and kept paddling on their way. Rylie smiled at Bella's antics. They walked at a brisk pace for a while and then walked more slowly on the way back.

When they got back to the SUV, she buckled Bella into the back seat and headed home to get something for lunch. She made herself a nice salad and took it out on the deck to eat while letting her gaze wander over the vineyard across the road.

After lunch she headed into St. Helena to wander around and check out the shops. She turned down the street where Vinterre was located looking for someplace to park. She didn't get far. The road was blocked off and there were police cars everywhere with their lights flashing. She pulled into someone's driveway and turned around to find parking elsewhere. As soon as she found someplace to park, she walked over to Vinterre to find out what was going on.

She wasn't able to get very close to Vinterre because the police had barricaded off a large area around the restaurant.

She saw Detective Michelson looking at something in a clear plastic evidence bag with a member of his team. She didn't see Lucien or anyone else that she knew so she headed back toward the main street of town.

She called Sophie right away. "Hi Sophie. Do you have any idea about what's going on at Vinterre?"

"No. What are you talking about?"

"There are police cars all over in front of Vinterre with their lights flashing. The police have barricaded off a large area around the restaurant. You can't even drive down that street right now."

"Oh my goodness! Is Lucien okay? Did you see an ambulance there?" Sophie asked.

"No, I didn't see an ambulance there. But that doesn't mean that there wasn't one there before I got there," Rylie said.

"I'll meet you in front of The Saint Wine Bar in about five minutes," Sophie said.

A few minutes later, Rylie saw Sophie hurrying in her direction.

"Let's go," Sophie said. She headed down the street toward Vinterre. Rylie sprinted to catch up.

When they got to Vinterre, Sophie called out, "Aaron! Detective Michelson!"

Detective Michelson turned to look at them. He said a few words to the guy standing next to him and then came over to talk to them.

"Aaron, what's going on? Is Lucien okay? Is he hurt?" Sophie asked.

"Lucien is fine, Sophie. No one has been hurt. This is a crime scene investigation," Detective Michelson replied.

"What? What are you talking about?" Sophie said.

"The Medical Examiner said that Lorenzo Marchetti suffered from acute liver failure and kidney damage consistent with some kind of toxin ingestion. Since he ate at Vinterre right before he started complaining of gastrointestinal problems, we need to search the restaurant to look for any kind of toxin that he might have ingested during the Chamber of Commerce awards dinner. I know that no one else got sick, but he may have been targeted and been the only one that was served something toxic. Someone could have added a toxic substance to his food," Detective Michelson said.

"The evidence technicians showed me a small packet containing a tiny amount of brown powdered material that they found on the floor in back of a trash can inside Vinterre. That's all we've come up with so far. They'll dust it for fingerprints and send the powdered material to the lab to be analyzed."

Sophie looked pale. "Are you arresting Lucien?"

"No. No one is being arrested right now, Sophie," Detective Michelson said. "Right now we're just looking for evidence. Please go home or go back to whatever home remodel you were working on. There's nothing you can do here right now."

"Come on, Sophie," Rylie said. "Let's go get something to drink."

She put her arm through Sophie's and steered her away from Vinterre. Sophie allowed herself to be guided away. Rylie led the way to The Saint Wine Bar. They sat at a small table outside in front of the bar.

"Did you have lunch?" Rylie asked.

"No, I didn't have time," Sophie said.

"Then let's get their Artisanal Cheese Board to go with our wine," Rylie said.

"Okay."

The waiter came and took their order. He was back in a few minutes with their glasses of wine.

"Your cheese board will be out in a few minutes." He disappeared back inside.

"Rylie, this is serious. What's going on?" Sophie said.

"Take a sip of your wine, Sophie. You don't look so good right now," Rylie said. She took a large sip of her own wine.

"The police are just doing their job, Sophie. We won't know anything until they analyze the packet of brown powdered material that they found. Maybe it's something completely innocent. But if it is some kind of toxic substance, then we'll deal with that when we know more. There's really nothing we can do about it right now," Rylie said.

Sophie slowly swirled the wine in her glass. "I know. I just need to talk to Lucien."

The waiter brought their cheese board. They nibbled at the cheeses as they drank their wine.

"I'm sure that Lucien isn't involved in this, Sophie," Rylie said. "There's just no way. Please don't worry."

"Whether he's involved in it or not, the police need to find someone to charge with Lorenzo Marchetti's murder. I'm afraid that Lucien might get caught in their crosshairs."

"Sophie, really. You know Detective Michelson personally. Do you really think that he would charge someone with murder if he didn't have airtight evidence to convict them?" Rylie said. "Even if he wanted to, it wouldn't hold up in court."

"You're right. I'm just going crazy. I have to calm down. I need to get back to work now, Rylie. I'll get the check," Sophie said. She went inside to pay the bill. Rylie swallowed the last of her wine and got ready to leave.

"Thanks, Sophie," Rylie said. "That was good wine."

"I'll call you," Sophie said. She walked quickly away in the direction of her car.

Rylie stared after her friend as she walked away. Then she turned around and headed for Lorenzo Marchetti's bar, Il Capriccio. She was instantly enveloped in the warm and cozy atmosphere of the bar as she stepped inside. She could tell that it wasn't a typical American bar. This was a place where families and friends hung out with each other. A local gathering place.

Behind the glossy dark wood bar, bottles of liquor were arranged on backlighted shelves enclosed within two decorative arches of exposed brick. A large flat screen TV hung on the brick wall between the two arches. Brown leather upholstered stools were arranged in front of the gold, brown, and cream-colored Italian tiles that lined the front of the bar. Rylie inhaled deeply of the luscious aroma of rich coffee.

Dark wood tables were scattered around the room. A group of men were playing cards at a table in the corner. A mother with two small children was seated at another table. Rylie took a seat at the bar and grabbed one of the menus. Even though she had already eaten a salad for lunch at home and some cheese with her wine at The Saint Wine Bar with Sophie, the food on the menu was enticing. They served an array of authentic Italian bar food such as panini, antipasto, and wood-fired pizza.

"And they have cannoli, too!" Rylie said. Then she realized she had said it out loud. She surreptitiously looked around to see if anyone had heard her. The bartender quickly moved to stand in front of her.

Rylie looked up at him. Very handsome. Very sexy. Very Italian.

"Hi! I'm Alessandro Marchetti, the manager. You can call me Alex. What can I get you?" His whole face lit up when he smiled at her.

Rylie paused a minute, then looked at the menu again as she tried to collect her thoughts. "I already ate lunch and just shared a cheese plate with a friend at The Saint Wine Bar. Everything on your menu sounds delicious. But I need some time to digest before I can eat anything more right now. Can I just have a Pellegrino with a slice of lime?"

"Sure. Coming right up," Alex said. He put a bottle of Pellegrino in front of her along with a tall glass of ice with a slice of lime on the rim. He poured the Pellegrino into the glass. Rylie was momentarily tongue-tied.

"So are you Lorenzo Marchetti's son?" Rylie asked quickly before he had a chance to walk away.

"Yes, I am."

"I'm sorry about your dad," Rylie said.

"*Grazie,*" Alex said. His face crumpled for a moment, then he recovered. He gave her a small smile.

"So are you going to take over the bar now that your dad is gone?" Rylie asked.

"I've been managing the bar for years. I'm not really doing anything different than I've already been doing. The only difference is that now I'll inherit the bar and it will be in my name," Alex said.

"It seems like a really nice place. It has a very homey feel," Rylie said.

"That's what bars are like in Italy. I was born and raised there. We didn't move to the U.S. until I was fourteen. I remember going to bars in Italy with my father and mother. They're places where everyone congregates. Children are welcome too. They're like a home away from home. You can go there for a light breakfast, lunch, or an aperitivo."

"What's an aperitivo?" Rylie asked.

"It's a drink served with a light meal at the end of the workday. Drinks served for aperitivo are usually low-alcohol drinks made with bittersweet liqueurs that are supposed to stimulate the appetite before dinner. A lot of people like Aperol Spritz. Have you ever had one?"

"No. But I'm interested in trying one sometime. I'm intrigued," Rylie said.

Alex smiled. "Just let me know when you're ready. I'll whip you up one anytime. You're going to love it."

A guy at the end of the bar signaled to Alex and he strode off. Rylie sipped her Pellegrino thoughtfully. A guy slid onto the bar stool next to her.

"Hi, Rylie! Remember me? Ashton Devereux. We met at Beringer Vineyards when you were there with Lucien and his wife."

"Oh yes, of course. Hi Ashton. How are you? You look a little more rested than the last time I saw you," Rylie said.

"I am more rested. I've had the last couple of days off." He gestured to Alex. "Hey, Alex!"

Alex came over and placed a beer bottle and a glass on the bar in front of Ashton before hurrying away to help another customer.

"I guess Alex knows what you like. You must be a regular. Lagunitas Little Sumpin' Sumpin', huh?" Rylie said.

"I've never heard of it."

"It's a pale wheat ale made by a craft brewery in Petaluma," Ashton said.

"I like Hefeweizen beer. Is it like that?" Rylie asked.

"Similar," Ashton replied. "So how are you enjoying St. Helena?"

"I love it here." Rylie smiled. "It's a beautiful area with so many fun things to do."

"I agree," Ashton said. "I've lived here all my life. I'm very happy here. So since you're a veterinarian, do you have any pets?"

"I have a golden retriever named Bella who is the love of my life," Rylie said.

"I have a golden retriever too! His name is Quinn. We should meet up at Wappo Dog Park sometime so our dogs can play with each other."

Alex walked over. "Did I hear something about you two getting your dogs together to play at Wappo Dog Park? I would love to have some dogs for my dog Amando to play with. Would you mind if I joined you?"

"Fine with me, buddy," Ashton said. The two men looked at Rylie.

"Sounds like fun. What kind of dog do you have Alex?" Rylie said.

"He's an Italian Spinone. Have you ever seen one? They're very popular in Italy," Alex pulled out his cell phone and swiped through some photos until he found what he was looking for. He turned the phone around so that Ashton and Rylie could see the photo of his dog.

"He's cute!" Rylie said. "I've never heard of that breed before. He has a very sweet face with those bushy eyebrows and fuzzy beard."

"He's very affectionate," Alex said. "He's the best dog I've ever had. So when do you guys want to get together at the dog park?"

"I'm free tomorrow," Rylie said.

"I don't have to go to work until tomorrow night, so I'm free during the day," Ashton said.

"I can get someone to cover my shift tomorrow. One of my bartenders has been asking for more hours," Alex said. "I'm in. What time?"

"10:00?" Rylie asked.

"Sounds good to me," Ashton said.

"Sounds good to me, too." Alex smiled. A curl of his dark brown hair flopped rakishly over his forehead. He turned to leave as a guy at the other end of the bar caught his eye.

"Dude, give me your cell phone before you take off so we can type our cell phone numbers into your contacts list," Ashton said.

Alex took his cell phone out of his pocket and handed it to Ashton before he hurried away. Ashton typed his cell phone number into Alex's phone and then handed it to Rylie. When they were done exchanging cell phone numbers, Rylie said she was going to call it a day.

"See you tomorrow, Ashton," she said. She left some cash to pay for her drink on the bar and smiled and waved to Alex as she left.

Chapter 4

The next morning, Rylie woke up to bright sun streaming through the French doors leading out to the deck off her bedroom. She bounced excitedly out of bed in anticipation of meeting Alex and Ashton at the dog park.

"Bella, we're going to have so much fun today!"

Bella jumped up out of her bed and came over to Rylie wagging her beautiful plumed tail. She panted happily.

Just before 10:00, Rylie bundled Bella into the back seat of her SUV and drove to the dog park. She snapped a leash on Bella and took her inside the park. She unclipped Bella's leash once they were safely inside the gate. Bella stayed by Rylie's side as she walked over to one of the benches on the far side of the park.

A big fluffy cream and tan colored dog bounded up to them. Rylie looked around to see who the dog's owner was and saw Alex walking quickly towards her. Her heart skipped a beat.

"Hi Alex!"

He smiled. "Hi Rylie!"

"Oh look. Ashton just got here," Rylie said. "Hi Ashton!"

Ashton's golden retriever bounded up to Rylie and Alex with Ashton close behind. He rushed up to Rylie wagging his tail with a big golden grin on his face. Bella quickly joined the fray. Rylie bent down to pet the excited dogs.

"It's a big doggie love fest!" Rylie said. "I brought a soft rubber frisbee for the dogs to play with. Do Quinn and Amando like to play frisbee?"

"Quinn's a pro," Ashton said.

"Amando's not a pro, but he likes to try," Alex said. "I don't think he's played with a frisbee very often. I usually throw a ball for him."

"I'll take the dogs out in the middle of the field with the frisbee," Ashton said.

"I always throw it just above Bella's head so she doesn't leap up into the air and come down and hurt herself," Rylie said.

"Okay. No problem. I can do that," Ashton said. He held the frisbee up out of the reach of the bouncing dogs as he headed to the middle of the field.

Rylie sat down on the bench. Alex sat down next to her. Rylie was intensely aware of his nearness. He was wearing a very intriguing masculine cologne with notes of citrus, herbs, and leather. She looked at the dogs playing with Ashton in the middle of the park.

"Oh, look! Quinn got there first! He is a pro," Rylie said. Bella and Amando were bouncing around Quinn excitedly.

"I wonder if Bella and Amando will have a chance," Alex said.

They watched Ashton throw the frisbee again. All three dogs tore after it. Amando was a big, strong dog, and now that he knew how the game was played, he outpaced the other two dogs and plucked the frisbee out of the air first. He chewed on the frisbee a few times to celebrate. Then he dropped it. Bella promptly picked it up and ran off.

Rylie and Alex laughed at the dogs' antics.

"You'll have to go get the frisbee from Bella, Ashton!" Rylie yelled. "She doesn't ever bring it back."

Ashton grinned and went to retrieve the frisbee from Bella. Rylie turned to Alex. "So how long have you lived in St. Helena?"

"We moved here when I was fourteen. My father opened Il Capriccio about six months after we moved here. Ashton was a year ahead of me in school, but he's been coming into the bar ever since my father opened it, so we've been friends for a long time."

"Did your mother move here with you?" Rylie asked.

"Yes, but she was killed in a car accident a couple years later. I still miss her," Alex said.

"I'm so sorry, Alex. And now you've lost your father too. I wish I'd had the opportunity to get to know him before he died. What was he like?" Rylie said.

"My father was very outgoing and fun to be around. He loved to tell stories. He had the perfect personality to bartend at an Italian bar. But he had a quick temper too. He didn't put up with anyone getting out of line at the bar. I'm sure he must have made some enemies over time," Alex said.

"Do you know who any of those enemies might be? Are we talking serious enemies - like people that you think might be capable of committing a crime - or just people who didn't like him?" Rylie asked.

Alex leaned forward with his elbows on his thighs as he stared out across the dog park. He clenched and unclenched his hands a couple of times.

"There's this one dude that's real trouble. Would he be capable of murder? I don't know. But I do think he's dangerous, and I know he had it out for my father," he said finally.

"Oh, Alex! Did you tell Detective Michelson about him?"

"No. I was so upset when I found my father dead on the floor in his house. It was horrible. I wasn't thinking clearly at the time."

"Detective Michelson hasn't been back to talk to you again since then?" Rylie asked.

"He called me the day before yesterday and told me that the Medical Examiner said that my father died from acute liver failure and kidney damage. He said that it looks like the cause of death was some kind of toxin ingestion. Since my dad called in sick the day after he ate at Vinterre, he said he was going to get a warrant to search the restaurant to look for any kind of toxin that my dad might have ingested during the Chamber of Commerce awards dinner. I know they were searching Vinterre yesterday. I heard some of the people that came into the bar yesterday talking about it," Alex said.

"I know Lucien. He comes in here for a drink after work from time to time," he continued. "He seems like a nice guy. He's always gotten along well with everyone at the bar, including my father. I think my father may have done some kind of business with him, but I don't know all the details. I don't believe Lucien killed my father. If someone poisoned my father's food at Vinterre, it had to be someone else."

Rylie was quiet for a moment. "I'm glad you feel that way, Alex. Lucien's wife, Sophie, is my best friend. She's beside herself right now because the police were searching Vinterre yesterday. She's afraid that the police are going to arrest Lucien for your father's murder so they can get this case wrapped up quickly. I know it's irrational, but she's really freaking out right now."

Alex reached over and took her hand and clasped it between his. His hands were warm and strong. "I'm so sorry, Rylie. This whole thing is such a mess."

Rylie startled as Ashton suddenly appeared in front of them. Alex quickly dropped her hand.

Rylie briefly looked down at the ground and clasped her hands together. They suddenly felt cold without the warmth of Alex's hands.

All three dogs were smiling.

"Hi, Bella! Did you have a good time with your new friends?" Rylie stroked Bella's head. Bella wagged her tail. Quinn nudged Rylie to get some loving too. Rylie chuckled and petted him. Then Amando pushed his way in. Rylie scratched Amando gently around his ears. She looked up and smiled at Ashton.

"I'm glad they all get along so well with each other. We'll have to do this again," Rylie said.

"Definitely," Ashton said. "I had as much fun as they did. Hey, do you guys want to drop our dogs off at our houses and meet for lunch somewhere? We could go to the Bakery Café at the Culinary Institute of America. They have really good food made by their students, and they're reasonably priced."

"Sounds good to me," Rylie said.

"I'm in," Alex said.

They decided to each take their own cars and meet at the café. Rylie left Bella comfortably settled in her rental house and then drove about a mile north of town to the Culinary Institute of America at Greystone. The massively long, three-story gray stone building set on the top of a hill dominated the landscape. She pulled into their driveway and found parking. Then she went inside to find the Bakery Café.

She found Alex and Ashton waiting for her just outside the entrance to the café. "Hi guys. This is fabulous! I want to explore this place a little after lunch."

"Have you ever been here before?" Alex asked.

"Once. A long time ago. But I've never eaten here," Rylie replied.

"They have an upscale restaurant called the Gatehouse that serves three and four course prix fixe meals. But the café is great for a casual lunch," Ashton said.

They went inside and found a table to sit down and peruse their menus.

"I'm going to have the four-cheese grilled cheese sandwich," Rylie said. "That sounds really good. And I'll try a glass of the Greystone Cellars Chardonnay."

"Do you know what you want, Ashton?" Alex said. "I'm buying. If you tell me what you want, I'll go up and order for all of us."

"I'm going to have the Winemaker's Cheese and Charcuterie Platter," Ashton said. "And a Lagunitas IPA."

"Great. I'll go up and order for us," Alex said. He went over to the counter and stood in line.

"So do you and Alex get together to do things very often?" Rylie asked.

"Not really. I've known him since he was fifteen years old when his father opened Il Capriccio. I've been hanging out at Il Capriccio ever since they opened even though I was only sixteen at the time. His father had no problem with children in the bar. But other than talking to each other at the bar, we haven't really spent much time together," Ashton replied. "I consider him a friend, but we're not super close."

Alex came back to the table and put the stand with their number on it on the middle of the table. A guy showed up a few minutes later with their drinks.

Rylie took a sip of her wine. "Oh, this is a nice chardonnay. I've never had their wine before."

"Rylie, I remember you told me when we met at Beringer Vineyards that you're only here for a month or so while you fill in for a local veterinarian that needs time off to recuperate from a surgery. Where are you from?" Ashton asked.

"I live in the East Bay in Brentwood. It's just over an hour and a half from here," Rylie said.

"How do you know Lucien and his wife?" Ashton asked.

"I've been best friends with Sophie since we were in college together. Lucien was one year ahead of us in college," Rylie replied.

"Lucien's a great guy," Ashton said. "I feel really bad that he's getting dragged into Alex's dad's murder investigation. I heard that the police found a small packet with a brown powdered substance in it on the floor in back of a trash can in Vinterre. They sent it to the lab for analysis."

"What?" Alex nearly choked on his wine. "Why didn't Detective Michelson call me to tell me that? How did you find out about it?"

"I hear things at work," Ashton said. "Maybe he's waiting to get the results from the lab before he bothers you with it. He might feel like you have enough on your plate right now just dealing with your father's death, planning your father's funeral, and taking up the slack at the bar."

"I don't need to be treated with kid gloves." Alex's jaw clenched. He gripped his wine glass so hard that Rylie was afraid it might shatter. She put her hand on top of Alex's free hand on the table. She watched as he tried to compose himself.

"It could also be that Detective Michelson has been so busy that he just hasn't gotten around to calling you yet," Ashton said. "They just found it yesterday when they searched Vinterre. You could always call him to find out more."

Alex put his head down and concentrated on eating his meal. Rylie ate her grilled cheese sandwich and sipped her wine.

"What time do you have to go to work today, Ashton?" Rylie asked.

"5:00. I'm going to have to go home right after lunch. I have some stuff to do before I go to work tonight," Ashton said.

Rylie turned to Alex. "Do you want to stay here with me after lunch and explore a little bit?"

Alex smiled at her in a way that looked almost grateful. "Sounds good to me."

They finished their lunches and said goodbye to Ashton.

"Thanks for lunch, Alex. See you around, Rylie," Ashton said.

After Ashton left, a guy walked up to their table with a tray of beautifully decorated chocolates in an assortment of shapes including some intricately designed little green turtles. "Would you like to try a sample of our homemade chocolates?"

"Oh, yes! Those look delicious! Can we buy these here to take home?" Rylie asked. She selected a chocolate in the shape of a pyramid with a ruby red top.

"Of course. You can look through our selection of chocolates in the display case over there and pick out whatever you want. Someone will make up a box for you to take home," the guy said.

Alex chose a round chocolate with green and gold swirls on top. "Yum. These are so good."

"Mine is delicious! Thank you," Rylie said. She turned to Alex. "I'm going to go pick out some chocolates to buy to take home. Do you want some?"

"Definitely," Alex said.

They each picked out an assortment of chocolates and bought a box to take home. Then they wandered over to the Spice Islands Marketplace and browsed through the cookware, kitchen tools, spices, and cookbooks. Rylie bought some black truffle salt from Italy.

"Have you ever had truffle fries, Alex?" she asked.

"I can't remember ever having them," he replied.

"They're delicious. I had them once in a restaurant in Guerneville when I was on vacation there. I asked them how they flavored their fries and they told me they use truffle salt. I don't ever make french fries at home, but I might be able to find something that I can use truffle salt for."

"Have you seen the corkscrew collection here?" Alex asked.

"A long time ago. I wouldn't mind seeing it again."

They went to look at the hundreds of corkscrews on display in glass cases.

"Oh, look at the dachshund with the corkscrew tail. That's so cute!" Rylie said.

"Yeah, the animal ones are the best," Alex said.

When they got to the end of the display, Alex grabbed her hand and said, "Let's get out of here. I know somewhere we can go for a nice walk through the redwoods along a creek. It's only five minutes from here. It's called the Redwood Trail, and it's at Bothe-Napa Valley State Park."

"That sounds great," Rylie said.

"Why don't you come with me in my car?" Alex said. "I can drop you off back here later to pick up your SUV."

"Okay."

Alex walked up to a navy-blue sports sedan and unlocked the doors. Rylie slid into the comfortable leather passenger seat.

"This is a cool car! What is it?" she asked.

"It's an Italian sports car called an Alfa Romeo Giulia," Alex replied. "Here, give me your box of chocolates. I have a cooler in the trunk that I can put our chocolates in. It doesn't have any ice in it right now, but at least our chocolates will be in an insulated container so they don't melt. And I'll try to find a shady place to park."

Alex put the chocolates in the trunk. He smiled as he got back in the car and drove out the driveway. "There. Now our chocolates are safe."

"Thank you. I love your car. Italy makes the best things. Cool sports cars, awesome food, designer fashions. I've been to Florence and Venice once, but I'd like to go back for an extended vacation. There are so many places that I would love to see in Italy," Rylie said.

"I would love to go back to Italy too. I still have a lot of family there."

"What part of Italy are you from?" Rylie asked.

"I'm from Montepulciano. It's in the southern part of Tuscany. We're famous for our Vino Nobile di Montepulciano wine. It's one of the best wines of Italy. And we're also known for our pici pasta."

"What's pici pasta?"

"Pici is a thick, hand-rolled pasta, like fat spaghetti. I'll make it for you sometime," Alex said. "You haven't lived until you've had Pici all'aglione. It's a traditional Italian recipe for pici with a garlic tomato sauce."

"That sounds wonderful. I love homemade pasta," Rylie said. "Can you get Vino Nobile di Montepulciano in the United States? I've never heard of it."

"Yes. I've seen it for sale here. But I have cases of it shipped to me from Italy. I have it by the glass at Il Capriccio if you want to try it."

"Definitely."

A few minutes later, Alex pulled into Bothe-Napa Valley State Park and parked the car.

"Ready for an adventure?" he asked.

Chapter 5

Alex pulled into a shady parking spot near the trailhead for the Redwood Trail. He went in his trunk and got out some bottled waters, put them in a small backpack, and hefted the backpack onto his shoulders.

"Wow, you really come prepared," Rylie said.

Alex grinned. "You wouldn't believe all the stuff I have in my trunk. It's like Mary Poppins' bag. You can pull almost anything out of it."

Rylie smiled. "Okay, then. I'll have to see if I can think of something to ask you for that you can't produce from your magical trunk."

They set off along the dirt hiking trail that ran along a creek through a redwood forest. Rylie inhaled the clean fresh air.

"The redwoods are so beautiful," she said.

"Yes. I love it here. It's a great place to clear your head," Alex replied. "I know a spot further up the trail where there are some boulders that we can sit on by Ritchey Creek to just relax and enjoy the beauty and peacefulness here."

They walked in comfortable silence for a while. Then Alex stepped off the well-worn trail onto a tiny, almost invisible foot trail through the woods. Rylie followed him. He turned back to her and pointed to a plant by the side of the trail.

"Watch out for poison oak," he said. "See the three shiny leaflets with scalloped edges? They're reddish in February and March and then they turn green in the summer. At this time of year, they turn yellow and red. Anything you see that looks like this, make sure you stay well away from it. Otherwise, you'll be suffering later."

"Okay. Thanks for the warning. I'll be careful," Rylie said.

They picked their way through the forest on the foot trail. Rylie was on the lookout for anything that looked like poison oak. She stayed far away from anything that looked suspicious.

"We can cross the creek here," Alex said.

He started carefully working his way across the creek balancing on some large rocks that protruded above the water. She watched Alex's progress. He seemed to be doing fine. She took a deep breath and started cautiously stepping from rock to rock across the creek.

Alex watched her from the other side of the creek.

"Doing okay?" he asked.

Rylie quickly made her way over the last couple of rocks.

"Yep. Fine," she said.

Alex led the way to some large boulders by the creek. "Want a lift?"

He put his strong hands around her waist and lifted her up onto the top of a boulder as if she were light as a feather. Then he scrambled up next to her.

"This is such a wonderful spot," Rylie said. "Do you come here often?"

"Not as often as I'd like," Alex said. "But I've been coming here since I was a teenager. I've always used it as my place to go when I needed some time alone. You're the first person I've ever brought here."

"Wow. Well thank you for bringing me here," Rylie said. "I can see why this is a very special place to you."

Alex suddenly looked serious. "So I assume that since you came to St. Helena alone that you're single?"

She gave him a small smile. "Yes, I am. I had a bad breakup with a guy about a year ago. I haven't been in a relationship since then. How about you?"

"I'm single too. I haven't been in a relationship for about two years now. I had a long-term relationship before that. We were together for three years. I thought she was "the one," but it didn't turn out that way."

"Could I ask what happened?"

"We just didn't want the same things out of life. I want to have children and a family. She didn't want that. She was very focused on her career. That was the most important thing to her. I thought she might change her mind and decide she wanted to have kids as our relationship grew, but she never did. I learned the hard way that you can't change people. You either have to accept them as they are or, if you can't, then move on," Alex said.

Rylie saw the sadness in Alex's eyes. "Are you still in love with her?"

"No. Looking back on it, I don't know if I ever really was in love with her. I think I was more in love with the idea of having a family, and I thought I could make her fit into my vision of the future. I haven't even thought about her for some time. I moved on a long time ago," Alex said.

He quietly watched the creek flow by for a few minutes, then he looked up at her. "Do you want to have kids someday?"

"Definitely. I think we share the same dream of having kids and a family. I just haven't found the right person to do that with yet. I haven't really even been trying to find someone since I broke up with Dylan. It was a painful breakup, and I guess I haven't been willing to put myself out there again. But I think I'm ready now. It doesn't hurt to think about him anymore. It just makes me mad at myself for wasting so much time on him," Rylie said.

She suddenly felt the sting of tears in her eyes. She tried to compose her features.

Alex noticed her moist eyes. "Do you miss him?"

"No, not at all," she replied. She quickly wiped the tears from her eyes. "I'm sorry. The reason I'm feeling emotional right now has nothing to do with my ex. It's a personal thing. I'm just not ready to talk about it right now."

"I understand. I'm here if you ever feel like you want to talk." Alex reached over and wrapped his warm hand around hers. It felt good.

They watched a scrub jay bouncing around on the ground looking for food.

"I know this is a hard time for you because of your dad's death. Is there anything I can do to help?"

"I think I have everything under control. Morrison Funeral Chapel will be taking care of all of the arrangements once the autopsy is finished and the Medical Examiner releases my dad's body. No one has told me yet when that's going to happen," Alex replied. His hand tensed on hers.

They sat quietly for a few minutes. "You told me this morning that you know a guy that you think is dangerous that had a problem with your dad. I think it's important that we tell Detective Michelson anything that we know, or that we find out about, that might help him with his investigation. The sooner Detective Michelson finds out who murdered your father, the sooner that person can be brought to justice. Who is that guy you told me about this morning, and why do you think he had it out for your dad?"

"His name is Sean Kavanaugh. He's a carpenter. He used to work for a construction company around here. He's a real piece of work. He was at Il Capriccio one night about six months ago. He got drunk and was making unwanted advances towards a woman who was sitting at the bar. The woman kept trying to get him to stop, but he wouldn't. My dad told him to get his hands off her or he was going to call the police. Sean got up in my dad's face and that was it. My dad called the police and Sean was forcibly removed from the bar a short time later. I think he may have spent the night in jail."

"I found out afterwards that when his boss heard about it, he fired Sean. Word gets around. No one wants to employ someone that's a liability like that. As far as I know, Sean's been unemployed ever since then. And I heard from several people that he was badmouthing my dad around town before my dad died."

"Why do you think he's dangerous?"

"There's just something about him. He's a loose cannon. He used to come to Il Capriccio fairly regularly before my dad had him forcibly removed that night. I know he has a bad temper. I've seen him when I was sure he was going to haul off and punch someone at the bar, but he managed to keep himself in check. Just barely," Alex replied.

"Promise me you'll call Detective Michelson and tell him about Sean," Rylie said.

"Oh, I will. I'll call him later today."

"Come to think of it, I heard something the other day that might be important to Detective Michelson's investigation when I was having lunch with a woman that I met at the

Chamber awards Dinner and some of her friends. You might know her. Patricia Davenport?"

"I don't think I've met her," Alex said.

"Patricia told me she gets together to do fun things with a group of local women once a week on Thursdays. She invited me along for their lunch on the Napa Valley Wine Train this past Thursday. While we were eating lunch in the dining car, a young couple named Derek and Stefanie Firth stopped at our table. They knew the woman that Patricia and I were sitting with, Liza Cresswell. Derek works in the tech industry in San Francisco, but they come to the Napa Valley for wine tasting several times a year. I guess they visit Liza and her husband at their winery when they're in the area."

"Oh, I know the Cresswells. Cresswell Wines is a nice winery. They make good wine," Alex said.

"Anyway, Derek told Liza that the last time they were in St. Helena about five months ago that Stefanie slipped in a puddle of water and fell down in the ladies' room at Il Capriccio. She was pregnant at the time and ended up having a miscarriage. Derek said they've been trying to get her pregnant again ever since, but they haven't been able to even though the doctor told Stefanie that she was fine and should be able to."

"I remember hearing about that woman falling in the restroom. It happened on a night that I was off. But the staff were talking about it the next day. I don't think any of them knew that she was pregnant though. Or that she had a miscarriage," Alex said.

"They probably could have filed a lawsuit against us," he continued. "Maybe they still will. Let's head back now. I'll call Detective Michelson as soon as we get back to the parking lot. I'll tell him that both you and I have some things we need to tell him that could be pertinent to his investigation and find out what he wants to do."

"Okay."

Rylie hopped down off the boulder. Alex handed her a bottled water and got one out for himself. They stood drinking their water for a few minutes, then headed back across the creek to the trail. Rylie kept her eye on the plants around them as they walked, trying to be careful not to brush up against any poison oak.

When they got back to the parking lot, Alex called Detective Michelson and told him that both he and Rylie needed to talk to him.

"He says we can meet him at the police department on Main Street in ten minutes," Alex said.

They got in Alex's Alfa Romeo and drove to the police department in St. Helena. Alex pulled into the parking lot of the sprawling single story red brick building and parked. Alex held the door open for her as they went inside.

"We're here to see Detective Michelson," Alex said to the middle-aged woman at the reception desk. "He's expecting us."

"Down that hall." The woman tilted her head slightly to her right. "Last door on your left."

"No warm fuzzies from that one," Rylie muttered under her breath as she and Alex walked down the hall. Alex smiled and put his arm around her shoulder. He gave her a small squeeze. Rylie smiled up at him.

The door was open to Detective Michelson's office, so they stepped inside. A large desk cluttered with paperwork took up most of the space in the small room. Detective Michelson got up from his desk and motioned for them to sit in the two uncomfortable-looking wood chairs in front of his desk.

"Rylie! For a newcomer in town, you sure do manage to get around," Detective Michelson remarked.

Rylie matched his gaze while she tried to figure out if he was accusing her of something or was just trying to be funny.

Good poker face.

"I met Alex at Il Capriccio yesterday," Rylie replied. "He and I and Ashton Devereux took our dogs to the dog park this morning so that they could play together. One thing led to another."

"I see," Detective Michelson said. "So what can I do for you two? You said you have some information for me that could be relevant to Alex's father's murder investigation?"

"There's a guy named Sean Kavanaugh. You may know him. My father had the police forcibly remove him from Il Capriccio one night about six months ago because he was drunk and making unwanted advances on a woman at the bar," Alex said.

"I remember something about that," Detective Michelson replied.

"I found out after that incident that when his boss heard about it, he fired Sean. I think Sean's been unemployed ever since then. And he blames my dad. Several people have told me that he's been badmouthing my dad since he got fired."

"Okay. I guess that could give him motive," Detective Michelson said. He wrote something down on a piece of paper in front of him.

"Alex thinks he's dangerous," Rylie said.

Detective Michelson raised his eyebrows as he looked at Alex.

"It's just that I know that he has a bad temper," Alex said. "I've seen him get really angry at Il Capriccio. There were times when I thought it was going to get out of control. But he managed to keep himself in check enough that I never had to intercede."

"Okay, Alex. I'll check into it. Thanks for the tip," Detective Michelson said. "Did you have something to tell me too, Rylie?"

"I met a woman named Patricia Davenport and her husband at the Chamber awards dinner at Vinterre. Then I ran into her and her husband a few days later at the dog park. Patricia invited me to join her and some of her friends for lunch on the Napa Valley Wine Train this past Thursday. While we were eating lunch, a young couple named Derek and Stefanie Firth stopped at our table to talk to the woman that Patricia and I were sitting with, Liza Cresswell. Derek and Stefanie live in San Francisco, but they come to the Napa Valley for wine tasting several times a year and visit Liza and her husband at their winery when they're in town."

"I'm familiar with Cresswell Wines," Detective Michelson said.

"I think that Derek and Stefanie may blame the management at Il Capriccio for the loss of their child. It was going to be their firstborn. Derek told Liza that the last time they were in St. Helena about five months ago that Stefanie slipped in a puddle of water in the ladies' room at Il Capriccio. The fall caused her to have a miscarriage. They've been trying to get pregnant again ever since then, but they haven't been able to. They both seemed pretty upset about it."

Detective Michelson held her gaze for what seemed like forever. Finally, he looked down at the paper on his desk and jotted down some notes. Rylie realized that she had been holding her breath. She slowly released her breath and concentrated on trying to relax the muscles in her shoulders and arms.

"Thank you for bringing this to my attention," Detective Michelson said.

"My friend Ashton Devereux is an EMT around here. He told me that the police found a small packet with a brown powdered substance in it on the floor in back of a trash can in Vinterre. I was kind of upset to hear about it secondhand instead of from you," Alex said.

"I'm sorry, Alex. I've been up to my eyeballs in this investigation as well as some other things that I have to deal with right now. I just hadn't gotten around to calling you yet. I'll make it a point to be better about keeping you informed going forward."

Alex clenched his fists in his lap. "So is there anything else that I need to know? Ashton told me the police sent the packet to the lab for analysis. When will you have the results?"

"I'm not sure when we'll get their report. It depends on how many tests they have to run to figure out what the powdered substance is and how backlogged they are. Hopefully I'll get it sooner rather than later," Detective Michelson said. "I do know several people over at the lab. I think I'm going to call in a favor to see if I can get that report faster. But you didn't hear that from me."

"That would be great," Alex said.

"They did find a partial fingerprint on the packet that had the powder in it," Detective Michelson said. "They're also analyzing that. I'll let you know as soon as I know anything more."

"Thank you, Detective," Alex said. He stood to leave. Rylie got out of her chair and stood next to Alex.

"Yes, thank you for taking the time to see us on such short notice," Rylie said. "I hope we've been able to be of some help to you in your investigation."

"If either of you learn of anything else that you think might be relevant to the investigation, please let me know," Detective Michelson said.

"We will," Alex said.

Rylie and Alex went back outside and got in Alex's car.

"Thank you for that," Alex said. "I feel a sense of relief knowing that some progress is being made in my father's murder investigation. I've been feeling kind of helpless and depressed about it."

"That's certainly understandable," Rylie said. "I can't even imagine how you're managing to continue running the bar and carrying on with your life so well after first finding your father dead in his home and then finding out that he was murdered."

"I think some of it has been that I can pretty much run the bar on autopilot. I've been working at Il Capriccio since I was a teenager. I've learned over the years to hide whatever I might be feeling while I'm working. I have to be able to give the customers what they want and keep them happy."

Alex drove back to the Culinary Institute of America so that Rylie could get her SUV. He parked his car near hers and popped open the trunk. He got Rylie's chocolates from his cooler and handed them to her.

"Yum. I can't wait to have some of these." Rylie smiled up at Alex. "Thank you for today, Alex. Even though we had to spend some of it at the police department, we still had a lot of fun. It was a good day."

Alex pulled her into a bear hug. Rylie inhaled deeply of his masculine scent and reveled in his warmth. Then he released her and quickly turned away.

"Bye, Rylie." He smiled at her before he closed his car door and drove away. Rylie watched him pull out of the driveway, then got in her SUV and headed home.

Bella greeted her enthusiastically at the door to her rental house.

"Hi, Bella! Were you a good girl for me while I was gone?" She got Bella a bacon, egg, and cheese dog biscuit. Bella made quick work of it. Her cell phone rang. She saw it was Sophie and picked up.

"Hi Sophie! What's up?"

"I talked to Lucien about the three of us spending the day together doing something fun tomorrow. I convinced him to go to the Solage Resort and Spa in Calistoga with us. I've never been there, but I've wanted to go there for a long time. Lucien's excited to eat lunch at their Michelin-rated restaurant, Solbar. He said lunch is his treat. I thought we could get spa treatments in the morning, then have lunch at Solbar. What do you think?" Sophie said.

"That sounds awesome. I think all three of us could definitely benefit from a spa day. I assume we'll have to call to make reservations for our spa treatments, right? I'll check out their website and pick out what I want to do and call you back, okay?"

"Sounds good."

Rylie immediately booted up her laptop and sat down at the desk to check out the Spa Solage webpage. Bella laid down on the floor next to her.

"Bella, this looks so nice! I'm excited!" Bella looked up at her and flopped her tail up and down a couple of times. She called Sophie back.

"Sophie, this looks so wonderful. I can't wait. Their website says that we should get there thirty minutes prior to our treatments for pre-treatment hydrotherapy in their geothermal pools. It says they have five different pools at different temperatures, an infrared sauna, and a eucalyptus steam room. I love the smell of eucalyptus. It doesn't say that they have separate saunas and steam rooms for men and women, so I assume they're co-ed. It does say that bathing suits are required."

"I was looking at that too. I saw that they have recommended bathhouse rituals depending on your goals. I thought the Vitality and Body Performance Circuit looked good. With that one, you start in the infrared sauna, then take a dip in the Vitality Cold Plunge Pool, then sit in the Eucalyptus steam room, then relax in the Restorative Mineral Jetted Pool," Sophie said.

"Let's do it!" Rylie said. "Except let's plan to get there an hour before our treatments so we don't run out of time. I'm going to get the 60-minute Organic Vibrancy Facial with the addition of the Neck, Back, and Shoulder Massage."

"I have been going back and forth with whether I wanted to get a facial or a massage. That sounds like a good compromise. I'll do that too," Sophie said. "I'll call to make reservations for our spa treatments and for lunch. Why don't you meet us here at our house at about 9:00 tomorrow and then we'll drive over there together in Lucien's SUV?"

"Sounds good. See you tomorrow."

Chapter 6

The sun was shining brightly when Rylie got up the next morning. It was typical October weather for the area. Brisk by Rylie's California girl standards with the temperature in the mid-60s. She wrapped her robe tighter around herself as she stood out on the deck outside her bedroom and looked out over the vineyard across the road. Bella stood next to her surveying the yard.

A squirrel leaped onto a tree branch at eye level with the deck. Bella jumped in surprise and started barking. The squirrel twitched his tail but stood his ground. Bella and the squirrel had a stare down. Eventually the squirrel bounded off the branch and disappeared into the trees. Bella kept watching for the squirrel to reappear.

"Come on, Bella. Let's go outside."

Rylie walked around the yard while Bella did her business. When they went back inside, Rylie got some coffee going and got Bella her breakfast. She toasted an English muffin and sat down at the kitchen table to enjoy her meal. She thought about the day she had planned with Sophie and Lucien. Then it occurred to her that she hadn't packed a bathing suit. She called Sophie.

"Hi, Sophie. It just occurred to me that I didn't pack a bathing suit. I never imagined needing one in October. Do you have one I could borrow?" Rylie said.

"I'm sure I do. I'll find something and pack it in my bag for you. See you soon," Sophie said.

Rylie left her house a little while later. Bella was lying down in front of the French doors in the bedroom keeping watch for the squirrel.

"Bye, Bella! You be a good girl today!"

Rylie drove to Sophie and Lucien's house and knocked on their front door.

"Hi, Rylie! We're all ready to go." Sophie stepped outside with a large tote over one arm. "I found a one-piece bathing suit for you. It's kind of cute. I think you'll like it."

"Hi, Rylie," Lucien said. "Ready for a relaxing spa day?"

"Can't wait."

It was about a fifteen-minute drive to the Solage Resort and Spa. Lucien parked and they walked over to the spa to get changed into bathing suits. A staff member showed them a map of the resort so they would be able to find the infrared sauna, the eucalyptus steam room, and the hydrotherapy pools.

"Are you going to do the Vitality and Body Performance bathhouse ritual too, Lucien? Or was there another ritual that you wanted to do?" Rylie asked.

"I'm down for whatever you two want to do."

"Okay. Let's go find the infrared sauna then and get started," Rylie said.

They found the sauna quickly and got comfortable inside.

"I've never been in an infrared sauna before," Rylie said. "I'd never even heard of it until I saw it on their website. Their website says that infrared targets the body directly with heat waves without warming the surrounding air. I'm used to hot saunas."

"Yes, this is definitely different. I think it's more comfortable than the traditional hot saunas," Sophie said. She leaned back and closed her eyes. Rylie did the same.

When the heat started to get to them, they headed to the Cold Plunge Pool.

"Might as well just go for it!" Rylie said. She took a deep breath and prepared herself for the shock of the cold water. She did a shallow dive out into the pool. After the initial shock, the cold water felt refreshing. She swam to the other side of the pool and back. Sophie and Lucien were both swimming when she stepped out and wrapped a towel around her torso.

After she warmed up enough to remove her towel, she laid the towel out on a chaise lounge and stretched out comfortably on it while she waited for Sophie and Lucien to join her.

Sophie got out of the pool first and wrapped herself in a towel. Lucien was close behind her.

"Wow, that was intense at first," Lucien said. "Then it felt good. Every single cell in my body is wide awake now."

Rylie smiled. "Now for the Eucalyptus Steam Room!"

They walked over to the Steam Room and stepped inside.

"Oh my goodness, the eucalyptus smell is really strong," Rylie said. "Their website said to do slow, deep breathing while you're in the steam room."

She put a towel down on the wooden bench and laid down on it. Sophie and Lucien did the same. She concentrated on relaxing and taking slow, deep breaths.

A while later, Lucien said, "I think I'm well done now. How about you two?"

Rylie opened her eyes.

"I'm ready to go if you are, Rylie," Sophie said.

"I'm ready," Rylie said. "Now to the Restorative Mineral Jetted Pool."

They dropped off their towels on the way and picked up some fresh ones. They sat and relaxed in the jetted pool for a while, then headed to the locker rooms to shower before their spa treatments.

Rylie and Sophie went to get their 60-minute Organic Vibrancy facials followed by neck, back, and shoulder massages. Lucien went to get a Shiatsu Swedish massage. Afterwards, they met in front of the women's locker room.

"That was amazing. I feel great. I'll meet you two in front of Solbar restaurant as soon as you're dressed," Lucien said. He headed off to the men's locker room.

In the women's locker room, Rylie inspected her face in a mirror. "That facial was incredible. So relaxing. The skin on my face feels so soft. And it looks brighter and healthier." She flexed her shoulders around. "And my neck and shoulders haven't been this relaxed in as long as I can remember."

"I know. It was awesome. We'll have to make it a point to come here more often," Sophie said.

After a refreshing shower, Rylie got dressed. She had brought a brown and white patterned fit-and-flare dress that she paired with a black belt and black ankle-length high-heeled boots. She blew dry her hair and brushed it into place. She saw Sophie looking at herself in the mirror.

"That's a cute dress," she said to Sophie.

"Thanks. Yours is cute, too. Where did you get it?"

"Banana Republic," Rylie said. "I'm starting to get hungry. Are you hungry yet?"

"Yes. I'm excited to eat at a Michelin-rated restaurant."

They joined Lucien in front of the restaurant and were quickly escorted inside by the hostess. The restaurant felt light and airy with vaulted ceilings and large windows that let in lots of natural light. Large, round, open mesh metal chandeliers with scattered twinkle lights hung from the vaulted ceiling. Many of the dark wood tables had curved, gray-blue upholstered sofas in addition to upholstered chairs. A large fireplace at one end of the room crackled with a cheerful fire. The hostess seated them next to a large window. Rylie and Sophie shared the long sofa, and Lucien sat on one of the upholstered chairs.

Lucien's face lit up as he opened the menu. "I'm so excited to finally eat here. We're so fortunate to live near so many fabulous restaurants."

Rylie and Sophie shared a smile.

"I'm going to have the Warm Maine Lobster Roll with butter poached lobster and béarnaise sauce on a toasted brioche bun," Lucien said. "It comes with a butter lettuce side salad."

"That sounds delicious," Rylie said. "I'm going to have that, too."

"Make that three, then." Sophie smiled. "I can't resist. I haven't had lobster in a long time."

They placed their drink and lunch orders with the waitress. Their drinks were delivered to their table a few minutes later.

Sophie looked at Lucien as she sipped her glass of chardonnay. "I haven't seen you look so relaxed in a long time, honey."

"This was a great idea," Lucien said. "I think it was good for all of us."

"You've seemed so distant and distracted for months now, Lucien. What's going on?" Sophie said.

Lucien took a sip of his sauvignon blanc and stared out the window for a minute. Then he sighed as he looked back at Sophie. "There's just been a lot going on at the restaurant. PGE turning off the power for four days during the busy tourist season in August because of the wildfire north of Calistoga resulted in a huge loss of income for all the tourist-related businesses in St. Helena. I got behind on some bills. I'm still playing catch up. I've also had some staffing issues. Then there's this really weird stuff that's been going on for a couple months now."

Lucien took a deep breath and continued. "One day towards the end of August when I came to work early one morning, there was a dead bird on the ground right in front of the door. I didn't think anything of it. I thought maybe a cat left it there. Then the following week there was another dead bird on the ground in front of the door when I got to work. This time there was a note tied to a string around the bird's neck that said, "Change is coming to meet you.""

"What the?" Rylie said. "Change is coming to meet you! What's that supposed to mean?"

"I don't know. But I looked it up online, and a dead bird on your doorstep is symbolic. It's supposed to mean that change is coming to meet you and you must be willing to receive it."

Lucien took another sip of his wine. "Several weeks later, when I got to work early one morning, the door to the walk-in refrigerator was wide open. It had been left open all night. Fortunately, everything inside was still cold, and I didn't lose anything. My sous chef that closed the restaurant the night before said he was certain that he didn't leave the door open. I checked all the windows and doors, but I didn't see any sign of a break-in."

"Oh my goodness, Lucien," Sophie said. "Why haven't you told me any of this before?"

"I'm sorry, honey. I didn't want to worry you," Lucien said. "But you asked why I've been distracted recently, so I'm telling you now."

"Then last Tuesday," he continued, "on the day after the Chamber awards dinner, I was getting ready to start dinner prep. I pulled my chef's knife off the magnetic knife holder on the wall and the holder and all of the knives came crashing down. One of the knives almost pierced my hand. I checked the magnetic knife holder, and someone had loosened all the screws."

"It sounds like someone has a beef with you and is targeting you," Rylie said. "I think you should tell Detective Michelson about all this. And the next time something weird happens, I think you should call him right away."

"You're right, Rylie," Lucien said. "I'll call Detective Michelson this afternoon."

The waitress came by with their warm Maine lobster rolls and salads.

Rylie rolled her eyes to the ceiling. "Oh my goodness. This is delicious."

"So good," Sophie agreed.

"Maybe I'll have a special at Vinterre featuring lobster," Lucien said. "I'll have to think about that."

"That would be great, Lucien," Rylie said. "I'm sure it would be popular. If you decide to do that, please let me know so I can plan to eat at Vinterre while you're running the special."

"I will," Lucien said.

After they finished lunch, they drove back to Sophie and Lucien's house, and Rylie got her car.

"This was so much fun," she said. She hugged Sophie and Lucien. "I'm going home to get Bella and take her to the dog park. See you guys later."

She drove home to change and get Bella.

"Hi Bella! Pretty girl. Would you like a treat?"

Bella wagged her tail furiously in response. Rylie got her a dog biscuit. Then she headed for her bedroom to get changed into a shirt, pants, and comfortable shoes.

"Want to go to the dog park, Bella? Maybe you'll meet some new friends." Bella bounced up and down excitedly.

She packed Bella's frisbee, tennis ball, and her portable water bottle with flip-open water dish in a tote. She added some bottled water for herself.

"Let's go, Bella!"

She buckled Bella into her seatbelt in the back seat of her SUV and drove to Wappo Dog Park. Once inside the gate, she let Bella off her leash. Bella bounded away to check out the other dogs at the park. Rylie walked over to where a bunch of people were sitting and found a place on a bench.

She turned to the girl with long red hair sitting closest to her. "Hi! I'm Rylie Sunderland. That's my golden retriever that's bouncing around over there. Her name is Bella."

"Hi. I'm Cara Burke and this is my boyfriend, Brian McKinney. The black lab over there is ours. His name is Willie."

"He's cute," Rylie said. "He seems interested in Bella."

"He's a big flirt," Brian said.

Rylie smiled.

"I'm going to go throw the ball for Willie," Brian said. He walked out past the excited dogs with the ball in his hand. Willie sniffed the ball in Brian's hand and followed him closely. Bella and a couple other dogs joined in. Rylie watched as Brian threw the ball as far as he could. All the dogs went tearing after it. Willie managed to get to it first. The other dogs pranced around Willie.

"I've never seen you here before," Cara said. "Did you just move here? Or are you just visiting?"

"I'm staying in a rental house for at least a month. I'm a locum veterinarian. I fill in for other veterinarians that need time off. I'm filling in for Dr. Corbyn at Valley View Veterinary Hospital while he's recovering from a surgery he had to have."

"Oh, I know Dr. Corbyn. We take Willie to Valley View for his shots," Cara said. "How do you like it here?"

"I love it here," Rylie said. "I've been exploring the area on my days off. And my best friend and her husband live here. I'm so happy to have the chance to spend more time with her while I'm here. I live in the East Bay, so I don't get up here very often."

"I live in Berkeley during the week. I'm getting my PhD at UC Berkeley in microbiology with an emphasis on mycology. I drive up here on the weekends to see Brian," Cara said.

"That's an interesting field. I don't know much about mushrooms other than that I love crimini mushrooms for cooking. But I've seen all kinds of interesting, weird-shaped mushrooms at the farmers' markets. I've never been brave enough to try any of them though."

"You should come visit me at the farmers' market here in St. Helena on Friday. I operate the stand for Marvelous Mushrooms. They're a local mushroom farm. I can show you all kinds of different mushrooms and make recommendations as to which ones you might like to try based on the kind of cooking you do," Cara said. "The farmers' market in St. Helena only runs from May to October though. So if you're interested in visiting my stand, this Friday will be the last day you could come this season."

"That sounds fun," Rylie said. "I'll definitely come to your stand on Friday. I'm game to expand my horizons on different mushrooms that I can use in cooking. I love to cook. Especially now that the weather is getting cooler. I like to make beef bourguignon and other comfort foods in the fall and winter."

Brian walked up with a bunch of panting dogs following close behind. "Hey Cara. I think Willie's burned off his energy now. I need to get back. I have some stuff to do before work tomorrow."

Cara got up from the bench. "Okay. It was nice meeting you, Rylie. Maybe I'll see you on Friday at the farmers' market," Cara said.

"Definitely. I'll see you then," Rylie said. Bella came up to her and put her head on Rylie's lap. Rylie stroked Bella's golden fur.

"Are you all worn out, Bella? Let's go home. Okay?"

Rylie put a leash on Bella and walked back to her SUV. She put Bella in the back seat and drove home. When they got home, Bella walked over to her water dish and took a long drink before walking into the living room and flopping down on the floor. Rylie got herself a mineral water and took it out on the deck. Bella followed her outside. She sipped her mineral water and let her mind wander for a while. She decided she wanted to get out and socialize rather than spending the rest of the afternoon alone in her rental house. She got out her cell phone looked for someplace in St. Helena where she could go out for a drink.

"This looks cool," she said. Bella raised her head and looked at her.

"I think I'm going to go check out The Charter Oak restaurant in St. Helena, Bella. They have a really pretty outdoor courtyard with tables where I can have something to drink and sit and read a book."

She brought Bella inside and left her curled up in the living room as she headed for town.

The red brick entrance of The Charter Oak restaurant was flanked with life-sized white marble lions. Rylie asked to be seated at a table outside in the courtyard. The hostess escorted her to a charming little table under a tree by the edge of the red brick paved courtyard. Rylie noticed some small white yurts off to one side.

"What are the yurts for?" she asked.

"Those are for dining in. They're just for fun. Some people really like sitting in them to have their meals. They provide a little extra privacy. Do you want to sit in one?" the hostess asked.

"Not right now. I want to enjoy your beautiful patio this time around. But I would definitely like to do that sometime," Rylie said.

"They're really pretty at night," the hostess said. "The yurts are lit up inside with small white lights that run along the top of the walls. They're very cozy inside. And all the trees outside are strung with sparkly white lights, too."

"Oh, that does sound nice," Rylie said. "I'll have to think about who I could invite to join me to eat in a yurt one of these nights."

Despite the fact that it was between lunch and dinnertime, they were still doing a brisk business. The hostess handed her a menu.

"What can I get you to drink?" she asked.

"Do you have lemonade?"

"Of course. We make it fresh in house. I'll get you some." The hostess walked quickly away.

Rylie slowly scanned the people at the tables scattered around the courtyard. She noticed a woman with shoulder length dark brown hair working on her laptop not far from where she was sitting. The woman looked up and caught her eye.

"Rylie? Is that you?" the woman asked. "It's Kinsley Logan. We met when you joined our group for lunch on the Napa Valley Wine Train. Remember?" She grinned at Rylie.

"Of course I remember you, Kinsley! You're the mystery writer. Are you working on writing a book right now?" Rylie asked.

"Yes, I am. I don't really have regular days off. I have a three book contract with my publisher, and I've got to finish this book by the end of November," Kinsley said.

"Well don't let me interrupt you," Rylie said. "I just came here to read a book and relax."

"You're not interrupting," Kinsley said. "I've kind of hit a wall and nothing creative is coming out of my brain right now. I'd enjoy the company. Would you like to join me at my table?"

"Sure," Rylie said. "Let me wait until the hostess comes back with my lemonade so I can tell her. I don't want her to think that I stiffed her and left."

As soon as the hostess came back with her lemonade, Rylie went over to join Kinsley at her table.

"Are you working on a murder mystery now?" Rylie asked.

"Yep. Sometimes the words flow out of me for hours, and sometimes I can't seem to come up with anything at all to write about. That's when I look for inspiration. I'll search the internet for interesting places for my characters to go, or I'll read news articles about real life murders. I try to take regular breaks to allow my brain to rest and recharge, but I'm not very good about it."

"You seem like such an upbeat kind of person. I'm finding it hard to equate that with someone that writes about murders," Rylie said.

Kinsley threw back her head and laughed heartily.

"I think mystery writers are similar to medical professionals who work in the ER. Those people see all kinds of horrible things. They have to compartmentalize and keep an emotional distance in order to cope with what they have to deal with. That's why they have what we would call "dark humor." They can joke about things that most people would think are disgusting," Kinsley said. "My brother is an EMT, so I've heard some of his jokes about things he's seen on the job. Definitely dark humor."

"I belong to a couple of different groups of mystery writers," Kinsley continued. "We talk about killing off our characters like it's no big deal because we're emotionally distanced from the reality of it. The kind of mysteries that I write are called "traditional mysteries." They don't have any graphic violence or sex. The murders happen "off stage," as it were. Readers like to read traditional mysteries because they connect with the characters and become invested in their relationships. And they enjoy the challenge of solving the mysteries."

"Interesting," Rylie said. "So how do you kill off your characters with no graphic violence?"

Kinsley chuckled. "I kill characters off in my books in all kinds of ways without going into any gruesome details. I'm especially fond of using poisons. Especially plant poisons because they're so readily available. I've become quite an expert on poisons over the years. The people in my writers' groups call me Professor Poison. They ask me to give talks on poisons several times a year."

"I see. Remind me to keep a close eye on my drink when I'm around you," Rylie teased.

"Oh, you're safe. Don't worry." Kinsley grinned. "But I do grow poisonous plants in my backyard. For research purposes only, of course. I'd be happy to give you a tour of my garden and show you my poisonous plants sometime."

Rylie raised her eyebrows. Kinsley giggled.

"Hmmm. I'll have to think about that," Rylie said. "I'll let you know."

Rylie took a sip of her lemonade. "I'm sure you've been following the news about Lorenzo Marchetti's murder."

Kinsley's head jerked back slightly. "Of course. Everyone in town is talking about it. What a horrible thing."

"Have you heard anything about how he was murdered?" Rylie asked.

Kinsley dropped her gaze. "This is a small town. It's hard to keep secrets around here. I heard that they think he ingested some kind of toxin."

"That's what I heard too," Rylie said. "Did you hear any details about why they think that?"

"Yes. I heard that the autopsy showed that he died from liver failure and that there was also kidney damage."

"Do you know of any plant poisons or other toxins that can cause liver failure as well as kidney damage?"

"I have some ideas," Kinsley said. "But I don't know enough about it to be able to come to any firm conclusions. Hopefully they'll be able to figure it out soon. I feel so bad for Alex losing his father like that."

"Have the police ever asked you to consult on a case because of your knowledge of poisons?"

"No. We never have murders around here. This is an extremely rare case. And with all the high-tech tests that they can perform at forensics laboratories, they're in a much better position to determine what toxin might have killed someone than I am."

"I'm sure you're right," Rylie said. Her phone buzzed on the tabletop. She saw it was Sophie.

"I'm sorry. I have to take this." She walked away from all the people in the courtyard to a place where she could have some privacy.

"Rylie! You need to come back to my house right away. Detective Michelson just took Lucien in for questioning!" Sophie said.

Chapter 7

Rylie quickly walked back to Kinsley's table. "I'm sorry, Kinsley. Something's come up. I've got to go. I enjoyed talking with you."

"No problem, Rylie," Kinsley said. "I enjoyed talking with you, too. We'll have to get together again sometime."

Rylie hurried to her SUV and drove to Sophie's house as fast as she could. She opened Sophie's front door and went in without knocking.

"Sophie? Where are you?"

Sophie came rushing out of the back of the house with tears streaming down her face. "Oh, Rylie! This is so horrible! They took Lucien away in the back of a police car!"

"What's going on? Did they say why?"

"They didn't tell us anything. Detective Michelson just said that he needed Lucien to come downtown and answer some questions," Sophie said. "I'm freaking out. I just started going through Lucien's desk to see if I could find out what they might be questioning him about. Look what I found."

Sophie's hands were shaking as she handed Rylie a stack of papers. Rylie started looking through them. Her mouth went dry.

"Lucien apparently took out a second mortgage on Vinterre when he was renovating the building. I knew he borrowed money from the bank. But he never told me that he also borrowed money from Lorenzo Marchetti. A significant chunk of money. Why didn't he tell me about this?" Sophie's voice cracked. She sat down quickly on the edge of the nearest chair.

Rylie looked at the promissory note from Lucien to Lorenzo. She swallowed hard.

"It's not a crime to borrow money from someone, Sophie. Just because Lucien borrowed money from Lorenzo Marchetti doesn't mean that he killed him," Rylie said.

"Look at the next paper," Sophie said.

Rylie quickly read the next paper in the stack. It was a letter dated last month from Lorenzo Marchetti's attorney to Lucien's attorney demanding immediate payment for two months' overdue mortgage payments. Lucien hadn't made a payment since July.

The next paper in the stack was another letter from Lorenzo's attorney stating the Lucien was now three months' behind on his payments. Lorenzo's attorney threatened to foreclose on the loan if payment was not made in full within thirty days. The letter was dated the week before the Chamber awards dinner at Vinterre.

"Okay, this doesn't look good. But I'm sure that Lucien didn't kill Lorenzo Marchetti. It's just not something I can even imagine him doing," Rylie said.

"Me either," Sophie said. "But if the police know about this, then they're going to be all over him because this could be used to show that Lucien had motive to kill Lorenzo."

"But we don't even know why they're questioning Lucien yet," Rylie said. "Maybe they're questioning him about something else entirely. We won't know anything until he comes back."

"What we need to do right now is try to calm down and collect ourselves," Rylie continued. "Let's go sit in the living room. Why don't you turn on the gas fireplace? A nice fire is always relaxing. Let me get us something to drink. Would you like some tea? Wine? Something stronger?"

She put her arm around Sophie and guided her into the living room. Sophie went over to turn on the gas fireplace, then curled up in an upholstered chair nearby.

"I think some chardonnay would be nice. There's some chilled in the refrigerator," Sophie said.

"Okay. I'll go get it."

Rylie came back with two wineglasses of chardonnay a few minutes later. She handed a glass to Sophie and then got comfortable on the sofa. She stared at the flickering flames in the fireplace for a few minutes.

"I love your fireplace. I really like the long contemporary gas fireplaces," Rylie said.

"Thanks, Rylie," Sophie murmured absently.

"Did you go through everything in Lucien's office to make sure you found anything that could possibly be relevant to Lorenzo's murder investigation?" Rylie asked.

"Yes. I think so," Sophie said. "I wonder who Lucien is supposed to make mortgage payments to now that Lorenzo is dead? I have some money in my savings that I can use to get Lucien caught up on his payments so he doesn't lose Vinterre."

"You can probably call Lorenzo's attorney tomorrow and find out."

"Good idea. I'll do that first thing tomorrow morning," Sophie said. "Are you getting hungry? I can make us a snack."

"Now that you mention it, I am getting a little hungry," Rylie said. "What have you got?"

"I have a lot of deli meats, cheeses, olives, and such. I can put together a charcuterie board pretty easily."

"That sounds great. Let me help you."

They went into the kitchen and busied themselves with making a charcuterie board. Rylie refilled their glasses of chardonnay. They took the charcuterie board and their drinks back to the living room and set everything out on the coffee table between them. They ate silently for a while. Sophie's cell phone rang. She glanced at the screen and picked it up.

"Hello?"

"Okay. I'll be right there."

Sophie turned to Rylie. "That was Detective Michelson. He said I can go to the police department and pick up Lucien now. You don't need to come. Why don't you just stay here and relax. We should be back in a few minutes."

"Are you sure you don't want some moral support?" Rylie asked.

"Yes. I'll be fine. I'm glad you're here. Lucien has some explaining to do when we get back home."

Rylie nibbled on some meats and cheeses while she waited for Sophie to return with Lucien. She heard the front door open. Lucien walked into the living room looking pale.

"Would you like something to drink, Lucien?" Rylie asked. "I'd be happy to get you something."

Lucien slumped into an upholstered chair in front of the fireplace. "Sure, Rylie. I'll have whatever you two are having."

Sophie put her purse away and sat down on her chair in the living room. Rylie got Lucien a glass of chardonnay and handed it to him. They sat quietly for a few minutes while Lucien took a couple sips of chardonnay.

"Well, that was fun," he said dryly. He looked over at Sophie.

"Sophie, you haven't said a word to me since you picked me up at the police department. I haven't done anything wrong. Want to tell me what's going on?"

"I'm waiting for you to tell us what the police were questioning you about," Sophie replied. "I've been freaking out while you were at the police department. Rylie came over for moral support and to help me calm down while we were waiting to hear why the police wanted to question you."

Lucien leaned forward and put his elbows on his thighs. He clasped his hands together in front of him and looked down between his arms at the floor for a few long minutes. Rylie and Sophie exchanged a look and waited patiently for Lucien to start talking.

"I think I might be in some real trouble, honey," he said finally. "I borrowed money from Lorenzo Marchetti when I was renovating Vinterre. The renovation costs were a lot more than I expected. I went back to the bank and asked for more money, but they wouldn't loan me any more. I used up all my savings, but it still wasn't enough. My contractor told me that he knew that Lorenzo had loaned money to some other people in town for real estate deals, so he suggested that I ask Lorenzo for the money. I knew Lorenzo because I go to his bar for a drink after work from time to time. He's always been very friendly. So I asked Lorenzo if I could meet with him. He said he would loan me the money but that the note would have to be secured with a second mortgage on Vinterre. It was a high interest rate, but I didn't have any other options. So I took the deal."

He took a sip of his chardonnay. "I told you that Vinterre lost a lot of business in August because of PGE shutting off the power for four days due to the wildfire north of Calistoga. That's when I got in trouble. I wasn't able to make my payment to Lorenzo in August. I haven't been able to make any payments to him for the last three months. His attorney has been sending threatening letters to my attorney. In his last letter, his attorney threatened to start foreclosure proceedings if I didn't pay all the past due payments within thirty days. As far as the police are concerned, that would have been enough to give me motive to kill Lorenzo."

Chapter 8

"Morning, Katie!" Rylie smiled as she walked into Valley View Veterinary Hospital for work the next morning. She went to the doctors' office and put her things on her desk. She put on her white lab coat and got out her stethoscope.

"Morning!" she said to the veterinarians, Cassandra and Addison, who were sitting at their desks.

"Good morning, Rylie," they replied one after the other.

Rylie scanned her appointment calendar on the computer to see what she had on her schedule for the day. She saw an afternoon appointment for Oliver Davison and his cat Oreo for a recheck exam after Oreo had been treated at the local veterinary emergency hospital for kidney failure. Rylie sighed inwardly. At least she hoped she hadn't sighed out loud. She surreptitiously glanced at the other veterinarians to see if she had attracted their attention. Nope. She breathed a sigh of relief.

Her room nurse, Miley, walked briskly into the doctors' office and stood next to her.

"Good morning, Dr. Sunderland. How are you doing today?" she asked.

"I'm great, Miley. How are you?" Rylie replied.

"It's Monday. What can I say?"

Rylie smiled. She got up and followed Miley down the hall while Miley gave her the rundown on her first appointment. She didn't get a chance to do much more than take an occasional sip of her coffee in between appointments for the rest of the morning. At lunchtime, she sat at her desk to write up her medical records from the morning while she munched on the sandwich she had brought from home.

She checked the time when she finished writing up her electronic medical records. She still had twenty minutes before afternoon appointments. She took off her stethoscope and lab coat and put on her jacket. She went outside for a brief walk around the area to get some fresh air and clear her head.

After she got back, she saw several more appointments before Oliver Davison arrived. She walked into the exam room where Oliver and his cat Oreo were waiting for her. She consciously made an effort to have a warm smile on her face as she entered the room.

"Hi Oliver. Hi Oreo." She stroked Oreo and allowed the cat to snuggle up against her. "I've been getting reports from the emergency hospital about Oreo. It sounds like she's responded well to treatment for her kidney disease."

Oliver smiled for the first time that she could remember. It was a radical transformation from the Oliver that she had seen up until that time. "Yes. She's doing really well. They told me to bring her back to you for a recheck exam."

"Is she eating for you?" Rylie asked.

"Yes. She's eating a little. Not a huge amount yet. They gave me an appetite stimulant for her. It seems to be helping," Oliver said.

"Did they talk to you about giving Oreo subcutaneous fluids at home?" Rylie asked.

"No. They said that you would work with me to develop a treatment plan going forward."

"Okay, then. The first thing I want you to do is to monitor her hydration status at home. When the kidneys aren't working properly, they don't retain bodily fluids like they should and so the pet gets dehydrated easily. Remember I showed you how I knew she was dehydrated when you came here last week? I pulled the skin up on the back of her neck and watched to see how quickly it went back down. Like this." Rylie demonstrated the skin tent test again.

"If her skin goes down slowly, then she's dehydrated," Rylie continued. "She'll always have problems with dehydration for the rest of her life because her kidneys aren't working well. So I'd like to have one of my nurses show you how to give Oreo fluids under her skin at home. You just pick up the skin between her shoulder blades like this to make a tent and then insert a needle right here in the middle of the tent. Trust me, it's not hard. You'll be a pro in no time. Just make sure that you make it a good experience for her. Snuggle her on your lap or pet her while she's getting her fluids. Or give her a treat when you're done."

"Okay. I'll give it a try," Oliver said a little hesitantly.

"I'd like you to give her subcutaneous fluids three times a week, if possible," Rylie said. "I'll write a prescription for the fluids. We'll send you home with a bag of fluids, an IV fluid line, and some needles."

"Okay." Oliver broke eye contact and looked away. "Look, Dr. Sunderland. I know I was a jerk to you when you were looking in the windows of my restaurant the other day. I'm sorry."

"I understand," Rylie said. "But thank you for that. I'm sure you're very upset about losing your business."

"It's hard not to be. I lost my restaurant and my reputation in this town. I have an empty building that I still have to make mortgage payments on. And I'm still working on paying off all the outstanding bills that the restaurant accrued when it was still open."

"I'm sorry, Oliver," Rylie said.

"I get angry every time I see Vinterre. They're responsible for me losing my restaurant. Especially after that article about Vinterre that came out in the Napa Valley travel magazine last year. Everybody wanted to check them out after that," Oliver said bitterly.

Rylie stood quietly petting Oreo on the exam table and waited for Oliver to finish his rant. His face was twisted with anger and bitterness.

"You're friends with the owner, Lucien, aren't you?" Oliver said. "I saw you sitting with his wife at the Chamber of Commerce awards dinner."

"Yes. Sophie and I have been best friends since college," Rylie replied.

"Well, your friend's husband is in some trouble now, isn't he?" Oliver sneered.

Rylie held her tongue with effort. She had to remain professional.

"I think Lucien and Lorenzo Marchetti were in it together," Oliver said. "I have reason to believe that Marchetti loaned Lucien money to get his restaurant up and running. I heard that Lucien ran out of money for the renovation and that the bank wouldn't loan him any more. Marchetti's been known to loan people around here money for real estate deals. Vinterre has been steadily growing since they opened four years ago while my restaurant was slowly dying. How could it not when they built Vinterre directly across the street from The Grapevine? My restaurant didn't have a chance."

Oliver fell silent. He stared at his hands on the exam table.

"I'll have one of my nurses come show you how to give Oreo subcutaneous fluids, Oliver," Rylie said. She walked quickly out of the room.

As soon as Rylie had seen her last patient and finished typing up her medical records, she packed up her belongings and went out to her car to call Detective Michelson.

"Hello? Detective Michelson? This is Rylie Sunderland."

"Rylie! Why am I not surprised?" Detective Michelson said wryly.

Rylie paused. "I learned some information today that could be relevant to Lorenzo Marchetti's murder investigation. Can I meet you somewhere to talk to you?"

"I'm at the dog park with my dog right now. Can you meet me here?"

"Isn't it kind of dark outside to be at the dog park?"

"They have the lights on. It's nearly bright as day," Detective Michelson replied.

"Okay. I can bring my golden retriever, Bella. She would love to get outside and play. She's been cooped up in my house all day today while I was working. Does your dog get along with other dogs?" Rylie asked.

"Max gets along with everybody," Detective Michelson replied.

"I'll go home and get Bella and meet you there in a little while."

Rylie drove home and went inside.

"Hi, Bella. Sweet girl! Were you a good girl today?"

Bella wagged her long, plumed tail so vigorously that her butt swayed back and forth with it. Rylie gave her a dog biscuit and went to get changed. She packed up Bella's things and a couple of bottled waters for herself.

"Come on, Bella! We're going to go meet a new friend! I have a new dog for you to play with at the dog park!"

Bella panted excitedly all the way to the dog park. She rushed inside the gate as soon as Rylie opened it. Rylie took off Bella's leash. Bella sprinted toward the large black dog in the middle of the park. Detective Michelson threw a ball and the two dogs raced after it.

Rylie couldn't help but notice how good Detective Michelson looked in jeans and a t-shirt. She hadn't noticed his muscular chest before. He looked over and grinned at her as she walked up to him. Sexy. She swallowed hard and tried to look casual.

The dogs came running back. Max had the ball in his mouth. He dropped it at Detective Michelson's feet. Bella excitedly bounced up and down.

"What kind of dog is he?" Rylie asked.

"He's a Belgian Sheepdog," Detective Michelson said. "He's a herding breed. They need lots of exercise. I come here a lot with him."

"There are some nice hiking trails around here, too," Rylie said. "Do you ever take him hiking?"

"Once in a while." He threw the ball far out into the field. The dogs took off after the ball.

"So what's up, Rylie? What have you got for me?"

"You remember that I'm a locum veterinarian and that I'm filling in for Dr. Corbyn at Valley View Veterinary Hospital, right?"

"Yes."

"Well today Oliver Davison came in to see me with his cat Oreo. I'm sure you know that he used to own The Grapevine restaurant right across the street from Vinterre until it went out of business about six months ago," Rylie said.

"Of course."

"Did you know that Oliver blames Lucien and Lorenzo Marchetti for his restaurant going out of business?" Rylie asked.

"How's that?"

"He thinks that Lucien and Lorenzo Marchetti conspired to put him out of business by building Vinterre right across the street from his restaurant. He told me that he has reason to believe that Lorenzo Marchetti loaned Lucien money for his restaurant renovation because he heard that Lucien ran out of money for the renovation and that the bank wouldn't loan him any more. He knows that Lorenzo has loaned money to other people around here for real estate deals," Rylie said. "He's very angry and bitter about the whole thing."

The dogs came running up to them. Bella's tongue was lolling out one side of her mouth as she grinned widely. Max dropped the ball at Detective Michelson's feet.

"I wish I could get Bella to do that," Rylie said. "For some reason she will not bring the ball or the frisbee all the way back to me when I throw them for her. She always drops them about ten feet away from me so I have to go get them."

Detective Michelson grinned. "She's got you trained."

Rylie grinned ruefully. "Yep."

Detective Michelson threw the ball again. The dogs took off.

"Thanks for bringing this to my attention, Rylie," Detective Michelson said. "I've heard rumors about Oliver Davison blaming Lucien for him losing his business, but I never had anything concrete to go on. I'll talk to Oliver tomorrow."

"I don't want him to know that I talked to you and told you everything he told me," Rylie said. "I don't want to get on his bad side. And I also don't want it to get back to anyone at Valley View Veterinary Hospital. That could get me in trouble."

"I know. Don't worry. I'll leave you out of it. I'll find a way to talk to him about it without him knowing where I got the information."

"Thanks."

The dogs came running back again, this time a little more slowly.

"I think Bella's getting tired. I'm going to have to get going now. I need to get something to eat and get to bed. I have to get up early for work again tomorrow," Rylie said.

"We'll have to do this again sometime," Detective Michelson said. "I think Max is sweet on Bella." He gave her a sexy grin that made her breath catch in her throat.

"That sounds like fun. See you later!" She smiled at Detective Michelson and snapped Bella's leash on. She turned and headed for her SUV.

When she got home, she unpacked Bella's bag and got comfortable on the sofa with a glass of red wine. She called Sophie and told her what she had learned about Oliver Davison today and about meeting with Detective Michelson at the dog park.

"He's kind of sexy," Rylie said. "I never really noticed it before. But you should see him in jeans and a t-shirt."

"I got to know him pretty well when I was doing a design remodel on his house last summer," Sophie said. "He's a good man. Any woman would be lucky to have him."

"So back to the subject of Oliver Davison," Sophie continued. "I'm going to ask Lucien if Oliver has ever said anything to his face about him being responsible for The

Grapevine going out of business. How could Oliver possibly think that Lucien and Lorenzo Marchetti conspired to put The Grapevine out of business? I think he's just trying to find someone to take the blame for his bad business decisions. His rotten personality and his mediocre chef are what caused The Grapevine to go out of business."

"I'm sure you're right, Sophie," Rylie said. "Unfortunately, I have to see Oliver at work. And I have to hold my tongue when he says nasty things about Lucien. He makes me very uncomfortable. I'm not sure what he's capable of, but I wouldn't want to find out."

"I understand. I'll let you know what Lucien says after I talk to him. But I think you've given Aaron enough informa-tion to hopefully take some of the heat off Lucien. Lucien is having a really hard time dealing with this. He's afraid the negative publicity could damage his reputation and make people not want to eat at Vinterre."

"I'm so sorry, Sophie. This whole thing is such a mess. At least you finally found out why Lucien has been so distant and distracted for the past few months. Maybe helping him deal with this will bring you closer in the long run."

"I paid off the last three months' past due mortgage pay-ments that Lucien owed Lorenzo today. I think Lucien had mixed feelings about it. He was relieved to get caught up so he doesn't have to worry about losing Vinterre. But I think it hurt his pride a little. He wanted to do it on his own. I told him that I love him and I will always support him no matter what. I said that I knew that he would do the same for me. I do think it brought us a little closer."

"That's great, Sophie. I'm happy for you. I know that Lu-cien seeming so distant and distracted for the past several months has been really upsetting you. Now we just need to find out who killed Lorenzo Marchetti so we can clear Lucien's name of any possible involvement."

"Let Aaron do his job, Rylie. He knows what he's doing."

"Of course. I'm not planning to meddle in his investigation. But I do think it's important that we keep our eyes and ears open and let him know about anything we learn that might help him solve the case."

"Yes, alright."

"I've got to get going, Sophie. I have to get something to eat and then get to bed. I've got to get up early for work again tomorrow. Talk to you later."

"'Night, Rylie. I'm really glad you're here right now."

"Me too, Sophie. Talk to you later."

Rylie headed to the kitchen to feed Bella and make a light dinner for herself. Her cell phone rang again.

"Hello?"

"Hi, Rylie. Sorry to bother you so late. This is Patricia Davenport."

"Oh hi, Patricia. How are you?"

"I'm great. Listen, the girls and I are taking a class on learning how to make artisan breads at the Culinary Institute of America in St. Helena this Thursday. Would you like to come? They still have openings the last time I checked. If you want to join us, you should go on their website and pay right away before the class is full," Patricia said.

"Oh, that sounds like fun," Rylie said. "I'll go on their website and sign up right now."

"Great! We're all meeting there Thursday morning at 9:00. It's an all-day class but we do get a lunch break. Our tuition covers lunch in their café. They have a special menu that we can select from that's just for the class participants. I'll let you go now. I know it's late. See you Thursday!"

Rylie got Bella her dinner and microwaved some lasagna she'd gotten at the grocery store. She made a small green salad to go with her lasagna and poured herself a glass of cabernet sauvignon. She absentmindedly watched a house remodeling show on HGTV while she ate. After dinner, she let Bella outside to do her business and got ready for bed.

She opened the back door and called for Bella. "Come on, Bella! Time for bed."

Bella loped inside. Rylie ruffled Bella's fur and wrapped her arms around her neck. She loved the feel of Bella's soft fur.

"You're such a good girl, Bella."

Bella slowly wagged her golden plumed tail.

Rylie's alarm jolted her out of a deep sleep the next morning. She groggily turned over and hit the button to turn it off. She got out of bed and slowly headed to the kitchen to make coffee. Bella followed her. She let Bella outside to do her business while she got the coffee going. The familiar gurgling of the coffeemaker and the aroma of fresh brewed coffee was comforting. She let Bella back inside and got her some breakfast.

As she munched on some toasted English muffins, she mulled over the people that seemed like they might have a motive for killing Lorenzo Marchetti. Oliver Davison. Derek Firth. Sean Kavanaugh. And Lucien. She wished that Lucien wasn't on the list. She had to make sure that Lucien didn't get charged with something that he didn't do.

She dressed quickly and got ready to leave for work. She felt guilty leaving Bella home alone all day while she worked, but she didn't have any choice.

"Bella, you be a good girl for me today, okay?"

Bella gave her sad dog eyes that broke her heart.

"See you later, Bella." She closed the door and walked over to her SUV.

As she was putting her things down on her desk at work, Katie, the receptionist, came in. Katie handed her a paper with a bunch of writing on it and a menu from Giugni's Deli. "Idexx is buying lunch for everyone today. Pick out whatever you want from Giugni's and write it down on the list," Katie said. "You can bring the list back to me when you're done with it."

Katie slipped out of the doctors' office.

"Oh, cool," Rylie said.

"Yeah, they have great sandwiches," Cassandra said. "You can choose whatever you want on your sandwich and they make it to order."

Rylie ordered a roast beef sandwich with horseradish and mayo, some salt and vinegar chips, and some iced tea. She dropped the list and the menu off with Katie on her way to her first appointment. The morning went smoothly. She got to see a couple of really cute puppies for their puppy shots. Cute puppies were the best part of her job. She loved to snuggle the puppies that came in to see her and the wonderful scent that puppies had.

At lunchtime, she went in the break room to pick up her boxed lunch. Katie was in there getting hers.

"I love your purse, Katie," Rylie said. "Where did you get it?"

Katie smiled proudly. "My boyfriend just got it for me. I've had my eye on it for a long time, but I could never afford it. He just surprised me with it yesterday."

"Nice boyfriend," Rylie said. "Sounds like a keeper. What does your boyfriend do?"

"He's a waiter at Vinterre."

"Oh really? My best friend is the wife of the owner, Lucien Marchand. What's your boyfriend's name?"

"Hector. Hector Briseno."

A wiry guy with an angular face, intense dark eyes, and a dark sweep of hair that hung over his forehead walked up.

"Katie, are you ready to go?" he said.

"Dr. Sunderland, this is my boyfriend, Hector. Hector, this is Dr. Sunderland," Katie said.

"Hi." Hector turned away from Rylie. "Katie, we've got to get going or we won't get you back before your lunch break is over."

"We're going to have a picnic lunch in the park," Katie said to Rylie.

"You look familiar," Rylie said. "Wait, I remember you. Weren't you one of the waiters at the Chamber of Commerce awards dinner at Vinterre?"

"Yeah," Hector muttered.

"Hector, what's wrong with you?" Katie asked. "Dr. Sunderland is just trying to be nice."

Hector remained stone faced and silent.

"We'd better go. See you after lunch Dr. Sunderland," Katie said.

"Hector Briseno," Rylie muttered to herself as she collected her boxed lunch.

The waiter that served Lorenzo Marchetti at the Chamber of Commerce awards dinner.

Chapter 9

Rylie forced Hector Briseno out of her mind so that she could focus on the patients she had to see that afternoon. Valley View Veterinary Hospital had a lot of very nice clients. She enjoyed talking with the pet owners and getting to know them. She saw patients every thirty minutes all afternoon. Two with ear infections, one with a broken nail, more than one with dental disease. Some pets were just there to update their vaccinations. She typed up her electronic medical records as quickly as she could at the end of the day so that she could go home as soon as possible.

Bella greeted her happily at the door when she got home.

"Hi, Bella! Were you a good girl today?" She got Bella a bacon, egg, and cheese dog biscuit. Bella inhaled it.

"Want to go outside, Bella?"

Rylie walked around the backyard with Bella while she did her business and sniffed everything in sight. When they went back inside, Rylie got a mineral water with lime and went in the living room to call Sophie.

"Hi, Sophie. How are you?"

"I'm fine, Rylie. What's up?"

"I met the waiter who served Lorenzo Marchetti at the Chamber of Commerce awards dinner at work today. Turns out he's the boyfriend of one of the receptionists at Valley View Veterinary Hospital. His name is Hector Briseno. Do you know him?"

"No. Why?" Sophie asked.

"He's creepy. And not very friendly. He could barely force out a "hi" when I tried to talk to him. I wonder if he knows something that could be useful in Lorenzo Marchetti's murder investigation."

"I'm sure that Aaron has questioned him already," Sophie said. "But if you're worried about it, you could call him."

"I want to, but I'm afraid he'll take offense and feel like I'm telling him how to do his job," Rylie said.

"It's all in the way you word it, I guess."

"Hmmm. Let me think about that. Maybe I can figure out a way to approach him without offending him. I've got to go. Talk to you later."

Rylie got Bella her dinner and made a light dinner for herself as she mulled over how she could ask Detective Michelson if he had questioned Hector Briseno without getting him upset with her. Finally, she decided she had to go for it.

"Hello? Detective Michelson?"

"Rylie! What's up? And please call me Aaron unless we're meeting at the police department or in some other official capacity," Detective Michelson said.

"Okay, Aaron. I met someone at work today. He's the boyfriend of one of our receptionists. His name is Hector Briseno. I recognized him as the waiter who served Lorenzo Marchetti at the Chamber of Commerce awards dinner," Rylie said.

"Yes. I know who he is."

"He wasn't particularly friendly," Rylie said. "He barely could manage to say "hi" to me. His girlfriend was embarrassed at the way he treated me."

Detective Michelson remained silent.

"Anyway, it just got me thinking that he might know something that could be useful in Lorenzo Marchetti's murder investigation. That's all," Rylie finished lamely.

"I've already spoken to him," Detective Michelson said. "He's on my radar, Rylie."

"Oh good," Rylie said.

"I'm bringing in Max to update his shots at Valley View Veterinary Hospital tomorrow. I asked to be scheduled with you since you already know Max and all."

"That's great. I'll see you tomorrow then," Rylie said.

"Goodnight, Rylie."

"'Night, Aaron."

Rylie stared at her cell phone after she hung up. She looked up at Bella.

"He wants me to call him Aaron, Bella."

Bella thumped her tail on the floor.

"That was Max's daddy. You remember that big black dog named Max? The one you played with at the dog park last night?"

Bella jumped up and rushed to Rylie wagging her tail.

"Yeah, Max. You liked Max, didn't you, Bella?" Rylie stroked the top of Bella's head. Bella broke out in a big doggie grin and started panting.

"Aaron said he thinks Max is sweet on you, Bella."

Rylie got out of bed as soon as the alarm went off the next morning.

"Hi, Bella. Want to go outside to go potty?"

Rylie let Bella outside and got the coffee going. A few minutes later, she let Bella in and got her some breakfast. She made herself a cup of coffee and took it with her as she headed for the shower. After she got dressed, she ate a quick breakfast and then packed up her stethoscope, lab coat, and other things she needed for work. Bella stood quietly watching her. Rylie felt a pang of guilt about leaving Bella alone while she was at work all day. She bent over and gave Bella a hug.

"You be a good girl for me today, Bella. Okay?" She pet Bella on the top of her head and then headed out the door. It was a short drive to Valley View Veterinary Hospital.

She walked through the reception area on her way to the doctors' office. "Hi, Katie!"

Katie looked up from the reception desk and smiled. "Good morning, Dr. Sunderland!"

She walked into the doctors' office and greeted Cassandra and Addison.

"Morning, Rylie."

Rylie put her things down on her desk and sat down to check her appointment calendar on the computer. She saw that Detective Michelson was bringing Max in at 10:00. She put on her white lab coat and draped her stethoscope around her neck.

"Good morning, Dr. Sunderland." Miley walked into the doctors' office holding a clipboard.

"Good morning, Miley," Rylie said.

"Our first appointment is in Room 2. It's Mrs. Parsons. She comes here a lot. She wants you to check a lump on her dog's side," Miley said. "She said it's been growing, and she's worried about it. She wants to make sure it's not cancer."

Ten o'clock rolled around quickly. Miley handed her the check-in sheet for Detective Michelson and Max.

"This is a new client. He brought his dog's previous vaccine records with him. They're under the check-in sheet," Miley said.

"Thanks, Miley. I'll take a look at them before I go in," Rylie said.

Rylie opened the door to the exam room with a smile. Max rushed up to her wagging his tail.

"Hi, Max! How are you?" Rylie pet Max as he bounced around excitedly. "Bella told me to say hi to you."

She looked up and saw the affection in Detective Michelson's eyes as he smiled at his dog. "He likes you."

"I like him, too. He's a sweetheart." Rylie gently scratched around Max's ears.

"Thanks for bringing Max's vaccine records, Aaron. That makes my job much easier."

"No problem. I figured you'd need them."

"I'm going to do a physical exam on Max to make sure everything's okay. Then one of the nurses will come in to give him his shots," Rylie said.

She did a physical exam on Max. She admired his shiny, healthy haircoat and his sparkling white teeth.

"His fur is very nice and shiny and healthy looking," she said. "That means he's getting good nutrition. What are you feeding him?"

"I've been feeding him Taste of the Wild."

"Oh, that's good. His teeth look great. I know he's only three years old, but usually dogs have built up some tartar by his age," Rylie said.

"He gets a Greenie every day," Detective Michelson said.

"That's great. Greenies really do work. They've done clinical trials that show that Greenies actually do help to keep their teeth clean."

"I think Max would like to play with Bella again," Detective Michelson said. "Could I interest you in a playdate with Max and Bella on Saturday?"

Rylie was afraid she might look like a deer in the headlights. She tried to arrange her facial features so she would appear calm. Like this kind of thing happened every day. Hot single men asking her out. Oh wait, was he single? And a playdate with dogs wasn't really a date. Was it?

"That sounds like fun. I'm sure the dogs would enjoy it. But aren't you married?" she blurted out.

Detective Michelson smiled. "Nope. Completely unattached. Very single."

"Oh. Okay then. Bella will be excited. Let me give you my cell phone number so you can call or text me with the details."

"That's okay, Rylie. You've called me enough times that I've already got your cell phone number in my contacts."

Rylie swallowed. "I hope I haven't been a pest."

"Absolutely not. You're a concerned citizen whose friend has unfortunately ended up in the middle of a murder investigation. I completely understand you wanting to do whatever you can to help your friend."

Rylie felt her shoulders relax a little. "Thanks, Aaron. I just don't want you to think that I'm trying to interfere or that I don't think you're doing enough."

"No problem, Rylie. I want you to come to me with anything that you find out that could be relevant to the case. It's always good to have eyes and ears on the ground. You never know when someone might discover something that turns out to be useful in an investigation."

Max stood quietly staring at them.

"Okay, Max. We haven't forgotten you," Rylie said. "Do you want to play with Bella again, Max?"

Max wagged his tail eagerly.

"Max checks out great on his physical exam, Aaron. I'll have one of the nurses come in to give him his shots. Talk to you later. I'm looking forward to our playdate on Saturday." Rylie slipped out of the exam room and on to the next appointment.

When she got home that night, she called Sophie to tell her about Detective Michelson asking her to meet him again for a playdate with the dogs. She could practically hear Sophie smiling through the phone.

"That's great, Rylie! It will be good for you and for Bella," Sophie said.

"I'm trying not to read too much into it," Rylie said. "It may be that Aaron really just wants the dogs to get together and has no interest in me whatsoever."

"Come on, Rylie. Get real," Sophie said. "You've been out of the dating scene for too long. You're getting rusty."

"That's me. Rusty Rylie," Rylie said. "I haven't wanted to be involved in the dating scene since I broke up with Dylan. Until recently, I guess."

"I didn't tell you about spending time with Alex Marchetti on Saturday," she continued. "I met him when I went to Il Capriccio on Friday afternoon. Lucien's friend that we met at Beringer Vineyards, the EMT, Ashton Devereux, was there too. Ashton asked me if I had any pets. When I told him I had a golden retriever, he told me that he has a golden retriever, too. He said we should get together to let our dogs play with each other at the dog park sometime. Then Alex walked over and said he would love to have some dogs for his dog to play with. He asked if he could join us at the dog park. So we all met up at Wappo Dog Park with our dogs the next day."

"Interesting," Sophie said.

"One thing led to another, and I ended up spending the entire day with Alex. He's a really nice guy. Sexy, too," Rylie said. "Ashton, Alex, and I took our dogs home after they were done playing and then we met up at the Bakery Café at the Culinary Institute of America. We had a nice lunch. Ashton had to leave after lunch. Then Alex took me hiking on the Redwood Trail. It was beautiful. We got to discussing his father's murder and found out that we both knew people who could possibly have motive to kill his father. So we called Detective Michelson and made arrangements to meet him at the police department so we could talk to him. I'm sorry I didn't tell you about all this before. When I got home from the police department that day and you called me about spending the day at the Solage Resort and Spa, I got so excited about having a spa day that I forgot to fill you in."

She told Sophie about Sean Kavanaugh and Derek and Stefanie Firth.

"Oh, wow, Rylie," Sophie said. "Thanks for telling me this. That gives Aaron some leads to follow up on. I'm sure he appreciated your coming to him. I was hoping the police would come up with some suspects other than Lucien to focus on. I've been afraid they might try to pin it on Lucien if they couldn't come up with anyone else."

"I'd like to hope that would never happen, Sophie," Rylie said. "Especially since Aaron is your friend."

"I know. I know." Sophie sighed. "It's terrible of me to even think it. But it happens. I trust Aaron. But I don't really know anyone else at the police department. I'm sure there's a whole team of people involved in this murder investigation. It's bad publicity for St. Helena and for the police department. I think they're going to want to wrap this thing up as quickly as possible."

"I hope that they do," Rylie said. "I've got to run, Sophie. I'm starving. I have to get some dinner for me and Bella and then call it a night. I'm meeting Patricia Davenport and her friends at the Culinary Institute of America tomorrow morning for an artisan bread making class."

"Oh, that sounds fun. Maybe you'll get to bring home the bread you make."

"I hope so. I'll share it with you if I do. 'Night, Sophie."

"'Night, Rylie."

Rylie walked out onto her deck early the next morning with a cup of coffee in her hands. It was a brilliantly sunny, crisp fall day. The vineyards across the street were starting to take on hues of red and yellow.

"Fall foliage in the Napa Valley, Bella. I can't wait to see it in full bloom."

Bella slowly wagged her tail as she stared at the trees to see if the squirrel would show up.

"Woof!" Bella started jumping up and down on her front legs as she spotted the cheeky squirrel in the tree near the deck. The squirrel flicked his tail back and forth and stood his ground as Bella barked at him.

Rylie went inside to make breakfast. The squirrel leaped from branch to branch until it was no longer visible. When she couldn't see the squirrel anymore, Bella followed Rylie inside. Rylie gave Bella her breakfast and toasted herself an English muffin. She ate quickly, then showered and got dressed.

"I'm going to learn how to make bread today, Bella. I might get to bring some of it home. That would be good, wouldn't it?"

Bella wagged her tail in agreement. She gave Bella a dog biscuit right before she left.

She pulled into the Culinary Institute's parking lot at about quarter to nine and found a parking space. She saw Kinsley Logan getting out of her car nearby.

"Kinsley! Hi!" she called out.

Kinsley looked over at her and grinned with that infectious grin that drew people to her. Rylie walked over to join her, and they walked through the parking lot to the Culinary Institute together. As they stepped inside, they saw Patricia, Liza, and Maggie talking to each other. Their eyes lit up as they saw Rylie and Kinsley walk in.

"Hi Rylie! Hi Kinsley!"

"Now the only one we're missing is Carolyn," Patricia said.

Carolyn walked in the front door. "Hi everyone. I'm not late, am I?"

"No, no. It's fine, Carolyn. We're a little early," Patricia said. "Let's go find the kitchen where the class is taking place. I think it's this way."

They filed into the expansive, spotlessly white kitchen classroom. There were four other people already in the room. A stocky man in a white chef's coat walked into the kitchen grinning broadly and stood in front of the class.

"Hi everyone! Welcome to the artisan bread making class here at the Culinary Institute of America. I'm Chef Kian Chantler. I've been a pastry chef here at the Culinary Institute for over ten years. Most people around here call me Chef Kian, but if you forget my name, you can just call me Chef. I'll know who you're talking to."

"I want each of you to choose a station to work at and stand at your station. The station you choose will be your station for the rest of the day. Each station has a mixer, measuring cups, all the ingredients you'll need, and the recipe for the bread we're making this morning. Don't worry about getting the recipe dirty. We expect that. All of the recipes that we're making today can be found in this wonderful book by Eric Kastel called Artisan Breads at Home."

Chef Kian held up a copy of the cookbook for everyone in the class to see.

"Eric Kastel was an associate professor at the Culinary Institute of America in New York for many years. You'll each receive a hard copy of this book at the end of the class."

"Whoop!" Someone yelled from the back of the class. Chuckles ran through the room.

"We'll start out today talking about the twelve steps of bread baking. Baking bread is not difficult. By the end of the day, you'll have made and baked two different breads that you can take home with you after class. I promise you that the aroma of baking bread will be so enticing that you'll want to snatch your breads out of the oven and eat them right away. I'll be making today's recipes right along with you, and my assistant will be preparing everything we need to make some delicious appetizers with the bread that I make that you can enjoy at the end of the day. We'll send you home with the recipes for the appetizers, too."

Rylie looked around the room. Everyone was hanging on Chef Kian's every word. She caught Kinsley's eye and smiled. Then she turned her attention back to the front of the room.

"This morning we're going to be making French baguettes. We'll break for lunch from 11:30 until 1:00. You'll have lunch in our Bakery Café. We have a special menu just for you today. While you're at lunch, we'll set up all the stations with everything you'll need for the bread we're making this afternoon. This afternoon we'll be making focaccia bread. We'll take a short break mid-afternoon, and we should be enjoying our focaccia appetizers by about 4:30."

"Let's begin."

Chef Kian went on to explain the twelve steps of bread baking.

Rylie felt a tingle of excitement when they finally got to start making their baguettes.

"This is so much fun," she whispered to Kinsley at the station next to hers.

"I think the best part will be eating it." Kinsley gave her a smile.

"I like making bread. I think it's very relaxing," Carolyn said.

"So you already know how to make bread?" Rylie asked.

"Just wheat bread. I've never branched out to anything fancy like baguettes or focaccia bread," Carolyn replied. "This is great."

Chef Kian walked up to their stations and observed them working for a few minutes.

"You guys are doing great. Your dough looks like it's ready to be kneaded, Rylie. Carolyn, I think you need to add a little more flour to your dough until it's not sticky anymore," he said. He moved on to the next group of students.

Rylie sprinkled some flour on her work surface. She took her bread dough out of the mixing bowl and put it on the floured work surface. She started kneading and found that she got into a rhythm as she worked the dough. When the dough was smooth and elastic, she formed the dough into a ball and put it in a lightly oiled bowl. She covered the bowl with a dishcloth and checked her watch. The first rising was supposed to take about thirty minutes.

"I'm going to go find the ladies' room," she whispered to Kinsley.

"No problem," Kinsley replied. "I'll tell Chef Kian if he asks where you went."

Rylie tried to slip out of the kitchen as unobtrusively as possible. She went in search of the nearest ladies' room. She saw a skinny guy with a dark sweep of hair that hung over his forehead walk out of a room down the hall.

"Hector!" she called out.

Chapter 10

"Hi, Hector!" Rylie said. "How are you?"

Hector mumbled something unintelligible as he kept walking.

"I'll be sure to tell Katie I saw you," Rylie said dryly.

"I'm sorry, Dr. Sunderland." Hector stopped walking and turned around to face her. "I was just here to talk to someone in the financial aid department. I'm trying to get enough financial aid that I can afford to go here for my associate's degree in Culinary Arts."

"You want to be a chef?"

"Yeah."

"Does Katie know?"

"She knows I'm interested in becoming a chef. But she doesn't know that I've applied here. I don't want her to know about it until I've gotten everything worked out and I'm sure that I'll be able to attend. Please don't tell her."

"I won't. Don't worry," Rylie said. "I'm glad I ran into you, Hector. My best friend is Sophie Marchand, Lucien Marchand's wife. She's really upset about the whole thing with Lorenzo Marchetti's death. There are plenty of suspects, but she doesn't want her husband to be one of them. Understandably. I was just wondering if you saw anything unusual on the night of the Chamber of Commerce awards dinner. Especially since you were the waiter that served Lorenzo Marchetti that night. Did you see anything that seemed odd or out of place that night?"

"I already talked to that detective," Hector grumbled irritably. "I told him everything I know."

"That's good," Rylie said. "But sometimes people remember things later that they didn't think about at first. Can you think of anything? Anything at all?"

"I didn't really see anything unusual. But Mr. Marchand seemed very concerned about Lorenzo Marchetti's dinner. He said, "This one is for Lorenzo Marchetti, the big Italian guy at Table 6. Make sure it gets to him right away so it's nice and hot. And be sure to ask him if he enjoyed his meal when he's done. He's a friend of mine.""

"Has he ever said anything like that to you before when friends of his came into the restaurant?" Rylie asked.

"Not that I remember. Oh, and another thing. I noticed that Lorenzo Marchetti's dinner smelled really good."

"Didn't all the dinners that night smell really good?" Rylie asked.

"I mean, yeah. But I think Lorenzo's smelled a little bit better than the rest of the dinners I served that night. Maybe it's just because I was really hungry at the time," Hector said.

"Hmmm, interesting. Thanks, Hector. I hope everything goes well with your financial aid and that you're able to attend CIA."

Rylie resumed her search for the ladies' room. Hector walked quickly away.

After using the ladies' room, Rylie went back into the kitchen classroom and took her place at her station. Her dough still had a few more minutes to rise. Chef Kian saw her walk back into the room.

"Okay, everyone. In a few minutes, it will be time to punch down your dough, divide it in half, and shape it into baguettes before the second, and final, rising," Chef Kian said.

Rylie worked on shaping her baguettes and put them on a sheet pan. After she was happy with the way they looked, she made several deep diagonal slits in the top of the dough before covering it with a dishcloth for the second rising. She looked at Kinsley's and Carolyn's baguettes.

"Carolyn, I can tell you're an artist. Your baguettes look so perfect," Rylie said.

Kinsley peered over at Carolyn's baguettes.

"Yeah, wow, Carolyn," Kinsley said. "Yours look so nice. Mine look like a twelve-year-old made them."

"I think yours look fine, Kinsley," Carolyn said. "I've made bread before, so I've had a little practice."

About fifteen minutes into the second rising, Chef Kian said, "You may have noticed that the baguette recipe calls for using steam in the oven when we're baking them. I'm going to show you how you can do this at home. Using steam helps to prevent the crust from forming too early. This allows the bread to rise as high as it can and makes the typical thin, crisp baguette crust that we all love so well."

"Fill the second rimmed baking sheet at your workstation halfway with water and carefully put it on the bottom rack of your assigned oven. Then turn the oven on to 450 degrees Fahrenheit so it can preheat while we're waiting for the dough to finish its second rising. This will heat the water in the pan and fill the oven with steam. Some recipes say to throw ice cubes into a hot pan just as you put in the bread into the oven. I don't recommend this. Ice cubes don't melt fast enough to produce the steam that you need when you put your bread in the oven."

The baguettes filled the room with an enticing aroma as they baked. Rylie's stomach grumbled. She was glad when Chef Kian told them they could break for lunch. She wistfully eyed the golden-brown baguettes sitting out to cool.

Kinsley put her arm through Rylie's. "Come on, girl. We'll be able to eat our baguettes later. Let's go get something to eat. I'm starved."

Rylie allowed herself to be led out of the kitchen classroom. The six women pushed two tables together in the Bakery Café and got seated. They perused the menu and decided what they wanted to eat. Patricia went up to the counter to order for all of them. She came back with a number on a metal stand and placed it in the center of her table.

"So, ladies, are you having fun?" Patricia smiled as she looked around the tables.

"Yes, this is great. I can't wait to eat our breads," Rylie said.

"I know. It's so hard to have to smell them baking and not be able to slather them with butter and devour them as soon as they come out of the oven," Liza said.

"So what do we want to do next week?" Patricia asked.

"Why don't you all come over to our winery next week? I can give you a tour and we can do a wine and cheese pairing at lunchtime," Liza said.

"That sounds fun!" Kinsley said. "I haven't ever been to your winery."

"Me either," Carolyn said. "Sounds good to me."

"I'm in," Rylie said. "If I'm invited, that is."

"Of course you're invited, Rylie," Patricia said. "You're one of us now."

"Yeah, Rylie," Maggie said. "You're one of us now."

Rylie felt a warmth spread through her body. She smiled around at the group. "Cool. I really enjoy doing things with all of you."

After lunch, they started making focaccia bread. It was similar to making baguettes except that before the second rising they had to stretch the dough out flat and make finger holes all over the dough to produce the typical bumpy surface of focaccia bread.

Around 4:30, when their focaccia breads were coming out of the ovens, Chef Kian's assistant laid out trays of focaccia appetizers cut in small squares.

"You all did great today. We want you to be able to take home the breads you created today, so we baked our own focaccia bread to use for these appetizers. We have focaccia with goat cheese, fig jam, and prosciutto, caprese focaccia, and focaccia with grapes and taleggio cheese. For those of you who haven't had taleggio cheese yet, it's similar to brie. If you like brie, you should like taleggio," Chef Kian said.

Rylie and the other women tasted each of the appetizers.

"Wow, these are amazing!" Rylie said. She saw Chef Kian nearby.

"Thank you, Chef Kian," she said. "This class was so much fun. I learned a lot. And these appetizers are so good. I'm definitely going to make these at home. They'd be great to serve when I have company over."

"You're welcome, Rylie," Chef Kian said. "I enjoyed having you ladies in my class today."

Chef Kian's assistant came around and handed them each a hard copy of Artisan Breads at Home and the recipes for each of the focaccia appetizers.

Rylie hugged each of the women in the parking lot before they went to their respective vehicles. She thought about her new friends as she drove home. She had never had so many friends before. All of the women in Patricia's group were so warm and welcoming. It was nice to feel like she belonged. She drove home and went in the front door. Bella excitedly bounced up and down on her front legs to greet her.

"Hi Bella! Sweet girl. Want to go outside?"

Bella ran to the back door. Rylie let Bella outside and headed for the kitchen. She put the baguettes and focaccia bread she had made in plastic food storage bags. She got Bella's dinner and then let her back inside. Bella ran to her dinner bowl, looked in it, and stopped. She looked up at Rylie.

"Oh, Bella, do you want a treat for being such a good girl today?"

Bella wagged her tail enthusiastically.

Rylie got Bella a bacon, egg, and cheese dog biscuit.

"I don't feel like cooking dinner for myself tonight, Bella. I'm going to Il Capriccio for dinner. Maybe Amando's dad, Alex, will be working tonight. Do you remember Amando? He's the big fluffy cream and tan colored dog that you played with at the dog park the other day. Remember? The dog with the fuzzy beard?"

Bella grinned her big golden grin and slowly wagged her beautiful, plumed tail back and forth. Rylie went into her bedroom and got changed into some nice dark blue pants and a cream-colored long-sleeved sweater. She put on a necklace and earrings and brushed her long blond hair. She grabbed a jacket and her purse and headed out the door.

"Bye, Bella! I'll see you later!"

Il Capriccio was starting to fill up with the after-work crowd. She slipped onto a barstool at the far end of the bar and pulled a menu out of the small metal stand on the bar in front of where she was sitting. She sensed someone's presence and looked up.

"Alex! Hi, how are you?"

Alex smiled warmly at her. "Hi, Rylie! What brings you to Il Capriccio?"

"I didn't feel like cooking dinner for myself tonight, so I thought I'd let you do the cooking."

"Great! Can I get you something to drink?" Alex said.

"I'll have a glass of cabernet sauvignon."

"Coming right up."

Alex poured her wine and delivered it to her. "Do you know what you want to eat?" he asked.

"Yes. I'm going to have one of your wood-fired pizzas. The combo sounds perfect," Rylie said.

"Pepperoni, salami, artichokes, mushrooms, green onions. What's not to love?" Alex's gaze lingered on her face. Rylie's breath caught in her throat. "I'll get my chef on that right away."

Alex hurried off. Rylie got out her cell phone to see if she'd missed any calls or texts while she was at the artisan bread making class. Just a text from her mother asking her how she was doing and if she was enjoying her job as a locum veterinarian. She shot a quick text back to her mother assuring her that everything was going well and that she was enjoying working at Valley View Veterinary Hospital.

Rylie could smell her pizza baking in the kitchen. She suddenly felt ravenous. She took a sip of her wine and looked around the bar. A tough-looking guy with red hair swept up off his forehead and a scraggly stubble beard walked in the front door. She saw him miss a step as he walked over to the bar. He sat on a barstool a couple of stools down from where she was sitting. She could smell the alcohol on his breath from where she sat.

Alex walked over and stood in front of the guy. "My father made it very clear that you're not welcome here anymore, Sean."

"Yeah, well your father's not here anymore, is he?" Sean replied with a sneer.

Rylie nervously scanned Alex's face. Those were fighting words. She saw Alex compose himself with difficulty.

"No one is going to serve you here, Sean. It's time to leave," Alex said.

"Come on, man. I lost my job because of your father. I can't get work in this town because of what he did to me. You owe me," Sean said.

"I don't owe you anything, Sean. Get. Out. Now." Alex spoke calmly but firmly. There was steel in his voice and a hard set to his jaw.

Rylie felt her shoulders and back tense. She sat rigidly on her barstool as she waited to see what would happen next.

Sean grudgingly got off his barstool and stalked out the front door. Rylie breathed a sigh of relief. She looked around at the other people nearby. Everyone had been watching the exchange between the two men. After Sean left, they all turned back to their families and friends and resumed talking and eating their meals.

A guy walked up and put her pizza down in front of her with a plate and silverware.

"Thank you," Rylie said. She sniffed the pizza appreciatively and dug in.

"Mmmm." She took another sip of her wine.

Alex walked over to her. "How's your pizza?"

"Absolutely delicious. Hits the spot," Rylie said. "So I assume that was Sean Kavanaugh?"

"Yes. A real charmer, isn't he?"

"I'm glad he left without a fight," Rylie said. "I was nervous for a while there."

"It was all I could do not to punch him in the face," Alex said. "But that's not my style. Plus, I have to be professional. I don't want my bar to get a bad reputation."

A guy at the other end of the bar held up a finger. Alex quickly walked away to help his customer.

Rylie thoroughly enjoyed her meal. Alex came back a while later. "All done?"

"Yes, it was delicious, but I can't eat the whole thing. Can I please have a box?"

"Sure thing. Are you interested in dessert? My chef makes fantastic cannoli."

"Yum! Cannoli!" Rylie said. " I love cannoli. Yes, I'll have a cannoli."

A cannoli was deposited on the bar in front of her by the same guy that delivered her pizza.

"Oh! It has little chocolate chips in it," she said. She bit into the cannoli and rolled her eyes to the ceiling. "Yum!"

When she was finished, she asked Alex for her check. She pulled out enough cash from her purse to pay the check and leave a nice tip and left it on the bar. She slipped her pizza box into the plastic bag the guy had left for her and stood to go. Alex quickly walked over to her.

"Are you leaving now?" he asked.

"Yes. Thank you for a delicious dinner."

"Wait here a second. My shift is about over. Greg is going to close tonight. I'll walk you to your car," Alex said.

Rylie waited for Alex to join her. They left the bar together and walked on the sidewalk along Main Street toward where Rylie had parked her SUV.

"The police have finally released my father's body to the funeral home," Alex said. "We're having a service at the Catholic Church at 10:00 on Sunday morning. It would mean a lot to me if you were there."

"Oh! Of course I'll be there, Alex. Thank you for inviting me."

"A bunch of my relatives are flying in from Italy tomorrow for the funeral. They'll be here through the weekend and leave on Monday," Alex said.

"After the service, we'll go to the cemetery. Then everyone will go to my house. There will be tons of food, I'm sure, knowing my family. You're welcome to come to the cemetery and to my house after the service."

"Thank you, Alex," Rylie said. She reached out and squeezed his hand. "I'm happy to go to the service at the church. But I think that the cemetery and the get together at your house afterwards are more for you and your family. They're only here for a few days. You should spend as much time as you can with them."

Rylie stopped when they reached her SUV. Alex grabbed both of her hands and twirled her to face him. He pulled her close and pressed his warm lips to her forehead for a long moment. She gasped softly in surprise. Then he stepped back.

"I'll see you Sunday, Rylie." Alex turned and walked quickly away. His masculine scent hung in the air for a few moments. Then it was gone. She got in her SUV and drove home.

Was Alex interested in her? Or was that just the way that Italian men acted?

Chapter 11

Rylie was enjoying a toasted bagel and a cup of coffee at her kitchen dining table the next morning when her cell phone rang. She didn't recognize the number, but it was a local area code. She answered the phone.

"Dr. Sunderland?" A man's voice asked.

"Yes?"

"This is Dr. Wesley Corbyn, the owner of Valley View Veterinary Hospital. How are you?" he asked.

"I'm fine, thank you."

"How's everything been going at the hospital?"

"Everything's been going very well. I really like the doctors and everyone on the staff. And Miley is a jewel. She's always cheerful and ready to do whatever it takes to keep things running smoothly," Rylie said.

"Well, good. I'm glad everything is going well," Dr. Corbyn said. "Listen, I think I was a little too optimistic about the time it would take for me to recover from my surgery. I was wondering if you could stay until the end of November? I know it's a lot to ask, but I'm hoping that you're still available and that you're not already booked up somewhere else. I'll be happy to pay for another month on your rental house."

Rylie looked out the window across the vineyards. Another month here in St. Helena with Sophie and all her new friends. And Alex and Aaron. Two relationships that she wanted to see where they went. And she needed to make sure that Lucien was cleared of any suspicion in Lorenzo Marchetti's murder. That would be a lot easier to do if she stayed in St. Helena.

"I'm still available for the month of November," she said finally. "I just started doing locum veterinarian work, so I haven't booked up my calendar yet. I'd be happy to stay on another month and help you out."

Dr. Corbyn let out a sigh of relief. "That's great, Dr. Sunderland. Thank you. I'll let my manager know to put you on the schedule through the end of November."

"Sounds good. Talk to you later," Rylie said. She hung up and put her cell phone down on the table.

"Bella! We're going to stay here for another month! You'll get to see your doggie friends at the dog park some more!"

Bella rushed up to Rylie wagging her tail. Rylie held Bella's face in her hands and gave her a quick kiss on the top of her muzzle. Bella's tail wagged furiously.

She showered, dressed, and got ready to go to the farmers' market. This would be the last farmers' market of the year in St. Helena. She didn't want to miss it. She wanted to see Cara's mushroom stand. She was hoping to find some interesting new mushrooms to try in her recipes.

She gave Bella a dog biscuit. "I'm going to the farmers' market, Bella. You be a good girl for me while I'm gone. I'll be back later."

She grabbed her backpack to carry any produce that she purchased and drove to the farmers' market in Crane Park. The farmers' market was bustling. She wandered down the wide aisle filled with people checking out the booths on both sides of the aisle. She liked to walk all the way through a farmers' market and check out everything on offer before she decided to purchase anything. Some booths had nicer produce than others. And some charged much less for the same produce that other booths were selling for more.

She spotted the booth for Marvelous Mushrooms and walked over to it. Cara was busy helping another customer. She browsed through the mushrooms on display while she was waiting. There were signs with the name of each type of mushroom for sale. King Trumpets, Shiitake, Lion's Mane, Tree Oyster. She always bought crimini mushrooms from the grocery store for her recipes. She hadn't really been brave enough to branch out into other kinds of mushrooms yet.

"Rylie!" Cara finished with her customer and turned to greet her. "Hi! I'm so glad you could make it! See anything that interests you?"

"I don't really know anything about the mushrooms you have here. As I mentioned the other day, I always buy crimini mushrooms. But I'm willing to try some other kinds of mushrooms if you can tell me a little about what they taste like and if they require any special cooking methods."

"Okay, let's start with shiitake mushrooms." Cara handed her a shiitake mushroom as she spoke. Rylie examined it. It looked fairly similar to the crimini mushrooms that she was used to.

"Shiitake mushrooms have a savory, earthy flavor. I think you'll like them. They have a meaty texture when they're cooked. Before you cook them, you should separate the caps from the stems because the stems take longer to cook. Cook the stems first and when they're starting to get tender, you can add the caps."

"Okay, I'll take some of those," Rylie said. "They sound good."

Cara put some shiitake mushrooms in a paper bag. Then she held up a thick-stemmed white mushroom with a small tan cap.

"This is a trumpet mushroom," Cara said. "If you like crimini mushrooms, you should like trumpet mushrooms. They have a slightly sweet, almost nutty flavor and a meaty texture when they're cooked. You can make a nice side dish with them by cutting them in half lengthwise and sautéing them in olive oil and fresh garlic. Just be sure to score the cut side so they'll cook evenly and soak up all the flavor of the garlic. You can use the tip of a paring knife to make shallow cuts in a crosshatch pattern on the cut side of the stems. They're good in salads, too. Here. I have some recipes you can try using shiitake and trumpet mushrooms."

Cara handed her some recipe cards.

"Okay, I'll take some of those, too," Rylie said.

Cara put some trumpet mushrooms in a paper bag. She weighed both the bags of mushrooms and told Rylie the cost. Rylie took off her backpack and put the bags inside. While she was getting out her wallet, she noticed a sealed, clear plastic display case at the far side of Cara's booth. She stepped over to look inside as she was getting some money out to pay Cara.

Inside the display case were some mushrooms with white stems and yellow-tinged caps. Next to the mushrooms was a typewritten paper. At the top of the display in large letters were the words "Beware the Death Cap Mushroom!" She read the paper next to the mushrooms:

In the San Francisco Bay Area, Amanita phalloides mushrooms, also known as Death Cap mushrooms, can be found growing in the wild at all times of year. Death Caps are most abundant during the fall and early winter, but they may be found through late spring. In areas of coastal fog, they may even be found in the summer. Amanita phalloides mushrooms grow throughout California wherever live oak is found.

These mushrooms are deadly. Ingestion of these mushrooms initially causes nausea, vomiting, and diarrhea which lasts for twelve to twenty-four hours. But the toxins in these mushrooms continue to cause problems even after the vomiting and diarrhea have stopped. Four to nine days after ingestion, people who have eaten this mushroom may develop acute liver failure and kidney failure which can lead to death.

The toxins in Death Cap Mushrooms are not destroyed by cooking. The lethal dose is very low. Ingesting even a single mushroom can be fatal.

Rylie took a photo of the display case contents with her cell phone. She looked up at Cara. Cara was busy helping another customer. After she checked out her customer, Cara came over to stand behind the display case.

"Pretty scary, huh?" Cara said. "It seems like every year I hear about people getting really sick from eating Death Cap mushrooms that they found growing in the wild. Some of them end up having to get liver transplants. I thought it was important to try to educate people about the danger of eating unknown mushrooms that they find in the wild."

"I can't believe that anyone would eat mushrooms they found growing in the wild if they weren't absolutely certain they were safe to eat," Rylie said. "But I guess it happens. That's great that you took the time to put this display together. Too bad there isn't a way to continue to get this information out there even after the St. Helena farmers' market is over for the year."

"Hmmm. I'll have to think about that," Cara said. "Maybe I can work something out with the city or the library or something."

"I think the library is a great idea. I think more people probably visit the library than City Hall. They might even let you put this whole display case somewhere."

"That's a great idea. I'll go talk to someone at the library after the market closes at noon and I get everything packed up. If they agree to have my display case there, then rather than breaking down the display case and putting it in storage, I could just move it over to the library," Cara said.

Rylie paid for her purchases and continued browsing. She bought some goat cheese at one booth and some fresh apple cider at another. She also picked up some fresh spinach and other fresh produce. Her backpack was bulging when she made her way back to her SUV. She went home to unpack her finds.

Bella was waiting at the door for her when she opened the door.

"Hi Bella! look at all the nice things I got at the farmers' market today!"

Bella wagged her tail and broke out in a doggie grin.

Rylie made a salad with the fresh spinach, goat cheese, and red bell peppers that she had just purchased at the farmers' market. She added some sprouts she had in the refrigerator and a couple spoonfuls of cottage cheese. She sprinkled fresh Parmesan and balsamic vinegar over everything.

"Yum! I'm starved."

She thought about what she might do after lunch. She mentally went through the clothes she had with her to see if she had anything appropriate for Lorenzo Marchetti's funeral on Sunday. She wondered if she was supposed to wear black or if any dark color would do. She got out her laptop and typed "are you supposed to wear black to a Catholic funeral" in the Goggle search bar. The first answer that came up said, "Black is traditional, but any dark color is usually considered appropriate."

After she finished her lunch, she looked through all the dresses hanging in her closet. Nothing really seemed appropriate for a funeral. Then she remembered Maggie inviting her to her boutique in St. Helena after their lunch on the Napa Valley Wine Train.

Perfect. I'll check out Maggie's store and see if she has anything I can use. What was the name of it again? Casual Chic, that's it. She remembered seeing it on Main Street as she drove through St. Helena one day.

She got her purse and headed downtown. She had to drive around the block to find parking. As she entered Casual Chic, a bell chimed overhead. She looked around to see if she could see Maggie anywhere.

"Coming!" Maggie called from the back of the store.

"Rylie! You made it! So nice to see you. Let me show you around," Maggie said.

"Hi, Maggie. I'd love to see your store. And I need to buy a dress that's appropriate for attending a Catholic funeral. Alex Marchetti invited me to his father's funeral this Sunday."

"I'm sure we can find something perfect." Maggie looked her up and down. "I have some dresses over on this wall that will look great on you. You need something in a dark color but that doesn't mean it can't be pretty."

Maggie held out a navy-blue A-line dress with three-quarter length sleeves.

"What do you think of this one?" she asked.

"I like it."

"Great. Let's get some accessories and then we'll send you to the fitting room," Maggie said.

Maggie held a necklace up to the dress.

"What do you think?" she asked.

"I think that will look great," Rylie said.

"Do you have some black heels?" Maggie asked.

"Yes. Thankfully. I brought some with me from home."

"Okay. Well, we'll pretend you're wearing black heels when you come out of the dressing room in this dress. You can go in this dressing room right here," Maggie said.

Rylie tried on the dress and turned back and forth in front of the mirror in the dressing room. It fit nicely and seemed like it would be appropriate for a funeral. She put on the necklace. The necklace made the outfit. This would do. She stepped out of the dressing room and twirled for Maggie.

"Looks great, Rylie!" Maggie said. "Do you like it?"

"Yes. I think it will be perfect for Sunday," Rylie said. "Now I'd like to look at some nice pants and sweaters. It's getting a little cool here now, especially at night."

Maggie guided her around the store and helped her choose some pants and sweaters.

"You have really good taste, Maggie," Rylie said finally. "You make it so easy to put outfits together. I usually have a hard time shopping for clothes."

"Thanks, Rylie." Maggie smiled warmly. "Let's get you rung up."

Rylie looked around the store and realized that there were several other women browsing the racks. She realized that Maggie had given her undivided attention even though she could have been helping the other women.

Maggie rung her up. Rylie looked at the receipt and saw that almost everything had been discounted.

"Were these things on sale?" she asked.

Maggie leaned over and whispered, "I gave you a special "Welcome to St. Helena" discount."

"Thanks, Maggie," Rylie said. "That was really nice of you."

Rylie drove home and put her new clothes away. Then she called Sophie.

"Hi, Sophie! Are you at work?" Rylie asked.

"Yes, but I should be done for the day in a couple hours. Why?" Sophie asked.

"Do you have plans for dinner?"

"No. I'm probably just going to reheat some leftovers," Sophie said.

"I have a better idea. Why don't you come over to my house for a light dinner of focaccia bread appetizers tonight? I want to share the focaccia bread that I made at the artisan bread making class with you. Chef Kian gave us the recipes for the appetizers that they made for us at the end of class yesterday. He made three different appetizers using the focaccia bread that he baked yesterday afternoon. They were delicious. They don't look too hard to make either. If you want to come over, I'll run to the grocery store and get the ingredients that I need to make them. We can have wine and focaccia bread appetizers for dinner."

"That sounds fantastic. What time should I come over?"

"Does around 6:00 work for you?"

"Perfect. I'll be there. I'll bring the wine," Sophie said.

Rylie got out the recipes for the focaccia bread appetizers and made a shopping list. Then she went to the grocery store to get everything she needed for the recipes. She also got black olives, capers, anchovy fillets, and the rest of the ingredients she needed to make olive tapenade to go with the baguettes she had made, some baby carrots and cherry tomatoes to serve on the side, and two slices of cheesecake with cherry topping for dessert. On impulse, she added a bouquet of sunflowers to her grocery cart. Sunflowers always made her feel happy.

She went home and unpacked her groceries. She found a vase for her sunflowers and set them on a table in the living room. She made the tapenade first so the flavors would have time to develop. Then she made the recipes for focaccia with goat cheese, fig jam, and prosciutto, caprese focaccia, and focaccia with grapes and taleggio cheese. Bella stayed close at hand in case anything dropped from the counter while Rylie was working. Rylie gave her a tiny bit of goat cheese. Bella made quick work of it.

Rylie arranged the focaccia bread appetizers on plates and set them on the dining table. She found an oblong glass serving dish that she used for the baby carrots and cherry tomatoes. She sliced one of the baguettes, put the slices in a small basket lined with a pretty kitchen towel, and set a small glass bowl of tapenade near the basket.

"Looks good, don't you think, Bella?"

She heard someone knocking and walked over to open the front door. Bella rushed to the front door alongside her wagging her tail.

"Sophie! Just in time. I just finished making everything and getting everything set up," Rylie said.

"I brought a nice zinfandel to go with our appetizers." Sophie leaned over to pet Bella who was looking up at her with big brown dog eyes and wagging her tail. "Hi, Bella! What a pretty girl you are!"

They walked back to the kitchen. "Where are your wine glasses? And a wine opener?" Sophie asked.

"Wine glasses are in that cabinet to the left of the sink. I'll get the wine opener," Rylie replied.

Sophie poured them both a glass of wine and then sat at the table.

"Wow, Rylie! This looks amazing!"

"Thanks, Sophie. I'll get us some plates." Rylie brought some plates to the table and handed one to Sophie.

"Help yourself. So what job are you working on now?" Rylie asked.

They both selected a few appetizers and put them on their plates. Rylie spread some tapenade on a couple of baguette slices and sat down at the table.

Sophie took a sip of wine. "I'm working on a kitchen re-design right now. The house is owned by a young couple. They saved up for a long time to be able to afford this. They bought a fixer-upper about a year ago and have been wanting to remodel the kitchen ever since. It really needs it. I don't think it's been updated since the house was built."

"Do you have to gut it?" Rylie asked.

"We start demo next week."

"Do you have any "before" photos to show me?" Rylie asked.

Sophie got out her cell phone and showed her the old kitchen. "If I had my laptop here, I could show you my design for their new kitchen. We're going to knock out this wall and open up the kitchen to the living room so they'll have an open plan. I'm adding a large island with seating on one side. It's going to be really pretty."

"That's great, Sophie. I can't wait to see what you do with the place."

"So I have some news," Rylie said. "Dr. Corbyn called me this morning and said he needs more time to recuperate from his surgery before he goes back to work. He asked me to stay until the end of November. I said yes, of course. He's going to pay for another month on this rental house."

"Oh, that's wonderful news, Rylie! I'm so glad you're going to be able to stay longer. It's been so nice having you around. I don't get to see you nearly enough with you living in Brentwood. And I really appreciate everything you've done to try to help clear Lucien's name in Lorenzo Marchetti's murder investigation. I know you won't stop until the police have arrested whoever did it. I don't know what I'd do without you," Sophie said.

"That's what friends are for, Sophie," Rylie said. "Alex told me that it would mean a lot to him if I went to his father's funeral at the Catholic church on Sunday. I told him I'd go. He said I was welcome to go to the cemetery and then to his house for a get together after the service. But I told him I think that those things are more for him and his family. He has a bunch of family members flying in from Italy today. They'll be staying here through the weekend and leaving on Monday. Are you and Lucien planning to go to the service at the church?"

"I don't know. I'm not sure how Lucien feels about it. I'll ask him later tonight when he gets home from the restaurant."

They finished their dinner and put away the leftovers.

"I got us slices of cheesecake for dessert!" Rylie said. "With cherry topping."

"That sounds delicious. But I need to digest for a little while. Let's go sit in the living room with our wine for a bit first."

"Okay."

They got comfortable in the living room and chatted for a while.

"You know, Sophie. We're not getting any younger. We're both thirty-two now. Do you think that you and Lucien will ever have kids?" Rylie asked.

"We've talked about it," Sophie replied. "I don't know. I think we both want kids, but it has never seemed like the right time. We're both so busy running our businesses and trying to make them successful. Neither of us has much free time. We'd have to make some major life adjustments in order to add a child to our lives."

"I feel like my biological clock is ticking, Sophie," Rylie said. "In my vision for my future, I always saw myself married with kids by now. I don't want to end up in my forties looking back and wishing I would have had kids when I was able."

"Life doesn't always work out the way we plan, Rylie. But look at you now. You have two men that you're attracted to that seem like they might be interested in you. I know Aaron is a keeper. I don't know Alex Marchetti very well, but from everything you've told me, he seems like a great guy. You never know. You could be married and pregnant with your first child a year from now."

Rylie thought about that for a minute. "It would be kind of hard for me to have anything serious with either Alex or Aaron since I live over an hour and a half away. You know how infrequently I've gotten up here to see you and Lucien since you moved to St. Helena."

"You could move up here too, you know," Sophie said. "There's nothing keeping you in Brentwood. Is there?"

"Not really. I've made more friends here in a short period of time than I've ever made in Brentwood. And I really do like it here. I'll give that some thought. But if I did move up here, it would be for you and Lucien and my new friends, not for the possibility of a relationship with Alex or Aaron. I wouldn't uproot my life and move up here on the chance that something might work out with one of them," Rylie said.

"Really? You'd consider moving here? That would be incredible!" Sophie beamed at her.

"Ready for cheesecake?"

"Sounds good."

Sophie left a little while later. Rylie's thoughts turned to the playdate she had scheduled with Detective Michelson and their dogs tomorrow. Her cell phone rang. Aaron Michelson's name showed on her caller ID.

"Hello?"

"Hi, Rylie. How are you?" Detective Michelson asked.

"Great. How are you, Aaron?" Rylie replied.

"I'm good. Look, Rylie, I'm afraid I'm not going to be able to make it for our playdate with the dogs tomorrow. I'm sorry. I was really looking forward to it. Something's come up at work."

"I hope that something means you're making progress on Lorenzo Marchetti's murder investigation," Rylie said.

"I'm not at liberty to say, Rylie," Detective Michelson said. "But I will say that things are about to get interesting."

Chapter 12

Rylie dressed carefully for the funeral on Sunday morning. The navy-blue dress with the teardrop-shaped white sapphire pendant necklace that Maggie had picked out was elegant in its simplicity. She chose some small diamond stud earrings to complete the look. She slipped on her black high heels and examined herself in the full-length mirror in her bedroom.

Bella was sitting nearby watching her dress.

"What do you think, Bella? Appropriate for a funeral but still pretty?"

Bella slowly wagged her tail. Rylie gave her a bacon, egg, and cheese dog biscuit and then went into her bedroom to get her small black purse.

"Bye, Bella. You be a good girl for me today. Okay?"

She parked her SUV in the Catholic church's parking lot. The massive stone church entrance was graced with tall double doors topped with pointed arch windows that matched the pointed arch windows in the rest of the building. The interior was well lighted with natural light from the stained glass windows. Tall cylindrical milk glass and metal lights hung from the vaulted coffered ceiling inlaid with blue stained glass. Wooden pews lined both sides of the aisle leading to the altar. People were milling about finding places to sit in the pews. Alex was standing in front of the first row of pews talking to an older woman with short reddish-brown hair.

Rylie quietly took a seat towards the back of the church. The perfume that the woman sitting in front of her had lavishly applied was overwhelming. She concentrated on trying to take shallow breaths. Patricia and Jonathan Davenport were sitting a few pews up from her with Liza and Harding Cresswell. She turned to look at the people in the back of the church and was surprised to see Detective Michelson. She felt her shoulders tighten. He gave her a small smile. She returned his smile and then turned back to the front of the church.

What's he doing here? Is he here watching everyone to see if he can get any clues that could help in Lorenzo's murder investigation? Or did he know Lorenzo personally and come to pay his respects?

She tried to concentrate on the front of the church and the altar. Finally, the priest walked in and stood at the front of the church. He had a deep voice that resonated throughout the church and commanded people's attention.

When the service was over, Rylie went outside to get some fresh air. She spoke to Patricia and Liza briefly on their way out. She waited for Alex to come out so she could pay her respects. Alex walked out with the older red-haired woman's arm looped through his. He smiled when he saw her.

"Rylie! I'm so glad you were able to come," Alex said. He gave her a quick hug. "This is my Aunt Rosa. She flew in from Italy on Friday."

"Hi, Rosa. I'm Rylie Sunderland. Nice to meet you."

"Awww, such a pretty girl, Alex. Nice to meet you too, dear," Aunt Rosa said. "You are coming to Alex's house for the reception, yes? You no want to go to the cemetery with us. It's too sad. But you come to the house and eat some good Italian food afterwards, yes? We were cooking all day yesterday. We have *molto cibo* - much food."

Rylie looked up at Alex. He grinned and shrugged. "I don't think Aunt Rosa is going to take no for an answer. I'll text you when we get to the house."

"Okay. Thanks, Alex. I'll see you both later."

Rylie smiled at them as she turned to leave and then headed home to wait for Alex's text. When she got home, she got a lime-flavored mineral water out of the refrigerator and went outside on the deck with it. She got comfortable in a chair with a nice view of the vineyard across the street. Bella curled up on the deck next to her. Rylie let her thoughts wander in the peaceful setting. A while later, her phone pinged with a text.

"Alex."

She read his text:

We're at my house now. Come on over. The address is 1857 Blue Oak Lane in St. Helena. It's a little bit out of town in the middle of a vineyard. The house is set back from the road, but the number is on the mailbox out front. See you soon.

"I've got to go, Bella. I'm going to go see Alex and his family and eat lots of yummy Italian food. I'll be back later."

Bella came over to her wagging her tail. Rylie stroked Bella's golden head. She stood up and checked to make sure she didn't have any dog hair on her navy-blue dress. Then she got her purse and headed out the door.

"Bye, Bella!"

With Alex's address in her GPS, she followed the directions until she spotted the house number on his mailbox. She drove down the long driveway that led to his house and parked in front of his two-car garage. The house was a stunning contemporary with flat roofs framed in rust-colored stucco accented by dark chocolate brown walls. The massively tall entryway roof was supported by a square stone pillar. She knocked on the door. A stocky older gentleman opened the door for her.

"Come in, come in!" he said. "Please make yourself at home." He wandered away towards the open plan living room.

Rylie breathed deeply of the luscious aromas emanating from the kitchen. The air was redolent with the smell of garlic, basil, tomato sauce, and pasta.

Alex saw her walking in and rushed to greet her.

"Rylie! Hi! Come on in," he said. He gave her a brief hug.

"It smells amazing in here," Rylie said.

Alex smiled. "My aunts have been cooking since yesterday. You're in for a treat."

He ushered her into the living room.

"Can I help out in the kitchen?" she asked.

"No, no. It's best to leave them to it," he said. "They're like a well-oiled machine. They've been cooking together like this all their lives. Let me introduce you to my Nonna."

Alex steered her toward a sofa in the living room where an elderly woman sat drinking a glass of red wine.

"Nonna, this is Rylie Sunderland."

"Ahhh, Alessandro, she is beautiful. She is your girlfriend, yes?" Nonna said.

"She's my friend, Nonna. We just met a little over a week ago when she came into Il Capriccio."

"Don't let this one get away, Alessandro." Nonna smiled. "She's a good girl. I can tell. You need to settle down with a wife and start a family."

Rylie swallowed hard.

"Smettila di fare la sensale, Nonna."

Nonna chuckled.

"What did you say?" Rylie asked Alex.

"I told her to stop trying to be a matchmaker." Alex smiled down at her.

He grabbed her hand and started introducing her to people around the room.

One of the aunts called out from the kitchen. "Alessandro, where are your manners? Get the poor girl a glass of wine!"

"Oh, I'm sorry, Rylie," Alex said. "Would you like a glass of Vino Nobile di Montepulciano? Remember I told you about it? The wine from where my family lives in Italy?"

"I'd love some."

Alex returned a few minutes later with a glass of red wine. Rylie took a sip.

"This is delicious," she said. "I love it."

Alex continued introducing her around the room. She smiled and chatted briefly with each person she met.

"You'll meet my aunts when they're done cooking," Alex said. "I don't want to interrupt them right now."

"That's fine," Rylie said. "Can you point me in the direction of your ladies' room?"

"Down the hall and to the right."

"Okay, thanks."

Rylie found the bathroom and closed the door. She leaned against the door and took a deep breath. She was sure she'd never remember the names of all the people she'd just met. She washed her hands and dried them on the thick hand towel hanging on the wall by the sink.

On her way back down the hallway, she noticed some framed photos on the wall. She stopped to look at one that appeared to be Alex when he was a young boy with his father and mother. Alex walked up and stood beside her.

"That's my favorite photo of my mother," he said. "That was taken shortly before she died in a car accident. That's how I remember her."

"She was beautiful, Alex," Rylie said.

She stepped over to look at the next photo. It looked like it was taken in an Italian restaurant. Plates of spaghetti were set out on a red-checked tablecloth. Lorenzo Marchetti was seated on the left side of the table. Opposite him was a man with a black fedora and a closely trimmed white beard. Seated next to the man with the white beard was a much younger man with dark brown hair wearing suspenders over a white shirt. The men were clinking their wine glasses together. An older woman with shoulder length dark gray hair in soft waves was standing at the head of the table. A man with a dark fedora was seated in back of her playing a violin. Everyone at the table looked happy like it was a celebration of some sort.

"That's an old photo," Alex said. "Look how young my father was. The man with the white beard is Leo Bernardi. He was my father's business partner in Il Capriccio for fourteen years. That's his son, Silvano, and his wife, Luisa. They moved away about three years ago."

"There you two are." Aunt Rosa came bustling down the hallway. "Come, come. *Tutti sono pronti da mangiare.*"

"She says everyone is ready to eat," Alex said.

Aunt Rosa herded them to one of the long tables set up in the dining area. Plates full of food and a glass of red wine had been set at each place and everyone was getting seated.

"Rylie, you sit here next to Alessandro," Aunt Rosa said.

Rylie obediently sat down in the chair next to Alex. She looked at all the wonderful food on her plate. Enough for a couple of meals, at least.

"We have lasagna, stuffed shells, and handmade pici pasta with freshly made pesto sauce. There's green salad on the side topped with shaved Parmesan and kalamata olives. And there's plenty of warm garlic bread in the baskets scattered around the table. When you're ready for more, please go out to the kitchen and help yourself," Aunt Rosa said.

Open bottles of Vino Nobile di Montepulciano were on the table in between the baskets of garlic bread and clear glass cruets containing olive oil and balsamic vinegar.

An elderly gentleman at the head of the table bowed his head and everyone followed suit. Rylie bowed her head.

"*Benedici, o Signore, questo cibo che ci siamo procurati usando i tuoi doni e la tua grazia.*

Dai a tutti il pane quotidiano: soprattutto ai poveri e ai bambini. Così sia."

Everyone started eating, talking, and drinking all at once. Rylie looked at Alex.

"It's an Italian prayer that we say before meals. In English, it's "Bless, O Lord, this food that we have procured using your gifts and your grace. Give everyone daily bread: especially the poor and children. So be it.""

"Oh, that's nice," Rylie said. She took a bite of the pici pasta with pesto.

"Oh, my goodness. This is so delicious," she said. She looked up and saw Aunt Rosa smiling at her.

"You like my pici pasta with pesto? You're a good girl. I will send some home with you in a container. We have too much food. Alex will have more leftovers than he knows what to do with," Aunt Rosa said.

Rylie devoured the wonderful meal. She was surprised at how much she was able to eat. Everything was so good, she just couldn't help herself. Aunt Rosa beamed at her when she saw that Rylie had eaten everything on her plate.

"Your girl, Alessandro, she's a good eater," Aunt Rosa said.

"It's all this good Italian food," Alex replied. "Mmmm. *Deliziosa.* Just like I remember eating when we lived in Italy. I'm going to get seconds."

"*Assicurati di risparmiare spazio per il dessert.* We have tiramisu and cannoli for dessert," Aunt Rosa called after him.

"Yum," Rylie said. "How did you have time to make all this food in one day?"

"We had many hands working." Aunt Rosa smiled. "We love to make food for our family."

After dessert and a cappuccino, Rylie went into the kitchen to see if she could help with the dishes.

"No, no. You are not to do dishes. You are our guest. Here, I am putting food for you in containers so you can have good Italian food at home," Aunt Rosa said. She put some of each dish into plastic food storage containers and stacked them all in a navy-blue fabric tote bag.

"Thank you, Aunt Rosa. I wish you were staying longer. I've enjoyed getting to know you," Rylie said.

"Ahhh, my sweet girl," Aunt Rosa said. "You must take care of my Alessandro. He is all alone here now. He needs someone to look after him."

"I will, Aunt Rosa."

"You are a good girl."

"I've got to get going now," Rylie said. "Thank you so much for the wonderful food."

Rylie found Alex in the living room and told him she had to go.

"Thank you for coming, Rylie. It really meant a lot to me," Alex said.

Rylie said her goodbyes to all of Alex's relatives. She bent over and gave Nonna a gentle hug.

"Bye, Nonna. I'm so happy I had the chance to meet you," Rylie said.

"You must come to Italy with Alessandro soon," Nonna said. "I'm an old lady. Don't wait too long."

Rylie looked up at Alex. He took her hand and squeezed it. He carried the tote bag full of food and walked with her to her SUV. He stood close in front of her as she stood with her back to the driver's side door. She could smell his masculine scent and feel the warmth that radiated from his body. He took her face in his hands and tilted it slightly upwards.

"My family loves you, Rylie," he said.

She caught her breath. "I love your family," she replied.

He bent down and kissed her on both cheeks. A twinge of disappointment briefly coursed through her when he stopped short of kissing her on the lips.

"Bye, Rylie. I'll talk to you soon."

He strode back inside his house. Rylie opened her SUV's door and put the tote bag and her purse inside. With one last look at Alex's house, she got in and drove back down the long driveway toward home.

She replayed the day's events in her mind as she drove. She had always secretly envied people with large families. Big families were loud and sometimes chaotic, but they seemed to have a special warmth and love for each other. They looked out for each other.

When she got back home, she carried her tote bag full of Italian food inside.

"Hi Bella!"

Bella's nose sniffed the air near Rylie's tote bag.

"I know! It smells good, doesn't it, Bella? But I don't think you'd really like Italian food. I'll get you a doggie health bar."

Bella wagged her tail as she accepted her treat. Rylie put the food in her refrigerator. She transferred everything in her small black purse back to her everyday purse and checked her cell phone. Two calls from Sophie. Sophie hadn't left any messages. She called her back.

"Hi, Sophie! I just got home. Sorry I missed your calls earlier. Alex's Aunt Rosa convinced me to go to Alex's house for the reception after the funeral. I just got home. What's up?"

"It's not good, Rylie," Sophie said. "Aaron finally got the results back from the lab for the powdered substance in the packet they found in back of a trash can at Vinterre. The packet contained dried Death Cap mushrooms."

Chapter 13

"Oh, my goodness," Rylie said. "How did you find out?"

"Aaron showed up at Vinterre this morning and told Lucien. He also told Lucien that they found a partial fingerprint on the packet containing the dried Death Cap mushroom powder. Aaron made everyone that was at work at Vinterre this morning go to the police department to get fingerprinted. Anyone that wasn't working today had to be called and told to go to the police department to get fingerprinted right away."

"Wow."

"Lucien is a wreck. His staff is panicking. He's trying to get his staff to concentrate on what needs to be done to get everything ready for dinner at Vinterre tonight," Sophie said.

"I guess that's why Aaron cancelled our playdate at the dog park for yesterday," Rylie said. "He called me to cancel on Friday night. He said something came up at work."

"He might have felt that spending time with you would be uncomfortable given the circumstances, Rylie. He knows that we're best friends. I don't know. I'm just guessing," Sophie said.

"So do they know that Death Cap mushrooms are what caused Lorenzo Marchetti's death?" Rylie asked.

"Aaron told Lucien that the autopsy results are consistent with Death Cap mushroom poisoning."

"Oh, okay. Not good," Rylie said. "Do you know when they'll have the results from fingerprinting all the staff at Vinterre?"

"Lucien asked Aaron that. Aaron said he should have the results by Wednesday," Sophie said.

"Oh, my goodness. Poor Lucien. I wonder if people are going to stop going to Vinterre because of this," Rylie said.

"Lucien says that business has been slower since the police blocked off the street and searched Vinterre. Now that all the employees have become involved, word will spread through this town like wildfire. This could have a huge impact on Vinterre's business. And Lucien was already having financial problems from when PGE shut off the power for four days in August," Sophie said.

"I'm so sorry, Sophie. Is there anything I can do?"

"I can't think of anything right now, Rylie. I'll let you know if I do. I think it helps just to have someone to talk to about it. I'll keep you in the loop. I've got to go."

Rylie went over to sit on the sofa. Bella came up to her and put her head in Rylie's lap.

She stroked Bella's head absentmindedly. Then she put her arms around Bella's neck and leaned into her. She loved Bella's doggie smell and the warmth of her soft golden fur.

She took a deep breath and put a smile on her face as she walked in the door of Valley View Veterinary Hospital the next morning. The head receptionist, Katie, wasn't at her usual spot to greet her.

"Where's Katie?"

"I think she's in the bathroom," the other receptionist replied. "All I said was "How was your weekend?" and she started crying. I have no idea what's going on, but I can't leave the reception desk unattended to go talk to her."

"I'll go talk to her."

Rylie went to the doctors' office to drop of her things. Then she went to find Katie. The bathroom door was shut and locked. She knocked on the door. She could hear snuffling inside.

"Katie? Are you in there?"

"Yes." Sniffle.

"Are you okay? Do you want to talk?" Rylie asked.

"I'm okay," Katie said in a small voice.

"Why don't you come out here so we can talk. I've got a little bit of time before my first appointment. We can go have a cup of coffee in the break room," Rylie said.

"I don't like coffee."

"Okay, then. I'll have coffee and you can have whatever you'd like to drink."

"Okay." Katie opened the door slowly. Her eyes were bloodshot. She held a wad of crumpled tissues in her hand. Rylie grabbed the box of tissues from the bathroom and ushered Katie to the break room.

"What would you like to drink, Katie?" Rylie asked.

"Is there any Coke in the frig?" Katie asked.

Rylie rummaged around the refrigerator until she found a Coke. She handed it to Katie and sat next to her at the table.

"What's going on, Katie?"

"I'm sure you've heard. It has to be all over town by now," Katie said.

"Heard what, Katie?"

"About the police making everyone that works at Vinterre get fingerprinted, including Hector. Hector was really upset about it. I told him not to worry about it. The police are just doing their job. He got mad at me when I said that. We had a big fight and he stormed out. I think we might have just broken up. I'm not sure. I've never seen him mad like that before," Katie said.

Rylie reached out and put her hand on top of Katie's. "I'm so sorry, Katie. I don't know what to say."

"That's okay, Dr. Sunderland," Katie said. "I know you're just trying to help."

"Did Hector tell you anything about what happened yesterday other than that everyone had to get fingerprinted?" Rylie asked.

"He freaked out when he had to go to the police station to get fingerprinted. I guess he got in trouble with the police about something a few years ago. He didn't give me any details. But he was afraid that the police were going to target him because he's gotten in trouble with them before," Katie said.

"Give him some time, Katie," Rylie said. "He's scared and upset right now. Maybe he just needs some time to be alone. You need to put him out of your mind the best you can so you can get through the day today. Then tonight when you go home, give him a call. Just ask him how he's doing. Don't get into all the details about the fight you had with him. Then see how it goes. Not that I'm a relationship expert or anything." Rylie grinned. "But I think it's worth a try. What do you think?"

"Thanks, Dr. Sunderland." Katie took a sip of her Coke. Then she took a deep breath and tried to force a small smile. "I can do this. All I have to do is get through today. Hopefully we have some cute puppies and kittens coming in today to distract me."

"That would be great." Rylie smiled encouragingly. "Puppies and kittens are the best part of my day, too."

After a busy day at work, Rylie was happy to go home for some rest and relaxation. Bella greeted her at the door wagging her tail and panting.

"Hi, Bella! Do you want to go outside?"

She let Bella out the back door and went to her bedroom to get changed into something more comfortable. Then she went out to the kitchen and got some of the Italian food Alex's aunts had given her out of the refrigerator to microwave for dinner. She put Bella's dinner in her dog dish and then let her back inside. Just as her kitchen was starting to smell like an Italian restaurant, her cell phone rang. Sophie.

"Hi, Sophie. What's up?"

"Hi, Rylie. I'm sorry to bother you when you just got home from work. I just thought you'd like to know that another weird thing happened at Vinterre today," Sophie said.

"Oh, really? What?"

"Lucien went to work a little earlier than normal this morning. As he drove up, he saw a guy in a black hoodie and blue jeans put something on the ground by Vinterre's front door. He parked as fast as he could and ran after the guy, but he wasn't able to catch him. The guy had his hoodie pulled up over his head, so Lucien wasn't able to see his face," Sophie said. "The guy left a flower on the ground in front of Vinterre's door."

Rylie poured herself a glass of wine and sat down at her dining table.

"What kind of flower was it?"

"Um, I don't know. I didn't ask," Sophie said.

"I just read a book about the language of flowers," Rylie said. "It was based on old Victorian flower dictionaries that the author had read. In the UK in the 1800's, it wasn't considered appropriate for people to talk freely about their emotions. So they developed a system of communication using flowers. Each flower had a different meaning. Maybe the guy that put the flower on the ground by Vinterre's front door knows about the meaning of the flower that he put there. Maybe he's delivering a coded message. Can you find out from Lucien what kind of flower it was?"

"Alright. I'll call him right now before he gets too busy with dinner at Vinterre."

Rylie made herself a small green salad to go with her lasagna and stuffed shells. She brought her food into the living room to eat and turned on the TV. Her cell phone rang, and she saw on the caller ID that it was Sophie.

"Hi, Sophie."

"Hi, Rylie. Lucien said it was a Black-eyed Susan."

"Does he still have the flower? He should give it to Detective Michelson so they can see if they can get any of the guy's DNA from it."

"I doubt if Aaron is going to put manpower into looking for DNA on a flower. It's not like it's a crime to give someone a flower."

"Good point. I'll see if I still have that book about the language of flowers on my e-reader. It had a small flower dictionary in the back of the book. If I don't have it anymore, I'll check it out from the library again and see if I can find out what a Black-eyed Susan means," Rylie said. "I'm going to finish eating my dinner first. I'll call you back later."

"Okay."

After she finished her dinner, Rylie downloaded the book about the language of flowers from the library again. She quickly found the entry for Black-eyed Susan. She called Sophie back.

"I found it. A Black-eyed Susan means justice."

"What's that supposed to mean?" Sophie said. "That guy's crazy."

"Maybe the guy thinks that Lucien is getting what he deserves since the police were at Vinterre again yesterday and all the employees had to get fingerprinted."

"Could be," Sophie said. "What a coward that guy is. Sneaking around at night, vandalizing things at Vinterre, and now trying to send a coded message to Lucien."

"Maybe Lucien should go to work a little early more often. Maybe he'll be able to catch the guy. Then he can call the police and have the guy arrested. Show him what justice really is," Rylie said.

"Good idea. I'll suggest it to Lucien. I'll sure never look at a Black-eyed Susan the same way again," Sophie said. "Have a good night. I'll talk to you soon."

When Rylie walked into Valley View Veterinary Hospital the next morning, Katie was in her usual place at the reception desk.

"Hi, Katie!" Rylie smiled.

"Good morning, Dr. Sunderland," Katie said.

Rylie went into the doctors' office to drop off her things. The other two veterinarians, Cassandra and Addison, were already at their desks.

"Morning, Rylie," Cassandra said. "There are warm cinnamon rolls in the break room, if you're interested. One of our clients brought them in for us. Better hurry if you want one. They won't last long."

"Oh, yum. I'll go get one right now." Rylie made a beeline for the break room. She put a warm cinnamon roll on a paper plate and made herself a cup of coffee with the Keurig coffeemaker. While she was waiting for her coffee to brew, she took a bite of the cinnamon roll. Heaven. Katie walked in as she was stirring milk into her coffee.

"Hi, Katie. Did you get one of these delicious cinnamon rolls? Oh my goodness. They're delicious," Rylie said.

"Just came in here to get one." Katie smiled at her.

"You look like you're feeling better today," Rylie said.

"Yes, I am feeling better. I talked to Hector last night and we worked everything out."

"That's great, Katie. I'm happy for you."

Rylie took her cinnamon roll and coffee back to the doctors' office. There was a small stack of labwork results on top of her computer keyboard. She went through them, took out the fecal test results that were negative for intestinal parasites, and put them in a separate stack. She would ask the techs to call the clients whose pets had negative fecal test results. She put on her white lab coat and draped her stethoscope around her neck.

She took another bite of her cinnamon roll. "These cinnamon rolls are amazing."

"Yes, we're lucky to have some very nice clients that bring us treats. Especially during the holidays. We get a lot of goodies over the holidays," Addison said.

"Did you decide what you're going to be for Halloween tomorrow, Rylie?" Cassandra asked.

"Yes. I went to Party City in Fairfield on Saturday. I'm going to be Hermione Granger from the Harry Potter books. I even got a wand. Hopefully it works, and I'll be able to perform some magic tomorrow." Rylie grinned.

Cassandra smiled. "Cool. It's always fun when everyone dresses up for Halloween."

Miley walked into the room carrying a clipboard in front of her. "Good morning, Dr. Sunderland. I have your first appointment for you."

She followed Miley out of the doctors' office to her first appointment. Her appointments were scheduled every thirty minutes. As she walked out of an exam room a while later, Dr. Cassandra Lambert was standing there with a clipboard in her hand.

"Hey, Dr. Sunderland, could I get you to look at these x-rays with me?" Cassandra asked.

"Sure." She followed Cassandra into the x-ray room to look at the digital x-rays on the computer monitor.

"So this is a fourteen-year-old Shih Tzu named Bitsy. The owner says that Bitsy hasn't been acting herself for the past couple weeks. She's not interested in playing with the owner or going for her walks. The owner says that Bitsy usually loves going on her walks. I had the techs take three-view met check x-rays of her chest and two views of her abdomen. What do you think?"

Rylie looked through all the x-rays on the touchscreen computer monitor. "Nothing's really jumping out at me. But I'd recommend that you send these out for a boarded radiologist to review. Sometimes the radiologists find things that we don't."

"Absolutely. I plan to. I just wanted to see if you noticed anything that I didn't. I couldn't find anything abnormal either," Cassandra said.

"Does she have a fever? Is she coughing? Does she have any clinical signs other than that she doesn't want to play or go on her walks?" Rylie asked.

"No fever. No other clinical signs. And she checked out fine on her physical exam," Cassandra said.

"Are you sending out bloodwork and a urinalysis?" Rylie asked.

"Yes, I'm sending out a Senior Profile."

"Well, maybe something will turn up on the bloodwork," Rylie said. "Did you check to see if she has any back pain? I do see a little bit of arthritis in her back on these x-rays. Did you flex and extend the joints in all her legs and watch her walk? Maybe she's having some back pain or joint pain that's making it uncomfortable for her to get around."

"Good idea. I'll go check that now. Thanks, Dr. Sunderland."

Rylie finished her morning appointments and went into the doctors' office to type up her medical records from that morning. She reviewed the lab results she had ordered the previous day and called the owners with the results and her treatment plans. She managed to slam down a quick lunch while she worked.

In the mid-afternoon, she started to think about what she was going to have for dinner. When she had a few minutes between appointments, she went online to the Goose and Gander restaurant's website to place an order for a burger that she could pick up on her way home from work. She read through the menu. The G & G Burger caught her eye: Grass-fed beef, Gruyère cheese, bacon, rémoulade, gem lettuce, Manhattan pickle, duck fat fries. Yum.

The smell of the hot burger tantalized her on the drive home. When she opened the door to her house, Bella's nose went into overdrive. Bella lifted her head and sniffed the bag that Rylie carried with the burger and fries.

"Oh boy, Bella. I've got a yummy, yummy burger for dinner. I'll share some of it with you."

Bella wagged her tail hopefully. She let Bella outside to do her business and then put her purse and other things away. She put Bella's dinner in her dog dish and then let her back inside. Bella stayed close while she sat down with her burger and fries at the dining table.

Rylie pulled off a small piece of her burger and gave it to Bella.

"You didn't even chew that, Bella. How could you possibly have even tasted it?"

Rylie reached over and stroked Bella's head. Then she took a large bite of the juicy burger.

"Wow. This is delicious." She loved burgers and considered herself somewhat of a burger connoisseur.

"This is one of the best burgers I've ever had."

Bella looked up at her with big brown eyes. Rylie chuckled and tore off another small piece of burger to give her.

Rylie sighed contently. She got up and poured herself a glass of cabernet sauvignon to go with her meal.

"What do you think, Bella? Maybe we'll have to stay in St. Helena just for the burgers."

The next morning, Rylie dressed carefully for her Halloween role as Hermione Granger from the Harry Potter books. She put on a white collared shirt and knotted a scarlet and gold-striped men's tie around her neck. She pulled on some black tights, stepped into a knee-length A-line black skirt, and buttoned a charcoal gray sweater with Gryffindor scarlet and gold stripes on the cuffs and waistline hem over her shirt. She examined the results in the full-length mirror in the bedroom. She pointed a wand at her reflection.

"Hmmm. I need a spell to say when I point my wand."

She went online and searched for Harry Potter spells and their meanings.

"Aparecium! Perfect." She read:

Aparecium (Revealing Charm):
Reveals secret messages written in invisible ink, or any other hidden markings. Also works against Concealing charms.

Bella stood nearby watching her.

"If only there actually was a Revealing Charm, Bella. It would make it so much easier to find out who really killed Lorenzo Marchetti. I hope this case gets wrapped up soon."

It was fun seeing everyone in their Halloween costumes at work. The clients seemed to enjoy it, too. But she was so busy all day that she was more than ready to head home when six o'clock rolled around.

Bella greeted her at the door, happy to see her. Rylie let Bella outside and went in the bedroom to change. Her cell phone rang. Sophie.

"Hi, Sophie."

"I thought you'd like to know that Aaron finally got the results of Vinterre's employees' fingerprints today," Sophie said. "The partial fingerprint on the packet of Death Cap mushroom powder belongs to the waiter who served Lorenzo Marchetti at the Chamber of Commerce awards dinner. Hector Briseno."

"Oh, no. Poor Katie," Rylie said.

"Who's Katie?" Sophie asked.

"Katie is Hector Briseno's girlfriend. She's the head receptionist at Valley View Veterinary Hospital."

"Oh. Well the police went to Vinterre to pick up Hector and take him in for questioning this afternoon. Aaron called

Lucien to pick Hector up at the police department a while later. Lucien asked Aaron what was going on. That's when Aaron told Lucien that the partial fingerprint on the packet belonged to Hector."

"Okay. So apparently they didn't charge Hector with anything since they let him go when they were done questioning him. What did Hector say when Aaron questioned him?"

"He said he didn't know anything about it. He said he must have seen a piece of trash laying around and tossed it in the trash can."

"So the murder investigation is back to square one?" Rylie asked.

"I don't think so. Aaron told Lucien that he wasn't anywhere close to being done with Hector. He said he's going to do some more digging," Sophie said.

"If Hector claims that he didn't know anything about the packet, then it would be pretty hard to prove that he did, wouldn't it?" Rylie asked.

"I guess we'll just have to wait and see what Aaron has up his sleeve. He's a really good detective, Rylie. Super smart. And very driven. He won't give up until he gets the answers he's looking for."

Chapter 14

Rylie was woken up the next morning by the sound of someone knocking on her front door. She jumped out of bed and put on some slippers. She hurried to the front door wearing her dark blue plaid flannel sleep pants and a navy-blue t-shirt. Her jaw dropped open when she opened the door. Aaron was standing there with a sheepish grin and a takeout cardboard tray containing two coffees. He held up a paper bag.

"I have chocolate croissants." He smiled hopefully.

"Well come on in then," Rylie said. "How did you find out where I live?"

"Sophie gave me your address."

"The kitchen is this way. There are plates in that cabinet over there. Make yourself comfortable. I'm just going to get dressed. I'll be right back."

She dashed into her bedroom and threw on some jeans and a cream-colored cable knit wool sweater with flower-shaped silver buttons on the shoulders. She quickly brushed her teeth, washed her face, and brushed her hair. She walked back out to the kitchen to see Bella staring adoringly at Aaron as he scratched around her ears.

"Come on, Bella. Let's go outside," Rylie said.

She let Bella out the back door, put some kibble in her dog dish and got her some fresh water, and let her back in a few minutes later. Then she sat down with Aaron at the kitchen table.

"I didn't mean to wake you up," Aaron said. "It should have occurred to me that you'd be sleeping in on your day off."

"Don't worry about it. I'm fine. Especially since you brought coffee and chocolate croissants. I love chocolate croissants."

"Oh good." Aaron smiled at her. "I was hoping you would. I wanted to tell you that I was sorry about having to cancel our playdate with the dogs on Saturday. I was hoping that coffee and croissants would convince you to meet me at the dog park for a playdate with the dogs tomorrow."

"You had me at coffee," Rylie said. "But the chocolate croissants didn't hurt, either. Sure, we'll meet up with you and Max at the dog park tomorrow."

"I saw you at the funeral on Sunday," Aaron said. "But I had to leave a little bit before it ended. Did you know Lorenzo Marchetti?"

"No. I never met him. But Alex told me that it would mean a lot to him if I was there."

"Did you go to the cemetery and the reception after the funeral?" Aaron asked.

"Just the reception. Alex's Aunt Rosa wouldn't take no for an answer."

Aaron took a sip of his coffee, then a bite of his croissant. He chewed it thoughtfully.

"Alex is a good man," he said finally.

"Yes, he is. His whole family was very warm and welcoming. And I got to eat lots of incredible Italian food. A bunch of his family members flew in from Italy for the funeral. His aunts were cooking food for the reception all day on Saturday."

"Lucky you. I love Italian food." Aaron smiled.

"They sent me home with a whole tote bag full of delicious leftovers."

"I'm glad Alex's family was able to fly in from Italy for his father's funeral. People need family around them when something like this happens," Aaron said. He paused for a beat. "I'm sure that you heard that it was Hector Briseno's fingerprint on the packet of Death Cap mushroom powder that we found in Vinterre. He claims that he didn't know anything about it. He said he probably just saw a piece of trash laying around and tossed it in the trash can."

"And you don't believe him."

"It doesn't matter whether I believe him or not. But I'm going to follow that lead until there's no place left to go with it. It's the best lead I've got right now," Aaron said.

"I understand. I hope you're able to wrap up this murder investigation as soon as possible. For everyone's sakes."

"Me too. Look, Rylie, I have to run. I'll see you tomorrow at the dog park, okay? How about sometime in the afternoon? Say around 3:00?"

"Okay."

Rylie walked Aaron to the front door and opened it for him.

"Bye, Bella." Aaron reached down and stroked Bella's head. Bella wagged her tail. He looked up at Rylie. "See you tomorrow."

Just before noon, Rylie drove to Cresswell Wines to meet up with Patricia Davenport and her friends for the wine and cheese pairing that Liza Cresswell was hosting for them. The entrance to Cresswell Wines was framed with dark wood with a large trellis on top. She followed the driveway through the vineyards until she arrived at the parking area. The main building was long with dark wood siding and lots of tall windows. It had a contemporary look with rustic charm.

"Hi, Rylie! Welcome!" Liza Cresswell greeted her at the door. Patricia, Kinsley, Maggie, and Carolyn were there waiting with her.

"Now that we're all here, I'll take you ladies on a little tour of our winery. Then we'll go to the barrel room for our wine and cheese pairing," Liza said.

The barrel room was warm and inviting. Soft toffee-colored leather sofas and upholstered chairs were arranged around tables down the entire length of the long rectangular room. The brown wood walls and vaulted ceiling matched the exterior of the building. Floor to ceiling windows ran the length of the room and flooded the room with natural light. There were stunning views of the vineyards ablaze in fall colors stretching across the valley to the softly rounded mountains in the distance. On the wall opposite the windows were massive oak wine barrels laying on their sides. Beautiful wood and glass light fixtures filled with tiny flame-shaped lights hung from the vaulted ceiling over the sitting areas.

"This is gorgeous, Liza!" Rylie said. The other women enthusiastically agreed.

Liza led them to a seating area with sofas and chairs arranged around a large square wood coffee table. A lazy Susan in the middle of the table contained artfully arranged salami, ham, gherkin pickles, green olives, red and green grapes, sliced red apples, strawberries, blueberries, pistachios, mustard, crackers, and crostini.

Wine glasses and rectangular plates containing five different cheeses had been set in front of each seat. Bottles of white wine in ice buckets were flanked by bottles of red wine on a hostess stand in front of the windows.

"Please make yourselves comfortable," Liza said. They all sat around the coffee table.

"Did you make all this yourself?" Rylie asked. "It looks delicious."

"No. We have staff that put together the charcuterie boards. We offer charcuterie boards as well as wine and cheese pairings to the public," Liza said. "Shall we begin?"

"Yes!" Patricia said.

"The first wine we'll be tasting is our 2017 Sauvignon Blanc," Liza said. She poured a small amount in each of the women's wine glasses.

"This lovely wine has aromas of white flower, orange blossom, and citrus. If you let it sit on your tongue for a minute, you can taste apple, pear, and lemon. Now for the cheese pairing. We'll be tasting the cheeses starting at the left side of your plates and working our way to the right. The cheese we've chosen to pair with our Sauvignon Blanc is the cheese on the far left of your plates. It's a soft, creamy brie called Mon Pere from France."

Rylie concentrated on the flavor of the wine and then spread some brie on a cracker and ate it. The flavors complemented each other nicely.

"What do you ladies think?" Liza asked. She took a sip of her wine.

"The wine is wonderful, Liza," Patricia said. "And the brie is great with it."

"Delicious," Maggie said.

"Amazing," Carolyn said.

"I second that," Kinsley said.

"I love it," Rylie said.

"That's the only white wine we're making right now," Liza said. "The next wine we're going to taste is our Cabernet Franc Reserve." Liza poured a small amount in each of the women's wine glasses as she continued.

"It has aromas of espresso, dark chocolate, and red cherries with flavors of blackberry cobbler, plums, and raspberries. The cheese we've paired with our Cabernet Franc Reserve is Sainte-Maure goat cheese from France. It's a smooth, buttery cheese with an edible rind."

"Oh my goodness. That's incredible," Rylie said. "Do you sell these cheeses here as well as your wines?"

"No, we don't sell the cheeses here. But we have a list of the cheeses that we use for our wine pairings with suggestions as to where you can buy them. Remind me to get that for you before you leave," Liza said. "We also have a list of all the wines that we serve in our tastings with descriptions of each. Here, let me get those for you."

Liza got some paper copies of their wine list and some pens from a shelf under the hostess stand and handed them out to the women.

"You can write your thoughts about each wine on the wine list as we go along. That way you'll know which ones you like if you decide to buy any of them later," Liza said.

Liza served them a nice merlot next paired with another cheese from France.

"The St. Helena AVA is well known for its cabernet sauvignon. We make several different cabs. We'll taste two of them today," Liza said.

"Our 2013 Cabernet Sauvignon has flavors of dark chocolate truffle, cherries, plums, and blackberries. We've paired it with Ossau-Iraty sheep's milk cheese from France," Liza said.

The second Cabernet Sauvignon that they tasted was paired with an aged gouda from Holland.

"Please, help yourself to the charcuterie board, ladies," Liza said. "And if you would like any more of any of the wines we've just tasted, just let me know, and I'll get you a full glass of whichever one you'd like."

"This was so nice of you, Liza," Rylie said. "I'd like to buy some of these wines before I go home."

"No problem, Rylie." Liza smiled. "I'm so glad you like our wines."

"I want to buy some of your wines, too," Kinsley said. "I have a glass of wine with dinner pretty much every night."

The women sipped wine and chatted as they helped themselves to the charcuterie board.

"Have you ladies heard what's been going on with Lorenzo Marchetti's murder investigation?" Patricia asked. "One of my friend's daughters works at Vinterre. A couple of weeks ago, the police showed up at Vinterre and said they needed to search the restaurant. I guess they thought that Lorenzo may have eaten something toxic during the Chamber of Commerce awards dinner. The staff found out later that the police found a packet with some brown powder in it on the floor behind a trash can in Vinterre."

"This past Sunday, the police showed up at Vinterre again," Patricia continued. "They told the staff that they found a fingerprint on the packet with the brown powder in it and that everyone that worked at Vinterre had to go to the police department to get fingerprinted. On Wednesday, the police went back to Vinterre and took one of the waiters that works there, Hector Briseno, in for questioning. When Hector got back from the police department a while later, he told everyone at Vinterre that the police told him that the fingerprint on the packet of brown powder was his. He said that he told the police that he didn't know anything about it. He said that if his fingerprint was on the packet, it was probably because he saw a piece of trash lying around and tossed it in the trash."

"Do they know what the brown powder in the packet was?" Carolyn asked.

"I heard it was dried Death Cap mushrooms," Kinsley said.

"Where did you hear that?" Carolyn asked.

"I do a lot of research about poisons for the murder mysteries that I write. I know people," Kinsley said.

"Hector Briseno. That name sounds familiar," Maggie said. "Wait, wasn't he the guy that pulled a knife on another guy at Gott's Roadside restaurant a few years back?"

"What?" Rylie's shoulders tensed.

"Oh, yeah! I remember that," Kinsley said.

"Oh, yes. I remember that now, too," Patricia said. "It was all over the news. It was all anyone could talk about for days."

A guy wearing a Cresswell Wines shirt came up and whispered something in Liza's ear.

"Okay. I'll be right there," she replied.

"Ladies, I'm sorry, but I have to go. I've got something that I need to take care of. I hope you all had a good time. Give me a call or text me after you decide what we're going to do next week. Anything you decide is fine with me. Rylie and Kinsley, and any of you who might want to purchase some of our wines, go through that door and down the hall. That will take you to our store. My staff will be happy to help you with anything you want."

"Thank you, Liza," Rylie said. "This was great."

Everyone chimed in with their thanks before Liza left.

"I'm going to have to leave now too," Patricia said. "Let's think about what we might like to do next Thursday. We can email or text each other with our ideas."

"I've got to go now too," Maggie said. "This was really fun."

Carolyn stood to leave. "I have some ideas as to what we can do next Thursday. I'll send an email to everyone. Bye now!"

Rylie and Kinsley headed down the hall to the store. A guy at the counter helped them with their purchases.

"I loved the Cabernet Sauvignons that we tasted," Rylie said. "I'd like two bottles of each. And Liza said you'd have a list of the cheeses that you use for your wine pairings with suggestions as to where we can purchase them?"

"Of course," the guy said. He handed a copy of the cheese list to each of them.

"Thanks," Rylie said. "Now I can invite people over to my house for wine and cheese pairings."

"I'd like two bottles of your Cabernet Franc, two bottles of your Merlot, and two bottles of the last Cabernet Sauvignon that we tasted," Kinsley said.

After they paid for their purchases, Rylie and Kinsley headed out to the parking lot with their wines.

"If you're not doing anything later this afternoon, I'd love to come and see your poisonous plants garden," Rylie said. "But if you're busy, that's fine. We can do it another time."

"I'd love to show you my poisonous plants garden, Rylie. I've got some things I need to do right now, but I should be free by about 3:30 this afternoon. Does that work for you?"

"That's perfect. What's your address?"

Chapter 15

Rylie drove to Vinterre and parked her SUV. She walked through the dappled sunlight under the beautiful grapevine arbor over the cobblestone path leading to the entrance and went inside. There were still a lot of people at the dining tables eating lunch.

The hostess stepped up to the hostess stand. "One for lunch?"

"Oh, no. I'm not here for lunch. I'm here to see Lucien Marchand. He's a friend of mine. I'm Dr. Rylie Sunderland. Could you please tell him I'm here?"

"Lucien is busy in the kitchen right now. We're right in the middle of lunch service," the girl said.

"I know. I'm sorry. But it's important. Could you please let him know I'm here?"

The girl turned on her heel and stalked away in the direction of the kitchen. She returned with an ingratiating smile on her face.

"Right this way, Dr. Sunderland."

Rylie followed the hostess into Lucien's kitchen. Lucien looked up from his cooking as she walked in and smiled.

"Rylie! What a surprise! What brings you here?"

"Hi, Lucien. I'm sorry to bother you right in the middle of lunch service. I was wondering if I could talk to you privately in your office for a few minutes. It won't take long."

Lucien held a spoon in front of her with a creamy soup in it. "Taste this and tell me what you think."

Rylie accepted the spoonful of soup. "Yum. Is it cream of broccoli?"

"Yes, except it's my special recipe with a secret ingredient. It's my soup of the day for our dinner service tonight. Would you like a takeout container of it to take home?"

"That would be great. Thank you!"

Lucien ladled some of his cream of broccoli soup into a takeout container and handed it to her. Then he wiped his hands on a towel. "Right this way."

Rylie followed him into his office.

"I was wondering if you know if anyone took photos at the Chamber of Commerce awards dinner," Rylie said. Lucien's smile faded.

"Are you playing amateur sleuth, Rylie?"

"You know that I've got to do whatever I can to help until you've been cleared of suspicion, Lucien. This murder investigation is causing you and Sophie a lot of stress. I can't just pretend like nothing's going on."

Lucien sighed. "I appreciate your wanting to help, Rylie. I really do. But I don't think there's anything you can do that the police aren't doing already. Sophie has assured me that Detective Michelson is very good at his job and that he'll get to the bottom of this as quickly as possible."

"I have no intention of interfering with Detective Michelson's investigation, Lucien," Rylie said. "I'm looking for any way that I might be able to help him with his investigation. That's all. If I happen upon any information that I think might be useful to him, I tell him about it right away. Please, Lucien. Do you know if anyone took any photos that night?"

"Yes. One of my waitresses is really into photography. She asked me if she could take photos of the awards dinner. I told her that was a great idea but that I would only agree to it if she allowed me to pay her for her time. She took tons of photos that night. I've already provided them to Detective Michelson."

"Are they on your laptop? Could you email them to me?"

"Alright, Rylie. But you have to promise me that you're not going to interfere in the investigation."

"I promise."

Lucien typed a few things on his laptop. "There. I just emailed them to you as a zip file."

"Thanks, Lucien. And thank you for the delicious soup."

"No problem, Rylie. I've got to get back to work now. See you later." Lucien hurried back to his kitchen.

Rylie headed home to take a look at the photos.

Bella greeted her at the door with a big golden grin. She wagged her tail happily as Rylie walked inside.

"Hi, Bella! Were you a good girl for me while I was gone?"

Bella's tail wagged faster as she looked hopefully up at Rylie. Rylie gave her a dog biscuit which she demolished in a flash.

Rylie set up her laptop on the kitchen dining table and opened her email. She downloaded Lucien's zip file and extracted all the photos to her laptop. Then she backed them up in her cloud storage. She started going through all the photos one by one, looking for anything that seemed unusual or out of place. She looked to see if anyone seemed to be staring at Lorenzo Marchetti. Nothing was leaping out at her as looking suspicious. She packed up her laptop in her carrying case so she could take it to Kinsley's house. She wanted Kinsley to look through the photos, too.

A little before 3:30, she headed over to Kinsley's house with her laptop.

Kinsley opened the door with a smile. "Hi, Rylie! Come on in! I'm so happy you were able to come today."

Rylie followed Kinsley through her house.

"You can leave your bags here on the kitchen table if you want, Rylie."

"Okay." Rylie set her laptop and purse on Kinsley's table. Kinsley was holding the back door open for her.

She stepped out into Kinsley's backyard. Flowers were blooming in a raised wood flower bed that ran along the back fence. A patio dining set with four chairs was arranged on the patio that was just outside the back door. There was an outdoor kitchen with a barbecue grill on one side of the patio. Over on the left side of the lawn, upholstered patio furniture was arranged around a rectangular fire pit. Fairy lights were strung around the fire pit area.

"This is amazing, Kinsley!" Rylie exclaimed. "This is such a beautiful backyard. You could have incredible parties here."

Kinsley grinned. "I've been known to have some great parties here from time to time. You'll be invited the next time I have one. Don't worry."

"Are the flowers along the back fence poisonous?" Rylie asked.

"No. I have a secret garden where I keep my poisonous plants," Kinsley said. "I don't want anyone mistakenly touching one of them. Some of the plants that I grow are poisonous to the touch. I have to use gloves to work with them."

Kinsley led the way across the lawn to the fence on the right side of the yard. She reached over the top of the fence and unlatched a concealed door. She pushed open the door and ushered Rylie inside. Rylie took a tentative step into the enclosed garden.

Raised wood flower beds ran along all four sides of the space. Many of the plants looked dormant, but there were still some in bloom. Weathered brick pavers in muted shades of red, brown, and gold were laid in a herringbone pattern over the ground between the raised flower beds. There was a blue-gray, two-tiered ceramic birdbath in one of the raised flower beds with a fountain splashing merrily over the small top basin into the larger fluted bottom basin. A blue-gray ceramic bird perched jauntily on top of the fountain.

"This is beautiful! What a special place," Rylie said. Her gaze continued to travel around the garden. There was an ornate metal bistro set with a small round table and chairs on the brick pavers near the birdbath fountain. On the other side of the garden, there were two dark brown wicker chairs with turquoise cushions, matching ottomans, and patterned turquoise accent pillows arranged on each side of a round metal and glass accent table.

"I like to come in here to write when the weather is nice," Kinsley said. "Or sometimes I like to just curl up in one of the wicker chairs and read a good book."

"There aren't many of my poisonous plants in bloom this late in the fall, but I still have a couple of late bloomers," Kinsley continued. "Just be careful not to touch any of them."

She led the way to a tall shrub with long slender leaves and pale pink flowers that sprawled about six feet along one of the fences.

"I'm sure you recognize this plant. You see it growing as large hedges in the center divide of many of the freeways around here. It's called oleander. It can grow up to twenty feet high, but I keep it pruned to stay below the top of the fence. Every part of the oleander, including its branches, leaves, flowers, and roots are toxic. Ingestion of any part of the plant can cause irregular heart rate, diarrhea, vomiting, headache, dizziness, and blurry vision. It can also cause respiratory failure, convulsions, coma, and in severe cases, death."

"Whoa. It seems strange that they would plant something so potentially dangerous all along the freeways," Rylie said.

"I guess they don't expect people to stop in the middle of the freeway to pick flowers," Kinsley said. "That's the only rationale I can come up with for why they would plant a highly poisonous plant along the freeways."

Kinsley walked over to a large shrub with pale yellow trumpet-shaped flowers hanging from its branches.

"These are Angel Trumpets," she said.

"They smell pretty," Rylie said.

"Yes, their smell helps to attract pollinators," Kinsley said. "Every part of Angel Trumpets are highly poisonous, including the leaves, flowers, seeds, and roots. The toxins can enter the bloodstream by being ingested or by being absorbed through mucous membranes like when someone touches the plant and then rubs their eyes or eats food. The toxins in Angel Trumpets can cause muscle weakness, rapid heart rate, fever, hallucinations, paralysis, and convulsions. They can also lead to coma and death."

"Okay, then," Rylie said. "This is very educational. I think I've seen these flowers growing on people's fences within easy reach of anyone walking by their houses. I'm glad I never tried to pick any of the flowers."

Kinsley walked over to a shrub with dark green leaves and purple bell-shaped flowers.

"This is Deadly Nightshade, also known as Belladonna," Kinsley said. "It's purple-black berries are called Devil's cherries. All parts of the plant are toxic. Deadly Nightshade can cause rapid heart rate, delirium, vomiting, hallucinations, and death from respiratory failure. The toxins can even be absorbed through the skin if someone touches the plant."

"Why do you grow all these poisonous plants, Kinsley? I know you said you like to use poisons to kill off some of your characters in the murder mysteries that you write, but couldn't you just look at photos of these plants?" Rylie asked.

"Yes, I suppose I could. But I'm an avid gardener, as you can tell from my backyard, and I just wanted to get a real feel for the toxic plants that I use in my books. How they smell, how they look up close. I take lots of photos when they're in full bloom and use them in the PowerPoint presentation about poisons that I give at the St. Helena library every year. I think I told you that I also give webinars about poisons for some of the writing groups that I belong to. Having so many toxic plants right here in my garden makes it easy for me to get a lot of the photos that I need for my presentations. But I still have to go out on hikes to find some of the toxic plants that I talk about in my presentations to get all the photos I want."

"Like to get photos of Death Cap mushrooms?" Rylie asked.

"Yes. I definitely don't grow Death Cap mushrooms here. They grow around oak trees in the woods," Kinsley said. "They're especially prolific in the early winter rainy season around here. I'll probably be going mushroom hunting again soon."

"What do you do when you find the Death Cap mushrooms?" Rylie asked. "Do you pick them?"

"No. I just take lots of photos."

"Speaking of Death Cap mushrooms," Rylie said. "I'm not sure if you know that Sophie Marchand has been my best friend since college. Lucien went to college with us, too. He was one year ahead of us. I want to do whatever I can to help clear Lucien's name of any suspicion in Lorenzo Marchetti's murder. The stress of this murder investigation is really taking a toll on Sophie and Lucien. I'm not planning to interfere with Detective Michelson's investigation, but I am on the lookout for anything that I can find that might help him with his investigation. And I'd like your help."

"Alright. What did you have in mind?" Kinsley said.

"I think fiction writers look at the world differently than other people," Rylie said. "I think you notice little details about people and the things going on around you that other people might miss. You have to write descriptions that enable readers to envision the places that you describe. You want your readers to feel the emotions that your characters are feeling. Little details are important to you. Am I right?"

"Absolutely."

"So I'd really appreciate it if you would look at some photos of the Chamber of Commerce awards dinner that Lucien's waitress took. Lucien has already provided the photos to Detective Michelson. I looked through them before I came over and didn't see anything that looked suspicious or out of place. But maybe there's something you will see that everyone else has missed. Would you mind?"

"Not at all," Kinsley said. "Do you have the photos with you?"

"Yes, they're on my laptop. That's why I brought my laptop with me."

"Okay. Why don't we go inside then? I'll make us some tea and we can sit at the kitchen table and look through the photos together."

Kinsley led the way inside to her kitchen.

"What kind of tea do you like? I have regular black tea, Earl Grey, chamomile, a nice one with chamomile and lavender, cinnamon spice. Here. Why don't you look through all the tea I have and pick one while I get the teapot going."

"I think cinnamon spice sounds good," Rylie said.

"Cinnamon spice it is then."

Rylie opened her laptop and pulled up the photos from the Chamber of Commerce awards dinner. Kinsley brought a chair over to sit next to Rylie. Rylie pushed the laptop over in front of Kinsley.

"You can look through them at your own pace," Rylie said.

Kinsley started going through the photos one by one.

"Wow. It looks like they had a good turnout," Kinsley said.

"I think everyone was looking forward to a good meal at Vinterre. Lucien is an amazing chef," Rylie said.

"Do you know who this guy is?" Kinsley said finally.

"Yes. That's Hector Briseno, the guy whose fingerprint was found on the packet with Death Cap mushroom powder in it."

"Well, if he hadn't left a fingerprint on the packet, this would be pretty incriminating evidence," Kinsley said. She pointed to a small packet falling to the floor below the two plates of food that Hector was holding in front of himself. Rylie looked at Hector's face. He looked like he had gotten caught with his hand in the cookie jar.

"Wow, Kinsley. You're good," Rylie said. "I wonder if Detective Michelson or anyone on his team has seen this. I'm meeting him at Wappo dog park tomorrow afternoon so our dogs can play with each other. I'll show him this then."

Kinsley raised an eyebrow.

"What?" Rylie asked.

"I don't have to have any special skills to see that something's going on with you and Aaron Michelson. Spill."

"There's nothing going on with me and Aaron Michelson, Kinsley," Rylie said. Her mouth felt a little dry.

"I called him last week with some information I found out about that I thought might be useful to him in his murder investigation. I asked him if I could meet him somewhere to talk. He said he was at the dog park with his dog Max and asked if I could meet him there. So I took my golden retriever Bella to the dog park to talk to him. Bella and Max had fun together. So Aaron said we should get the dogs together again for a playdate sometime. No big deal." She swallowed a lump in her throat.

"Surely you've noticed that Aaron Michelson is really hot?" Kinsley teased.

"I'll be honest with you, Kinsley. I never really noticed it until I saw him in jeans and a t-shirt at the dog park that night," Rylie said. "Every other time I saw him before that was in his capacity as a police detective. When he's off duty and relaxed, he's a totally different person."

Kinsley raised her eyebrows and remained silent.

"Okay. And hot." Rylie smiled. "Now can we get back to business here?"

Kinsley continued pouring through the photos.

"Here's something interesting," she said finally. "Do you know this guy?"

Rylie looked at the man she was pointing to at Lorenzo Marchetti's table. "No."

"That's Viktor Bergman. He and his wife own the local hardware store. He was involved in a bit of a scandal this past summer. He was in a boating accident on Lake Berryessa in which another man nearly drowned. The circumstances surrounding the incident were kind of sketchy, but no charges were filed," Kinsley said.

"Look at these photos. He's taking photos of each person at Lorenzo Marchetti's table. But I don't think he's actually interested in the people as much as what's on their plates. He has his camera aimed at the plates, not at people's faces. And everyone's plates are nearly empty. So it's like he wants to see what each person ate," she continued.

"Oh, my goodness. You're right." Rylie stared at the photos of Viktor Bergman. "This could be really important. Thank you so much, Kinsley. You're amazing."

"It was no trouble at all, Rylie," Kinsley said. "You're talking to a woman who writes murder mysteries for a living. Murder mysteries are kind of my thing."

Chapter 16

Rylie allowed herself the luxury of sleeping in the next morning. She had decided to stay home and relax until it was time to meet Detective Michelson and his dog Max at the dog park later that day. When she finally rolled out of bed, she let Bella outside to do her business and went into the kitchen to get her coffee brewing and get Bella's breakfast.

"Bella! Come! Breakfast!" she hollered out the back door. Bella trotted up with an eager expression on her face. She whisked through the back door and headed straight for her dog dish full of food.

Rylie ate a leisurely breakfast and then went to shower and get dressed. She slipped into some jeans and a t-shirt, then pulled on a sweater over the top of her t-shirt. She was brushing her hair when her cell phone rang.

"Hi, Sophie. What's up?"

"Rylie, I have to talk to you. It's important. But I can't get away. I have contractors working here and I have to stay on top of things or things won't get done right. Can you come over to where I'm working?"

"Sure, Sophie. Just text me the address, and I'll be right over."

Rylie drove over to Sophie's latest house renovation project and parked on the street out front. The front door was ajar, so she let herself in.

"Sophie? Where are you?"

Sophie emerged from a room at the back of the house.

"Rylie! Thanks for coming. I have contractors all over this house. Let's go sit outside on the back patio for a few minutes."

"Okay."

Sophie strode toward the back of the house and let them out the French doors that opened onto the back patio. She sat down at the patio table. Rylie sat across from her.

"You're kind of scaring me, Sophie. What's going on?"

Sophie's hands were trembling where they rested on the table. She reached over and put her hands over Sophie's.

"Aaron called Lucien this morning. Hector Briseno has been charged with involuntary manslaughter in the murder of Lorenzo Marchetti! He's in jail until he can post bail," Sophie said.

"What does involuntary manslaughter mean? He killed Lorenzo Marchetti by accident?"

"Lucien asked Aaron the same question. Aaron says it's an unplanned, unintentional killing," Sophie said.

"Okay. I think you need to start from the beginning. This isn't making any sense."

Sophie took a shaky breath.

"Aaron got access to Hector's bank account. There were two unusually large deposits to Hector's bank account. One for $2,000.00 on the Saturday before the Chamber of Commerce awards dinner and one for $3,000.00 on the Monday after Lorenzo died. Apparently, someone paid Hector to mix the Death Cap mushroom powder into Lorenzo's dinner," Sophie said.

"What?" Rylie gasped.

"Hector said that he found an envelope with his name on it on his windshield after work on the Friday before the Chamber of Commerce awards dinner. There was a note inside with a small packet of brown powdered material and $2,000 in cash. Whoever wrote the note said that he wanted to play a little prank on his friend Lorenzo Marchetti. The note said for Hector to make sure that he was the waiter for Lorenzo's table during the Chamber of Commerce awards dinner. His instructions were to mix the contents of the packet in the brown sauce for the steak if Lorenzo ordered the steak, the cream sauce for the salmon if Lorenzo ordered the salmon, or the risotto if he ordered risotto," Sophie said. "It said if Hector pulled it off and did a good job, he'd get another $3,000 in cash."

"So Hector just thought someone was playing a prank on Lorenzo Marchetti? How does Aaron know he's not lying? Maybe there was no note and Hector is just trying to shift the blame," Rylie said.

"Aaron said that Hector saved the note in a plastic ziplock bag. Hector turned it over to Aaron this morning after Aaron confronted him about the two unusually large deposits to his bank account. Aaron is sending the note in to the lab to have it dusted for fingerprints and to see if there is any DNA on it."

"So Hector is in jail until he can post bail?" Rylie asked. "Does he have to have a hearing where the amount of the bail is set?"

"Aaron said the bail amount for involuntary manslaughter is automatically set at $100,000.00 in the bail schedule for Napa County," Sophie said.

"Hector will never be able to come up with that kind of money," Rylie said. "Unless he has some wealthy friends or relatives."

"Or unless he gets a bail bondsman to post bail," Sophie said. "But he would still have to come up with quite a bit of money to do that. I think you have to pay ten percent of the total amount of the bail to the bondsman to get a bail bond."

"Wow. What a mess," Rylie said. "So at this point we know that Hector is the one who put the Death Cap mushroom powder in Lorenzo Marchetti's dinner. But we still don't know who the real killer is."

"That's right," Sophie said.

Rylie drove home slowly after her talk with Sophie, her mind sorting through all the things she had just learned. She heard Bella panting as she opened her front door.

"Hi, Bella!"

Bella grinned and wagged her tail.

"Do you remember the big black dog Max, Bella? We're going to the dog park this afternoon so you can play with Max. I'll bring your frisbee this time, okay?"

She packed up Bella's frisbee, ball, and flip-top water bottle dish in a tote bag along with a couple bottles of water. She checked the time on her cell phone. She had plenty of time before the playdate at the dog park.

She made herself a salad and sat down at the kitchen table with her laptop, her salad, and a lime-flavored mineral water. She searched to see where the jail was for St. Helena and discovered that the Napa County jail was in Napa. She read that the Napa County jail houses both male and female inmates serving sentences for all types of misdemeanors and felonies as well as people trying to get out of jail on bail.

She wondered how Katie was taking all this. Would Katie break up with Hector once she found out what he did? She hoped so. Katie deserved better.

Still, she couldn't help but feel bad for Hector. He wasn't the nicest guy she had ever met, but Katie loved him so he must have some redeeming qualities. He did something incredibly stupid, but if everything that he told Aaron was true, he never meant to kill Lorenzo Marchetti. He just thought he was helping someone pull a prank. Would he have to sit in jail for months waiting for a trial because he couldn't post bail?

A little before 3:00, Rylie put Bella in the back seat of her SUV and buckled her into her seatbelt. She was deep in thought as she drove the short distance to the dog park. Bella dashed off as soon as she unclipped her leash and bounded over to the big black dog standing with Aaron Michelson. The two dogs sniffed each other and wagged their tails excitedly. Rylie walked up with Bella's frisbee in her hand.

"I brought Bella's frisbee. Has Max ever played frisbee?" Rylie asked.

"I don't think so. I usually just bring a ball for him," Aaron said.

"Great! Then maybe I can level the playing field a little for Bella," Rylie teased. "Bella, Max, want to get the frisbee?"

She held the frisbee in front of her chest. The two dogs bounced up and down excitedly. Rylie sent the frisbee flying out just over the dogs' heads. Both dogs tore after it. Bella plucked the frisbee neatly out of the air and celebrated with a few good chews on the soft rubber. Max looked a little confused. Bella slowly walked towards Rylie and Aaron, then stopped about ten feet away and dropped the frisbee. Then she sat down to wait for Rylie to retrieve it.

"See! I told you! She never brings the frisbee all the way back to me," Rylie said.

Max sat down next to Bella. Rylie walked over and got the frisbee, then walked back to join Aaron.

"Do you want to throw the frisbee for them? I like to throw it just over Bella's head so she doesn't have to leap into the air to get it. I'm afraid she might hurt herself coming back down," Rylie said.

"No problem," Aaron said.

He expertly threw the frisbee out just over the dogs' heads. The dogs went racing after it. This time, Max caught on. He beat Bella to the frisbee by a nose, grabbed it out of the air, and shook it violently back and forth a few times. Bella nudged him. He trotted back to Aaron and deposited the frisbee at his feet.

"Good job, Max! You learn quickly!" Rylie said. She reached over and petted Bella on the head. "You did a good job too, Bella."

They took turns throwing the frisbee for the dogs until the dogs started looking worn out.

"I think Bella's done in, Aaron. Max is looking a little tired, too," Rylie said. "Sophie called me this morning and asked me to go talk to her at her latest renovation project. She filled me in on everything that's happened with Hector Briseno."

"I figured she would."

"I have some things to show you that you might be interested in," Rylie said. "You may have already seen them, but if you haven't, then you should. Can you come over to my house for a little while so I can show you some things on my laptop?"

"Okay. I'll follow you there."

Rylie let Bella, Aaron, and Max into her house. Bella headed for her water bowl. Rylie got another dog dish and filled it with water for Max. After drinking their fill, Bella and Max went into the living room and laid down a short distance from each other where they could keep an eye on Rylie and Aaron.

"Have a seat," Rylie said. She indicated the table in the dining area. "Can I get you something to drink?"

"Anything cold and wet will do."

"Lime-flavored mineral water, bottled water, orange juice?" Rylie asked.

"I'll have a mineral water. Thanks."

Rylie got a mineral water for each of them and sat down in the chair next to Aaron. She opened her laptop to the photos of the Chamber of Commerce awards dinner.

"I know that Lucien already gave you these photos that his waitress took of the Chamber of Commerce awards dinner. Did you see anything unusual or out of place when you looked through them?" Rylie asked.

"Not really," Aaron said. "There were some photos with Hector Briseno in them that at least prove that he was working that night. Other than that, neither my team or I found anything useful."

"I looked through them yesterday. I didn't see anything unusual either," Rylie said. "I have a friend who's a published murder mystery author. You might know her. Kinsley Logan?"

"The name sounds familiar."

"She likes to use poisons to kill off her characters in her murder mysteries. She's become quite an expert on poisons," Rylie said. "She gives a PowerPoint presentation on poisons at the St. Helena library about once a year."

"That's why her name sounds familiar!" Aaron said. "I went to her presentation on poisons one year. She really does know her stuff."

"Anyway, I asked Kinsley to look at these photos to see if she saw anything unusual or suspicious. I think writers are very tuned in to noticing little details, and I hoped that she might see something that no one else had seen."

"Okay," Aaron said. "So did she find anything?"

"Yes."

Rylie pulled up the photo of Hector Briseno with the packet falling from his hands under the two plates full of food.

"I know you already know that Hector was the one who mixed Death Cap mushrooms into Lorenzo Marchetti's meal," Rylie said. "But here's some incriminating evidence. See the packet falling from his hands below the two plates of food he's holding?"

"Well, what do you know?" Aaron said. "I'll print out that photo to use at his trial. What else did your friend see?"

Rylie scrolled to the photos of Viktor Bergman taking photos at Lorenzo Marchetti's table.

"Kinsley said that she doesn't think Viktor Bergman was taking photos of the people at Lorenzo's table. See the way his camera is angled towards the plates rather than towards people's faces? And he waited to take these photos after everyone was done eating like he wanted to see what everyone had eaten," Rylie said.

"Wait, what?" Aaron pulled the laptop over in front of himself and peered at the photos.

"I think she's right!" he said finally. "It looks like I need to have a little chat with Viktor Bergman. Thanks, Rylie. This actually was very helpful. And thank your friend for me."

He sipped his mineral water thoughtfully.

"So are you going to be going back home soon, Rylie? You told me that you were doing locum veterinarian work here for about a month."

"Oh, didn't I tell you?" Rylie said. "Dr. Corbyn needs more time to recuperate from his surgery. He asked me to stay until the end of November. I told him I'd be happy to help him out. So you'll have to put up with me for at least another month." She grinned at him.

"Ahhh. That's great, Rylie." Aaron smiled warmly at her. "I like having you around. I'd like to have the time to get to know you better. Unfortunately, I haven't had a lot of free time since I got thrown into the middle of a murder investigation."

"I'd like to get to know you better too, Aaron," Rylie said. "But it seems like it could be a little bit sticky until Lucien is cleared of suspicion in Lorenzo Marchetti's murder since I consider him a friend and his wife has been my best friend for years."

"I know, Rylie," Aaron said sadly. "I can't wait to get this investigation wrapped up so things can get back to normal. I'll tell you what. As soon as I wrap up this murder investigation and the killer has been charged, I'll take you out to dinner at whatever restaurant you want to celebrate."

"Sounds good, Aaron."

After Aaron left, Rylie busied herself around the house. She got out the vacuum and vacuumed the whole house. Then she dusted and straightened and reorganized things. When she ran out of things to do, she sat down at the kitchen table, her mind a million miles away. She drummed her fingers on the table. A thought came to her. She stood up quickly.

"I'm going to Il Capriccio for dinner, Bella," she said.
"I'll get you your dinner before I go."

She dressed carefully in some nice dark gray pants and a
soft pale pink sweater. She curled her hair into long waves
and put on some mascara and face powder. She had never
liked using a lot of make-up. She rarely took the time to
apply it. Only for special occasions.

This wasn't a special occasion, really. She just wanted to
look and feel pretty. She added a necklace and earrings to
her ensemble.

"Too much?" she asked Bella. Bella walked over to her
and nudged her hand. She stroked Bella's soft golden head.

"You have to stay here, Bella. I won't be out late. I just
need to get out of here. And I don't feel like cooking."

Rylie drove into town and found parking. She walked
the short distance to Il Capriccio and opened the door. She
was immediately surrounded by the sounds of friends and
families talking, laughing, teasing. As she walked in, she
felt like she was included in the warmth and conviviality of
the room. The tension in her shoulders melted away. She
took a deep breath. The air was redolent with the aroma
of garlic and tomato sauce.

She found a seat at the far end of the bar. Alex appeared
in front of her almost immediately.

"Rylie! I'm so glad you came!" Alex leaned across the
bar, put his hands on each side of her head, and kissed
her on both cheeks. "What can I get you? Are you hungry? We're having a special tonight. Spaghetti with my
world-famous meatballs. I felt like cooking today. Would
you like to try my spaghetti and meatballs?"

"That sounds amazing, Alex."

Rylie looked deeply into his eyes and smiled. This was a good man. Simple, straightforward. Someone who always made her feel good.

"And to drink? May I recommend a glass of Vino Nobile di Montepulciano?"

"Sounds perfect."

Alex hurried off. Rylie looked at the people sitting at the bar to see if she recognized anybody. Then she tried to discreetly look around the room. She didn't see anyone she knew. Alex appeared with her wine.

"Here you go. Salute!" Alex said. He pulled a glass of sparkling water out from under the counter and clinked glasses with her.

"Salute!" Rylie said.

She took a sip of her wine. "Mmmm. So good."

"Your spaghetti will be up shortly." Alex strode to the other side of the bar where a guy was beckoning him by holding up his index finger.

A guy came out from the kitchen with a small salad and a basket of warm garlic bread. Rylie opened the towel covering the garlic bread, took out a slice, and bit into it. Sinfully delicious. The guy came back with a plate of spaghetti and meatballs for her a little while later. Rylie sampled one of the meatballs. Amazing. A hot Italian man who can cook, too. This was definitely worth exploring.

Alex showed up as she was about halfway through her meal.

"What do you think? Do you like it?" he asked.

"Your meatballs are amazing. I've never had meatballs like this. Is it a family recipe?"

"Yes. It was one of my mother's recipes," Alex said. "The reason they taste different than anything you've ever had before is because I use three kinds of meat: ground beef, ground veal, and ground pork. I also mix in freshly grated Parmesan."

"A handsome Italian man that can cook." Rylie smiled. "What's not to love?"

Alex's face shone with his broad smile. He leaned on his arms across the bar so that his face was close to hers. He spoke softly in a voice that only she could hear.

"I'm so glad you came here tonight, Rylie. I was going to call you later tonight. I need to get away from here. From all the stress of dealing with my father's murder investigation. My family has a house in Lake Tahoe on the north shore near Tahoe City. I'm driving up there tomorrow morning. I'm planning to spend the weekend there. Will you come with me? I'd really like to have some time alone with you."

Rylie stared at Alex for a minute. She was afraid her jaw might have dropped open. She tried to appear casual. Like hot Italian men asked her to spend the weekend with them all the time. She looked down at her plate and tried to compose her thoughts. Alex reached out and grasped both of her hands.

"I'm not trying to get you in the sack, Rylie," Alex said earnestly. "We have four bedrooms. You'll have your own bedroom. You can pick whichever bedroom you want. Except mine, of course. What do you say?"

Rylie cleared her throat as quietly as possible. "I'd like that, Alex. Can I bring Bella?"

"Of course!" Alex said. "She can keep Amando company. Pack warm clothes. You never know when it might snow in Tahoe at this time of year."

"Wait a minute. You can't drive to Tahoe in your Alfa Romeo," Rylie said.

"Don't worry, Rylie. I have an SUV. And I always carry chains in the back."

"Oh good," Rylie said. "What time will you pick me up in the morning?"

"It's about a three and a half hour drive from here so I'd like to get an early start," Alex replied. "Can you be ready by 7:00 tomorrow morning?"

"No problem. We'll be ready." Rylie smiled.

"Hey, Alex, want to stop making goo-goo eyes at the pretty lady and take care of your other customers?" a guy hollered from the other end of the bar. "We're getting thirsty over here."

"Gotta go," Alex said. He pulled her hands to his lips and kissed them lightly before he strode to the guy at the other end of the bar.

When she had finished eating, Rylie left some cash on the bar to pay for her meal as well as a nice tip. She called Sophie as she walked down the sidewalk to where her car was parked.

"Hi, Sophie. I just had dinner at Il Capriccio and Alex invited me to spend the weekend with him at his family's house in Lake Tahoe this weekend. Do you have a warm winter jacket and some snow boots that I could borrow?"

"Wait, what? You're spending the weekend with Alex? Did I miss something here?" Sophie asked.

"Nope. We haven't even kissed. He's feeling overwhelmed by everything going on with his father's murder investigation, and he just wants to get away. He has a four-bedroom house. I get my own room. Nothing to worry about," Rylie said.

"Oh, I'm not worried, Rylie. I'm happy for you. When do you want to pick up the jacket and boots?"

"Can I come over right now? I have to pack tonight. He's picking me up at 7:00 in the morning tomorrow," Rylie said.

"No problem. Come right over. I have a winter jacket that will look really cute on you," Sophie said.

Rylie drove to Sophie's house to get a winter jacket and snow boots for her trip.

"I love this jacket, Sophie. It's really cute. Thanks for letting me borrow it. I've got to run now. I've got to get everything packed tonight so I'm ready when Alex shows up at 7:00 tomorrow morning," Rylie said.

"No problem. I hope you have a great time with Alex this weekend."

"Thanks, Sophie. I'm sure I will."

Chapter 17

Rylie perched on the edge of one of the chairs at the kitchen table. Her suitcases were packed and ready to go by the front door. Bella sensed the anticipation in the air. She knew an adventure was in the offing.

She heard Alex's SUV come up the driveway. She forced herself to stay in her chair until Alex knocked, then sprang out of her chair to answer the door.

She grinned widely as she flung the door open.

"Hi! Bella and I are ready to go! Bella's excited."

Alex scooped her up in a big hug. "Amando's excited too. You're all packed?"

"Yep. My suitcases are right here."

Alex eyed the suitcases. "You know we're only going to be gone for two days, right?" he teased.

"You never know what you might need when you go on a trip," Rylie countered. "I like to be prepared."

"Great."

Alex smiled as he picked up her suitcases and carried them out to his SUV. Rylie snapped a leash on Bella and followed him outside. Amando had his head out the window in the back seat of Alex's SUV. He started panting and wiggling happily when he saw Bella.

Rylie got Bella buckled into her seatbelt in the back seat and climbed up into the front seat next to Alex. They chatted happily on the drive up to the north shore of the lake. Alex drove through Tahoe City towards Tahoe Vista. He pulled into a nearly invisible driveway in the middle of a dense stand of tall pines on the lake side of the road. He stopped to open the wrought iron gate at the entrance to the property with a remote on his visor. They followed the driveway as it curved through the trees until they reached a dark brown wood house in the middle of a large clearing. She caught a glimpse of the sparkling lake in back of the house.

Alex opened one of the garage doors with a remote on his visor and they pulled in. Bella and Amando could barely contain themselves.

"We're here!" Alex said.

"I think the dogs might need to go potty. Is your property fenced in so it's safe to let them loose here? Or should I put a leash on Bella?" Rylie asked.

"The entire property is fenced. We've got about five acres. Plenty of room for the dogs to run around."

"Great!"

Rylie unbuckled Bella from her seatbelt. Bella leaped from the SUV and ran a short distance away before she squatted in the underbrush. Amando was close behind.

"Poor Bella! You really had to go, didn't you?"

Bella loped back inside the garage where Alex was getting their suitcases out of the back compartment. Amando appeared a minute later.

Alex led the way inside. They walked through a large great room with a kitchen on one side and the living room on the other. A wall of glass opened onto views of the shimmering blue lake stretching out to the mountains in the distance.

"Wow! What fantastic views!" Rylie said.

She followed Alex down the hallway where the bedrooms were located. Alex showed her the four bedrooms. His was on the right at the end of the hall. She chose the bedroom next to his. Each bedroom had its own bathroom. The house was charmingly rustic with an old Tahoe feel. She got unpacked and went to find Alex.

She found him sitting on the deck gazing out over the lake with a hot chocolate in his hands. He smiled when he saw her.

"Would you like some hot chocolate?" he asked.

"Sure. I can make it. You can just stay here and relax. Just tell me where everything is," Rylie said.

"The cocoa powder is in the pantry. Mugs are in the upper cabinet to the right of the sink."

Rylie made herself a hot chocolate and joined Alex and the dogs out on the deck. She sat down on the cushioned loveseat next to Alex.

"What a gorgeous home, Alex. The views of the lake are spectacular. No wonder you wanted to spend the weekend here. This is a very special place."

Alex put his arm around her shoulders and pulled her close. She could feel the warmth of his body next to hers. It warmed her all over. They sat quietly for a while, and she let herself relax into the moment. So peaceful. She sipped her hot chocolate and let her mind wander.

"Do you mind being homebodies this weekend, Rylie?" Alex said finally. "I just need some time and space away from everybody. Except you, of course. I haven't had time to really process everything surrounding my father's death. Maybe by tomorrow I'll have my head on straight and we can go out and do something. But today, I just want to stay here. There's a nice path that runs along the lake where we can take the dogs for a walk. I'll go to the grocery store and get us some food. I'll make you my special Pici all'aglione for dinner. I brought some Vino Nobile di Montepulciano from home to go with it."

"I'm absolutely fine with hanging out around the house," Rylie said. "This place is so beautiful and peaceful. And I can't wait to have some of your famous Pici all'aglione."

Alex pulled her close and kissed her forehead. Rylie held her breath.

"Okay, then. I'm going to go to the grocery store. You can stay here with the dogs so they don't get nervous being alone in a strange place. I'll be back soon."

Alex got up and walked back through the house to the garage. Amando followed him and whined at the door to the garage after he left.

"Amando!" Rylie called. "Come out here on the deck with me and Bella!"

Amando walked slowly back outside on the deck. He whined again. Rylie stroked his head. Bella got up and pushed her nose into Amando's neck.

"Are there any dog treats here, Amando?" Rylie asked.

She looked around the pantry to see if she could find any dog biscuits. Nothing. She searched all the cabinets in the kitchen and couldn't find anything. She texted Alex and told him that the dogs would like a treat, but she couldn't find any. She asked him to buy some dog treats while he was at the store.

No problem. What kind of treats do you want me to buy?

The healthiest ones you can find. I usually buy Bella bacon, egg, and cheese health bars, but I'm sure you won't find them in the grocery store. So whatever kind of dog treats you can find that look like they're made with wholesome ingredients.

You got it.

"I'm sorry guys," Rylie said to the dogs. "Alex doesn't have any doggie treats here right now. But he's going to buy some and bring them home in a little while. Okay?"

Bella wagged her tail. Amando looked sad. Rylie ruffled the cream-colored fur on his fuzzy head. She went to her bedroom to get her e-reader, took it out onto the deck, and got comfortable in a loveseat. Amando walked over and put his head in her lap.

"You want to come up here, Amando?" Rylie asked.

She patted the loveseat cushion next to her. Amando's face perked up. He quickly leaped onto the loveseat next to her and put his head in her lap. Bella came over and pushed against Rylie's legs. She lifted her head up to Rylie to be petted.

"Who's a jealous girl, Bella?" Rylie smiled.

She stroked Bella's head and scratched her gently around her ears. She opened her e-reader to see what books she hadn't read yet.

"Let's see. Cozy mystery? Historical fiction?" She browsed the books on her e-reader and chose a cozy mystery by one of her favorite authors. She had just opened the book and started reading when she heard the garage door open. When she heard Alex slam his SUV door shut, she ran to put her e-reader away and help Alex with the groceries.

Alex was walking into the house with his arms full of bags of groceries when she got back to the kitchen.

"Are there more bags in the car?" she asked.

"Nope. This is it."

Alex set the bags of groceries on the floor.

"Did you find dog treats?" Rylie asked. She saw the dogs' ears perk up at the word "treats."

"Yes, I did. Healthy ones, too. They're in here some-where."

Alex dug through the grocery bags until he found the dog treats. Rylie opened the dog treats and got two of them out.

"I told you Alex was going to bring you guys some treats," she said. Amando and Bella were sitting patiently in front of her. She gave each of them a treat.

"Whoa! Gentle, Amando," Rylie said.

Amando tried again to get his treat, going slower this time. He gently plucked the treat from Rylie's hand.

"Good boy, Amando. And you're a good girl, Bella," Rylie said.

"Can I help you put the groceries away, Alex?"

"Sure. You can take the things I've stacked on the counter and put them away in the pantry for me."

"No problem. I can do that."

When she got back from the pantry, Alex had finished putting the rest of the groceries away.

"Are you hungry? I got us some turkey pot pies from the deli for lunch," Alex said.

"I'm starved. And I love turkey pot pies."

"Great. They won't take long to cook in the microwave," Alex said. "Would you like a glass of wine with lunch? I got some chilled sauvignon blanc at the store to go with our pot pies."

"Sounds good to me. Why don't I open the wine while you get the pot pies going? Where's your wine opener?" Rylie asked.

Alex opened a drawer, pulled out a wine opener, and handed it to her. "Wine glasses are in the cabinet over there."

Rylie poured their wine and handed a glass to Alex.

"Salute!" He clinked his glass with hers.

"Salute!" Rylie took a sip of her wine. "Oh, this is a nice wine. I like it."

"I'm glad you like it." Alex smiled and took a sip of his wine. "That's the thing about us Italians. We know good food and good wine."

"And good cars and clothes," Rylie added.

"And good women," Alex said. He pulled Rylie into a quick hug and then held her away from himself. "Thank you for coming here with me, Rylie. It means a lot to me."

The microwave beeped. He stepped away to take the pot pies out of the oven. Rylie slowly released the breath she didn't know she'd been holding.

They took their plates and silverware to the kitchen dining table in front of the floor to ceiling windows looking out over the lake. Bella and Amando curled up on the floor near the table in the hope that something good might come their way. Rylie pulled a couple of chunks of turkey out of her pot pie and set them to cool on the side of her plate for the dogs.

"Yum, this is good," she said.

"Comfort food," Alex said.

They chatted comfortably over lunch. Rylie gave Bella and Amando each a chunk of turkey which they quickly swallowed without even taking the time to chew.

"I'm sure you guys couldn't even taste that turkey, you ate it so fast," she said to the dogs. Bella and Amando both wagged their tails hopefully. "That's it. That's all I've got."

They rinsed their dishes and put them in the dishwasher.

"Okay. Time for a walk along the lake. What do you say?" Alex said.

"Great! I'm sure the dogs will be happy to go on a walk," Rylie said. "Just let me get a jacket."

The sun was shining brilliantly in a clear blue sky as they headed down the dirt path that ran along the lake in back of the house. Amando and Bella had their noses to the ground sniffing everything in sight. A Stellar's jay squawked a noisy rebuke at the dogs for venturing onto his turf. He bounced from branch to branch keeping a close eye on the dogs as they passed. The dogs ignored the jay and continued on.

Rylie inhaled deeply and stretched out her shoulders as she walked. The air was crisp and clean and scented with the smell of the alpine lake and forest. The path was narrow so they had to walk single file. Alex kept up a brisk pace. She followed close behind. He veered off the path onto a footpath heading towards the lake. The dogs kept heading down the main path.

"Bella, Amando, come!" Rylie called.

The dogs turned quickly and ran towards her. She waited until the dogs caught up with Alex before she followed. Alex led the way to a redwood bench near the water's edge. He took her hand and pulled her onto the bench next to him.

"Wow, I never would have guessed there was a bench out here. I would have walked right by that little footpath," Rylie said.

"My father built this years ago," Alex said. "He liked to come here when he needed to get away."

Rylie put her arm through Alex's and snuggled up next to him. They sat quietly looking out over the water. The dogs kept busy sniffing the underbrush nearby.

Rylie looked up at Alex's face. She saw tears glistening in his eyes. She turned her attention back to the lake.

"I'm so sorry about your father, Alex," she said quietly. "Would you like to be alone?"

"No. I want you here," Alex said firmly. "Please. Stay with me."

"Okay. No problem."

They sat quietly for a few minutes.

"You know, sometimes my father could be a real jerk. But he was always a good father to me. I'd be proud to be half the father he was to me to my kids someday," Alex said finally. He rubbed a hand over his face.

"I'm exhausted. I haven't been sleeping well since my father was killed."

"I love afternoon naps on the sofa. Want to curl up on the sofa together for a nap?" Rylie asked.

"That's the best offer I've had in a long time. Let's go," Alex said.

They walked back through the woods along the lake to the house. Rylie went to her bedroom and got a pillow. She found a spare blanket in the closet. She brought them out to the living room and set them on the sofa. Alex was sitting on the sofa staring at his hands.

"I'm going to take off my shoes. Do you want to take off your shoes before we cuddle up together?" Rylie said.

"Oh, yeah. Good idea."

Alex laid down on the sofa with his head on the pillow. Rylie pulled the blanket up over him and then crawled under the blanket with him. She stretched out alongside him facing away from him with her body tucked comfortably into the curve of his body.

"This is nice," she said.

Alex wrapped his arms around her waist. "Definitely."

She felt Alex's body relax as his breathing slowed. She closed her eyes and allowed herself to drift off to sleep.

"Ugh! What the?" Rylie pulled away from the edge of the sofa closer to Alex. The light was dim in the room when she opened her eyes and saw Amando staring at her. Bella pushed up next to Amando and started wagging her tail as she looked at Rylie expectantly.

"What's wrong?" Alex asked. He pulled her closer.

"I think Amando just licked my face. I was in a deep sleep and suddenly something warm and wet was on my face. It woke me up," Rylie said. "Wow, how long have we been sleeping? It's getting dark already."

"Well, it's not totally dark yet, so it's probably around 5:00. I was in a deep sleep too. I haven't slept like that in months." He stretched his arms and legs out.

"Maybe Amando has to go potty," Rylie said.

"Or maybe his internal dinner bell is going off. He knows exactly when it's time for his dinner every night," Alex said.

"Amando!" Rylie chided. "Did you wake us up so you can get your dinner?"

Amando looked at her delightedly. Both dogs started wagging their tails faster.

Rylie forced herself out from under the nice warm blanket and got up. She went into her bedroom and put her shoes away. She put on some slate blue suede slippers and went back to the living room.

"Come on Amando, Bella! Let's go outside to go potty," Rylie said.

She opened the front door for the dogs to go outside. Bella stopped cold as soon as her front legs were out the door and started barking loudly. Amando rushed out just past Bella and started barking ferociously.

Rylie saw the huge black bear at the edge of the driveway nosing around in the underbrush. The bear looked over at the dogs and stood up on his hind legs.

"Bella, no!"

She grabbed Bella's collar and tried to pull her back inside. Alex was there in a split second. He grabbed both dogs by their collars and pulled them inside. He slammed the door and locked it.

"Holy crap!" Alex said. "That is one enormous bear!"

Rylie looked at Alex in shock. Then she started giggling. Alex broke into a wide grin. They both dissolved into fits of laughter.

Rylie put her hand on her stomach. "Ow, my stomach hurts, I've been laughing so hard."

She wiped the tears streaming down her face. "What are we going to do now? The dogs have to go potty."

Alex composed himself and pulled her into a warm hug. Then he released her. She took a tiny step back.

"I think the dogs can wait. We'll get them their dinner now. I'll check in a little while to see if the bear has moved on. I don't think he's going to want to stay around here very long with two big dogs barking at him," Alex said. "Do you want to feed the dogs while I start making pici?"

"Okay."

She filled the dogs' food bowls with kibble and got each of them a bowl of fresh water. She watched Alex measure out two kinds of flour onto the square butcher block island in the middle of the kitchen. He mixed the flours together and then formed them into a mound. He made a well in the center of the mound and slowly poured a mixture of water and olive oil into the well as he mixed everything together until it formed a smooth dough. He flattened the dough slightly, wrapped it in plastic wrap, and left it to rest on the butcher block.

"Pici all'aglione is a very simple recipe to make," Alex said. "The sauce only has three ingredients: olive oil, fresh garlic, and canned plum tomatoes. I let the pasta dough rest while I make the sauce. Then I hand roll the pici. It only takes about four minutes to cook the pici. The hardest part is hand rolling each strand."

Soon the house was filled with the aroma of garlicky tomato sauce.

"Would you like to make each of us a small green salad?" Alex asked.

"Sure."

She searched the refrigerator to see what she had to work with. She made two salads with red leaf lettuce, sliced cucumbers, chunks of Campari tomatoes, Kalamata olives, and alfalfa sprouts. She sprinkled freshly grated Parmesan over each salad.

"Do you have balsamic vinegar?" she asked.

"There are glass cruets of balsamic vinegar and olive oil in the pantry," Alex replied.

He put a large pot of salted water on the stove to boil. He rolled out the pasta dough with a rolling pin until it was about a quarter inch thick and then cut it into thin strips. He used the palms of his hands to roll each strip into a strand that looked like thick spaghetti.

"What else can I do?" Rylie asked.

"You can slice up that baguette into one-inch-thick slices and arrange the slices on this sheet pan. I already melted some butter and mixed minced garlic and Parmesan cheese into it. Here's a pastry brush to brush the melted butter onto each slice. Then put the pan in the oven at 450 degrees for about five to eight minutes until the bread is lightly toasted."

"No problem."

Alex poured them each some Vino Nobile di Montepulciano. He handed her a glass of wine. As he handed her the wine, he leaned in and gave her a quick kiss on the lips.

Rylie looked down at her hands. "Hmmm. Not exactly the kind of kiss I would expect from a hot Italian guy. I think that was the kind of kiss that you give your aunts."

She lifted her head and smiled coyly at him.

Alex put down his wine glass. He took Rylie's wine glass from her and set it down. He put his hands around her face and gave her a long kiss.

"Better?" He smiled tenderly at her.

"Hmmm." Rylie held out one hand and rocked it back and forth. "I'd say that was at least an eight out of ten." She grinned at him.

"Well, that will never do," Alex said. He pulled her close and kissed her long and passionately. Rylie felt a little dizzy as he pulled away.

"Well?" he asked.

"Oh, that was definitely a ten out of ten."

"Now we're talking!" Alex gave her a sexy grin.

Oh, my goodness. I'm in trouble.

Alex turned, put his pici in the boiling pot of water, and gave it a stir. Rylie set the kitchen dining table with plates, napkins, and silverware. She set a salad in front of each plate. She found a basket in one of the cabinets and a kitchen towel to line it with for the garlic bread. She waited for her breathing to return to normal and for her heart to stop beating out of her chest.

Alex put some Pici all'aglione on each of their plates and sprinkled it with freshly grated Parmesan. Rylie pulled the garlic bread out of the oven and arranged the slices in the towel-lined basket. She folded the towel over the bread to keep it warm and put it in the center of the table.

They sat down across from each other at the table.

"Oh my goodness, Alex," Rylie said. "This looks and smells amazing!"

She took a bite of the Pici all'aglione. "Yum. Delicious."

Alex smiled happily. "I'm glad you like it."

They chatted comfortably over dinner and then worked together to get the kitchen cleaned up afterwards.

"This was so much fun, Alex. Thank you for having me here this weekend with you."

Alex pulled her into a warm embrace and kissed her thoroughly.

"I wouldn't want to be here with anyone else," he said earnestly.

"Well, we're here so you can rest and recuperate from everything that you've been through lately, so I opt that we go to bed early so you can catch up on your sleep. I'll cuddle with you if it helps you sleep better. As long as you promise to behave," Rylie said.

"How about I get a movie going and we cuddle up on the sofa like we did this afternoon?" Alex asked.

"Perfect. I'm going to get changed into my pajamas and get ready for bed in case I fall asleep during the movie. Do you want to get in your pj's?" Rylie asked.

"You don't have to ask me twice," Alex said. "I want to let the dogs out to go potty first. Then I'll go get changed and get ready for bed."

Rylie went to her bedroom to put on her pajamas and then went back to the living room. She plumped up the pillow they had used earlier and straightened the blanket.

"What kind of movies do you like?" Alex asked.

"I like mysteries, rom-coms, and movies set in places that I'd like to visit like France or Italy. I don't like anything with violence or gore."

"Hmmm, okay. You should like this one."

Alex got the movie going and then laid down on the sofa. He reached for her hand and pulled her towards him. She laid down on the sofa with her back to him and wiggled around until her body fit nicely into his. His body felt comfortable and warm. Alex wrapped his arms around her waist and kissed her neck.

She turned around to face him. He pulled her close and kissed her soundly.

"You're getting better at this," she teased.

"You think so?"

She giggled. He kissed her again. Slightly breathless, she turned around to face the television and snuggled close to him.

Chapter 18

Rylie woke up to the smell of coffee and bacon. And something else that smelled delicious.

She went into the kitchen where she found Alex doing something at the stove. She wrapped her arms around his waist. He put his utensil down and turned around.

"Good morning, beautiful," he said. He leaned down and kissed her deeply.

"Good morning," Rylie said. "It smells incredible in here. What are you making?"

"I have a frittata in the oven with spinach, mushrooms, onions, and cheese. Just like my mother used to make. Do you like frittatas?"

"I love them. Do I have time to take a quick shower and get dressed before breakfast?" she asked.

"Of course. I already took mine. Breakfast will be waiting whenever you're ready. Do you want a cup of coffee to take with you?"

"Yes. I can get it. You're busy."

She made herself a cup of coffee with milk and took it with her to her bedroom. After her shower, she put on a bathrobe and went back out to the kitchen.

"What are we going to be doing today so I know what to wear?" she asked.

Alex's eyes raked over her body. "Nice outfit. I thought we could go hiking on a short loop of the Tahoe Rim Trail. There's a trailhead just outside of Tahoe City off of Fairway Drive that goes to Twin Crags. It's only about a three-mile hike there and back. And it has some fantastic views of the lake. I'm sure the dogs will enjoy it."

"Sounds good. I'll get dressed and be back in a few minutes."

Rylie dressed in jeans and a t-shirt and then pulled a warm sweater over the t-shirt. After she put on her hiking boots, she went back out to the kitchen. Alex had put plates of crispy bacon, wedges of frittata, and buttered toast on the table for each of them.

"Wow, this looks amazing. I'm so hungry. Thanks for making all this." She sat down at the table with Alex.

"I think I'm going to need to go on that hike to burn off all of the calories I've eaten this weekend," she teased.

"Making delicious food for our loved ones is a very important part of the Italian culture. I will always feed you well." Alex looked deeply into her eyes and smiled warmly. She swallowed hard.

After breakfast, they loaded the dogs into Alex's SUV and strapped them into their seatbelts. Alex had filled a backpack with bottled water for themselves and the dogs. He found a place to park near the trailhead. Bella and Amando whined and bounced up and down in their seats.

"I'm not comfortable letting Bella off leash here," Rylie said. "She doesn't know where she is, and she might wander off."

"No problem. We can keep the dogs on leashes. They'll still have fun," Alex said.

They followed the dirt trail up the mountain through a forest of tall pine trees. Bella strained at her leash as she tried to sniff everything in sight. Eventually the trail leveled off and opened to stunning views of the lake.

Alex found a large flat rock for them to sit on. He handed Rylie a bottle of water and poured water in bowls for the dogs. She quickly downed half the bottle. Bella and Amando lapped up their water and then flopped down on the ground panting and smiling.

"This was definitely worth the hike," Rylie said. "What incredible views!"

"I love coming to the lake. It always helps me clear my head and get re-centered," Alex said. He reached for her hand and held it.

"You're a very special woman," he said finally. "I've never met anyone like you. You're smart. You're funny. You're gorgeous and very sexy."

She looked in his eyes as he spoke.

"I think we have something special here, Rylie. I'm falling for you hard."

"I'm falling for you too, Alex."

"I'm absolutely ready to be in a committed, monogamous relationship with you. I see a future with you. I hope you feel the same way," Alex said.

The intensity in Alex's eyes was unnerving. She looked down at Alex's hand holding hers and took a deep, steadying breath.

"I'll be honest with you. I'm a little scared. But it feels right. I'm ready to commit to a monogamous relationship with you, too." She smiled at him. "So does that mean that you're my boyfriend now?"

"Yes, I think it does." Alex smiled a sexy smile. "And that makes you my girlfriend now. I like the sound of that."

He leaned in and kissed her passionately. Then he wrapped her in a warm hug for a few minutes while their breathing slowed.

"I'm feeling better than I have in a long time. I feel rested and like I have the energy of both of our dogs combined. I'm the luckiest man in the world right now. The woman I love has just agreed to be in a committed relationship with me. I couldn't be happier," Alex said.

Love? How did we go from "falling for me hard" to "love?" Her head was spinning. She took a long swig of her bottled water.

"Wait. You just said you love me," she said.

"I do love you, Rylie. I've loved you since the first time I saw you. That's no joke. It's the truth," Alex said. "And I've never believed in "love at first sight." I always thought that was ridiculous. But I guess it really can happen."

"I'll never hurt you, Rylie. Please don't be afraid."

She studied Alex's face. His dark good looks. His thick black wavy hair with one of his curls flopped rakishly over his forehead. This was a man she could trust. A man she could love. She leaned in to kiss him. Amando came over and shoved his nose in between their faces.

"Ugh! Amando! You've got to quit doing that!" Rylie laughed.

They got up and continued on the trail for a little while before turning to go back. Bella and Amando were having a great time running around and sniffing things. Amando ran up to Alex with a smelly mass of something rotten.

"Oh, Amando! No! That's disgusting." Alex pulled whatever it was from Amando's mouth and threw it far into the woods.

Rylie giggled. "Dogs seem to love things that smell disgusting and rotten."

When they got back to the house, Rylie filled both of the dogs' water bowls with water. Bella and Amando took long drinks and then flopped down on the living room floor.

"We probably ought to start getting packed up and head back to St. Helena," Alex said. "I want to get you home early enough that you have time to do whatever you need to do to get ready for work tomorrow."

"Okay. That's a good idea. I'll go get packed."

On the drive back to St. Helena, Alex told her about his life growing up in Italy and then his teenage years in St. Helena. She told him about growing up in the East Bay area, going to college, and then to veterinary medical school. The three and a half hour drive passed quickly.

When they got to Rylie's house, Alex carried her suitcases inside. Amando stared forlornly from his seat in the SUV.

"Have a good day at work tomorrow," Alex said. "I'll talk to you soon."

He kissed her deeply and then got in his SUV and drove away. Rylie watched until she couldn't see his SUV anymore. Bella stood close by her side.

"Who knew, Bella? I left here a single woman yesterday morning, and I came back in a committed relationship with a guy I'm crazy about. It feels surreal."

She stroked Bella's golden head and turned around to go inside. She called Sophie to let her know about everything that had happened.

"You're what? In a committed, monogamous relationship? How is that possible? You've known the guy for all of two minutes," Sophie said.

"I've actually known him for a couple of weeks. And we've spent quite a bit of time together during that time. I've already met his family. I spent a whole day with him and his family at his house after his father's funeral. He treats me like a queen. He's one of the nicest, kindest men I've ever met. The fact that he's incredibly sexy doesn't hurt either. I'm crazy about him. Please, Sophie. I need you to support me in this. It's really important to me."

"You know I'll support you in whatever you do, Rylie. No matter how crazy it sounds. I think I just need a little time to process all this. I'm happy for you. You deserve to have a man that really loves you," Sophie said. "I am worried that Alex might not be ready for this though. He needs time to grieve and heal from everything he's gone through."

"I know, Sophie. I agree with you," Rylie said. "I saw his grief when we were in Tahoe together. He went to Tahoe specifically because he hadn't had the time to process everything that's happened or deal with his grief. I think getting away from everything for a weekend helped him a lot."

"So does this mean that Aaron is out of the running?" Sophie asked.

"Um, yeah."

"Too bad. I was kind of rooting for him. He's a great guy."

"I wouldn't feel comfortable getting involved in a relationship with Aaron because he's investigating Lucien as a suspect in Lorenzo Marchetti's murder."

"I understand. Thank you for that," Sophie said. "What happens when you go back home at the end of the month?

Are you going to try to maintain a long-distance relationship with Alex?"

"I don't know, Sophie. We haven't gotten that far. It's all too new. Right now I just want to enjoy our time together. We'll figure out the future later."

"Fair enough," Sophie said. "So when do I get to meet this guy? How about you and Alex come over for dinner on Thursday night? Lucien's part-time chef told him that he needs more hours, so Lucien's going to be taking Thursdays off starting this week. He can't afford to lose his part-time chef, or he'll have to work seven days a week."

"That sounds great. I'll check with Alex and get back to you."

She hung up with Sophie and called Alex to tell him about the dinner invitation.

"So what do you think? Are you comfortable having dinner with Sophie and Lucien in view of the fact that Lucien is under investigation for your father's death?"

"Yes, I am. Lucien has been coming to Il Capriccio for years. I like him. My father liked him. I don't believe he's responsible for my father's death."

Rylie breathed a sigh of relief. "Great! I'll text Sophie and let her know we'll be there on Thursday."

Chapter 19

Rylie wasn't surprised to see that Katie wasn't at work the next day after Hector had just been thrown in jail.

"Where's Katie?" she asked the receptionist as she walked through the reception area on her way to the doctors' office.

"She called in sick today."

Her first appointment had arrived early and was already waiting for her. She quickly put on her white lab coat and draped her stethoscope around her neck. Miley stood waiting in the doctors' office doorway with her clipboard in hand.

She was slammed for the rest of the day. After finishing her last appointment for the day, she rushed to write up her medical notes for all the patients she'd seen that afternoon as quickly as possible.

"Wow, today was crazy," she said to Cassandra.

"No kidding," Cassandra replied. "I'll be lucky to get out of here by 7:00 tonight. I have a ton of charts to write. And I still haven't had time to call back my labs from yesterday."

Rylie logged off the hospital's veterinary software program on her computer. "I'm sorry, Cassandra. I hope you get out of here soon. See you tomorrow."

Rylie headed home to let Bella out to do her business. Bella bolted out the back door and then trotted quickly back inside.

"I'm sorry I was late getting home, Bella. I tried to get home as soon as I could. You were such a good girl today."

She gave Bella a dog biscuit. Then she got Bella her dinner and some fresh water.

"I'm too tired to cook anything tonight, Bella. I'm going to go check out the burgers at Gott's Roadside restaurant. I shouldn't be gone long."

She changed into some jeans and a sweater, put on a warm jacket, and took off in her SUV. She got to Gott's Roadside a few minutes later. She quickly realized that they didn't have any indoor seating. Long communal picnic tables with large, square beige umbrellas were lined up in front of the restaurant. Small patio heaters had been hung inside the umbrellas to keep the diners warm. She stood in line to place her order.

After she ordered a burger and fries, she scanned the tables looking for a place to sit. She spotted Viktor Bergman at the end of one of the long tables. She walked over and sat down across from him.

"Hi," she said.

Viktor glanced briefly at her and continued eating.

"Aren't you the guy that owns the hardware store in town?" she asked.

Viktor stopped chewing and swallowed. "Yes."

"I thought you looked familiar. I'm Rylie Sunderland. I'm a veterinarian from the East Bay. I'm filling in for Dr. Corbyn at Valley View Veterinary Hospital while he recuperates from surgery. I remember seeing you at the Chamber of Commerce awards dinner. I was sitting with my friends Sophie Marchand and Patricia Davenport and her husband. They were pointing out some of the businesspeople in town since I'm new here and don't know a lot of people."

"I know Patricia and Jonathan very well," Viktor said.

"Sophie Marchand has been my best friend since college," Rylie replied. "I'm worried about her husband Lucien being considered a suspect in Lorenzo Marchetti's murder. Do you happen to remember what Lorenzo Marchetti talked about at the awards dinner? I'm just wondering if he might have said anything that might help Detective Michelson in his investigation."

Her restaurant pager started to flash and vibrate on the table. She went up and got her burger and fries, then returned to her seat across from Viktor.

"I already told Detective Michelson everything I could remember about that night," Viktor said. "I know Lucien. He's a good guy. I don't believe for a second that he had anything to do with Lorenzo's death."

Rylie sat quietly looking at Viktor for a minute. Then she started in on her dinner.

"Look, I just found out last night that I must have accidentally pressed the record button on the voice recorder app on my cell phone at some point during the awards dinner. There's a recording on my cell phone of a few minutes of conversation between the people at my table that night. I can send you the recording if you want. What's your cell phone number?"

"Oh, great. Thank you." She gave Viktor her number. "Are you going to send the recording to Detective Michelson too?"

"Yes, I guess I'll have to. Something about that guy really irritates me, but I want to do whatever I can to help Lucien. Detective Michelson came to talk to me on Saturday. I think he's trying to pin something on me. He said he has photos that show me taking photos of the empty plates of everyone sitting at my table at the awards dinner. I told him I was just taking photos of everyone for my memory book. I didn't want to bother them when they were eating. So I waited until everyone was finished eating before I took their photos."

Rylie's phone pinged with a text. Viktor's voice recording from the awards dinner. Rylie felt a thrill of excitement course through her body. She couldn't wait to listen to it.

Viktor finished his meal and left. She quickly finished her burger and then headed home. As soon as she got inside, she went in the living room and curled up on the sofa to listen to Viktor's voice recording. Bella laid down on the floor nearby.

"So Lorenzo, how did you happen to move to California from Italy and open a bar here?"

"My wife and I wanted our son, Alessandro, to have more opportunities for colleges to attend and jobs after he graduated from college. My family in Italy had a bar. I grew up in that bar. I felt like running a bar was in my blood. So I started my own bar here in the U.S."

Garbled noises.

"Whatever happened to your business partner, Leo?"

"We had some disagreements."

Garbled noises.

"We dissolved our business partnership and he and his family moved away."

"I heard that Leo had a stroke after he left St. Helena."

"I don't know. I haven't spoken with him since he left."

Rylie called Detective Michelson. "Hi Aaron. This is Rylie."

"Rylie! Nice to hear from you! What's going on?"

"Did you get a text from Viktor Bergman tonight?"

"No. Why?"

"I went to Gott's Roadside for a burger tonight and happened to sit across from him," she said.

"I doubt that your sitting across from Viktor Bergman was accidental, Rylie," Detective Michelson said dryly.

"Well, it may have been accidentally on purpose. I told him that Sophie Marchand is my best friend and that I'm worried about Lucien being considered a suspect in Lorenzo Marchetti's murder. I asked him if he remembered what Lorenzo talked about at the awards dinner. I was hoping that Lorenzo might have said something that could help you in your investigation."

"Don't you think I already asked him those questions, Rylie?"

"Well, of course. But I was hoping that he might remember some new piece of information," she said. "He told me that he already told you everything that he could remember about the awards dinner. I didn't respond. I just sat there quietly and took a bite of my burger. Then he told me that he just found out last night that he must have accidentally pressed the record button on his cell phone at some point during the awards dinner. He found a recording of a few minutes of conversation between the people that were sitting at his table, including Lorenzo Marchetti."

"What? Now I'm wondering where my text is from Viktor."

"I asked him if he was going to send you the recording. He said he would. He doesn't believe Lucien killed Lorenzo. He said he wants to help Lucien in any way he can. He told me there's something about you that rubs him the wrong way. He said he thinks you're trying to pin something on him because you told him that you have photos of him photographing the empty plates of everyone that sat at his table during the awards dinner. Anyway, I'll send you a text with the voice recording so you have it. Call me after you listen to it."

Detective Michelson called back shortly.

"Hi Rylie. Thanks for sending that to me."

"Don't you think it's a little bit fishy that Viktor "accidentally" pressed the record button on his voice recorder app?" Rylie said. "I've never accidentally pressed mine. Have you?"

"I don't know, Rylie. But I'm definitely going to have another chat with Viktor."

"And what about Lorenzo's former business partner, Leo? It seems like there may have been some bad blood between them, don't you think?" Rylie asked. "Maybe Leo should be on the list of suspects."

"It's been three years since Leo and his family left town, Rylie. If Leo was angry about their split, I think he would have done something about it a long time ago. I'll look into it. But I have to tell you, Rylie, that things are not looking good for Lucien. I have several witnesses who saw him having a heated argument with Lorenzo at Auberge du Soleil on the day before the awards dinner. And I have an eyewitness who saw him in the woods mushroom hunting with Kinsley Logan the week before the dinner."

Chapter 20

Rylie sat staring into space after Detective Michelson hung up. Now what? Should she call Sophie and tell her what Aaron had just told her? Or wait for Aaron to tell Sophie or Lucien himself? She wished Alex was there so she could talk to him about it. But she was pretty sure that he was working right now. Her cell phone rang. Alex.

"Hi Alex!"

"Hi. Are you home from work now?"

"Yes, I got home a while ago. Then I went out to Gott's Roadside for a burger and fries. Now I'm just hanging out on the sofa."

"Want some company? I'm having one of my staff close tonight so I'm off in a few minutes."

"I would love some company. Come over whenever you're ready."

"Bella, what are we going to do? Poor Lucien."

Bella walked over and pushed herself against Rylie's legs. Rylie bent over and wrapped her arms around Bella's neck. She ran her hands through Bella's soft golden fur. When Alex knocked on the door, she jumped up off the sofa and rushed to greet him.

"Alex! Come in!"

Alex swept her up in a warm hug. Then he pulled back a little and looked at her face.

"I missed cuddling with you last night, *cara mia*. I didn't sleep a wink," he said.

"I was a little lonely last night, too."

"I'm changing my work schedule effective tomorrow. It occurred to me that if you're working days and I'm working nights, we would never see each other. So I changed my schedule to work 7:00 to 3:00 Monday through Friday. That way we'll have evenings and weekends together," Alex said.

"Oh, that's great, Alex. But I don't want you to change your life for me. Isn't it important that you be at the bar at night when it's busiest?"

"No. I have good staff. People I trust. They can handle it. And if they run into something they can't handle, they know they can call me on my cell any time," Alex said.

Rylie moved in closer to Alex and put her head on his chest.

"What's wrong, *cara mia*?"

Rylie stayed where she was with her head on Alex's chest. It felt warm and safe.

"I just spoke to Detective Michelson. I gave him some information that I thought might be useful to him in your father's case. But it seems like he's narrowing in on Lucien. It's crazy. I know that Lucien would never hurt anyone. I've known him since he and Sophie and I all went to college together. Sophie is my best friend. Lucien's not a murderer, Alex."

Alex wrapped his arms firmly around her. He kissed her on the top of her head.

"I'm so sorry, Rylie. I think we just have to let this whole thing play out. Detective Michelson is not going to be able to make a case against anyone without some solid proof. It'll take him some time to investigate everything and go through all the evidence. We just have to hope that he finds the real murderer soon."

"Let's try to focus on some positive things. Why don't we cuddle up on the sofa and try to relax a little?" Alex asked.

"Okay. Good idea. Would you like a glass of wine? I don't have any Italian wine, but I have some good Napa Valley cabernet sauvignon," Rylie said.

"That sounds great."

Rylie poured two glasses of wine and went in the living room to sit with Alex on the sofa. Alex put his wine down and put his arm around her.

"We need to talk," Alex said.

"Uh oh. That's never good," Rylie said.

"Well, this time it is, I think," Alex said. "I would like to ask you to move in with me. Otherwise, we'll be driving to each other's houses every night. It just makes sense that you move in with me so we can spend more time together and not spend all our time driving back and forth between our houses."

"Dr. Corbyn paid for this rental house until the end of November," Rylie said.

"So keep it. If you find out that you can't stand living with me, then you'll have someplace to go," Alex teased.

"You do know that I'm only here as long as Dr. Corbyn needs me, right? He originally only asked me to help him out for one month. Then he extended it until the end of November. He should have recuperated from his surgery by then."

"So we have until the end of November before we have to worry about that," Alex said. "In the meantime, I want you in my bed with me every night."

Rylie raised an eyebrow. Alex gave her a sexy grin.

"Well, you are my girlfriend. I think couples do that sort of thing."

Rylie laughed. "I think you need to be more specific. What sort of thing are you talking about?"

"This sort of thing." Alex pulled her close and kissed her long and passionately.

When they came up for air, Rylie said, "Oh, okay. I'm cool with that."

"Great! Let's get you packed up and moved over to my house right now," Alex said.

"Um, you're kidding, right? I can't be up late tonight. I have to work tomorrow."

"We'll get you packed up in no time. All you have with you is clothes, right? And some food in the frig? Piece of cake," Alex said. "I brought some boxes with me on the chance that you said yes."

Alex went out to his SUV and came back with some boxes. "Is all the food in the cabinets yours?" he asked.

"Yes, all the food in the cabinets, the refrigerator, and the freezer is mine."

"Okay. I'll pack up all the food while you pack your clothes. We'll knock this out in no time."

An hour and a half later, Bella was buckled into the back seat of Rylie's SUV and her clothes and food were safely stored in the back. She hopped up into the driver's seat. Alex stood next to her. She grinned at him.

"You should know that I've never been comfortable with change in my life. So this type of spontaneity is so not me," she said.

"Life's an adventure. You have to enjoy it in the moment." Alex smiled warmly at her. "So now we're on this adventure together. I'm very happy."

He reached out and pulled her hand to his lips and kissed it. "Ready? You can follow me."

He closed her SUV door and got into his SUV. Rylie started her SUV and followed Alex out the driveway to his house.

The next morning, Rylie pulled herself out of a deep sleep when the alarm went off at 6:00 a.m. She was momentarily confused when she opened her eyes. She couldn't figure out where she was. Then she became aware of Alex's warm body next to hers and it all came back to her.

Alex pulled away from her to roll over and turn off the alarm. Then he quickly turned back and wrapped his arm around her again.

"You feel so good," he said. He nuzzled her neck and kissed it. "I wish I didn't have to be at work by 7:00. I'd rather stay here in bed with you."

"Unfortunately, we both have to get up. I don't have to be at work until 9:00, but by the time I feed Bella, get some breakfast for myself, read my email, and take a shower, it seems to take about that long for me to get ready in the morning," Rylie said.

"I usually just make some coffee and get something to eat once I get to work," Alex said. He rolled out of bed and put on some flannel sleep pants and a t-shirt. He looked very sexy in a "just got out of bed" rumpled sort of way.

"The en suite bathroom is all yours," Alex said. "I'll use the en suite bathroom for the guest bedroom down the hall. That way we won't be tripping all over each other when we're trying to get ready in the mornings."

He disappeared out the bedroom door. Rylie put on her flannel sleep pants and a t-shirt and went to brush her teeth so she wouldn't gross Alex out with her morning breath. When she walked out of the bathroom, Bella and Amando were standing side by side looking at her and wagging their tails.

"Do you guys need to go outside?"

The dogs' tails wagged faster.

"I'll take that as a yes."

She headed to the kitchen with the dogs bounding ahead of her. Alex was in the kitchen making coffee.

"Is the property totally fenced in so I can let the dogs out?" she asked.

"Yes, and the front gate closes automatically after a car drives through."

Rylie opened the front door. Bella and Amanda sprinted outside to do their business. She waited at the door for them to return. They rushed back a few minutes later with eager looks on their faces.

She inhaled deeply of the aroma of fresh coffee brewing as she walked back to the kitchen.

"I'll feed the dogs. What does Amando get to eat in the morning?" she asked.

"He gets two cups of kibble. His kibble's in here."

Alex showed her where he stored Amando's kibble. She got bowls of kibble and fresh water for both of the dogs.

"How do you like your coffee, *cara mia*?"

"About half warmed milk and half coffee. I usually warm the milk in my coffee cup in the microwave and then add coffee."

"No problem."

Alex handed her a steaming cup of coffee a few minutes later. He took his coffee with him and went to shower and get dressed for work. He came back about half an hour later looking clean and refreshed. He pulled her out of her chair at the kitchen dining table into his arms and kissed her thoroughly.

"I've got to get going. I'll see you tonight, okay?"

"Okay. Have a good day."

She wasn't sure if Sophie would be up yet, so rather than calling, she sent Sophie a text to let her know that she had moved in with Alex. She smiled to herself as she pictured Sophie's jaw dropping when she read the text.

Katie was at her usual place when Rylie got to work at about 8:30 a.m.

"Hi Katie! I hope you're feeling better," Rylie said.

"Hi Dr. Sunderland. I am feeling better today. Thank you," Katie said. Something about her tone of voice said she was not okay.

"I'm going to go drop off my things in the doctors' office. Do you have time for a quick coffee with me in the break room before the first appointments get here?" Rylie asked.

"Sure. I'll meet you in the break room in a few," Katie said.

Katie was standing by the Keurig making coffee when Rylie walked into the break room. Rylie selected a coffee from the Keurig pods and got a coffee mug out of the cabinet.

"I heard Hector got put in jail," Rylie said finally.

"I figured you would. I'm sure everyone knows about it by now. The gossip grapevine around here is faster than lightning," Katie said. She stirred some non-dairy creamer into her coffee and stepped aside so Rylie could use the Keurig.

Rylie put her coffee pod in the Keurig and pressed the start button. She looked over at Katie.

"Is he still in jail? Or did he manage to post bail?" Rylie asked.

"His parents put up the money for a bail bondsman to post bail. He's getting out today. I moved all my stuff out of his apartment over the weekend. We're through. He doesn't know it yet. When he gets home and finds all my stuff gone, he'll be texting me to find out what's going on," Katie said.

"I'm not sure what to say or how I should handle it," she continued. "I just know that I don't want to be with someone who could do something like that. Even though he didn't know that he would end up killing Lorenzo Marchetti, he should have been smart enough to figure out that something bad could happen."

Katie's voice cracked and tears sprung to her eyes. Rylie reached out and grasped Katie's hand.

"I can only imagine what you're going through, Katie. But you're a strong person. You can get through this. If you ever need to talk, I want you to feel free to call me. Give me your cell phone. I'll type my number into your contacts list."

Katie wiped her eyes and managed a small smile. "Thank you, Dr. Sunderland."

Rylie's cell phone buzzed with a text message. Detective Michelson.

"I've got to get this and get ready for my first appointment, Katie. I'll talk to you later."

Are you free for lunch today? I'd like to talk to you. Nothing to do with the investigation. I'll make reservations for us for in a private yurt at The Charter Oak restaurant.

Rylie stared at the text in surprise. What could Aaron possibly have to talk to her about that he couldn't talk to her about on the phone? Was this his version of a date?

I have a lunch break from 12-1. I'll meet you there a few minutes after 12.

She told Cassandra that she had to do something over lunch and wasn't sure if she'd get back in time for her 1:00 appointment.

"Any chance you could do my 1:00 appointment?" she asked. "It's just a wellness exam on a three-year-old Aussie. It shouldn't take too long. I'll be happy to return the favor for you sometime."

"Sure, Rylie. No problem. Hot date?" Cassandra grinned.

Rylie returned her grin. "Something like that."

She had a hard time focusing on her appointments that morning. When she finished her last appointment, she hurried out to her SUV and drove quickly to The Charter Oak. She told the hostess that she was meeting Detective Aaron Michelson for lunch and that he had reserved a yurt.

"Oh, yes. Right this way."

She followed the hostess to a small yurt on the other side of the large courtyard. Aaron was sitting inside sipping an iced tea. He'd ordered one for her, too.

"Hi Rylie! Thanks for coming."

He stood up and hugged her briefly, then pulled out her chair for her. She sat down and waited to hear what he had to say.

"How are you doing? I'm sorry if I upset you last night. There was just no easy way to say what I had to say. And I knew you'd find out from Sophie as soon as I told her anyway," Aaron said.

Rylie took a sip of her iced tea. "So did you tell Sophie and Lucien what you told me last night?"

"Yes. I called Lucien at work late yesterday afternoon. And I called Sophie right before I called you."

The waitress walked into the yurt with her order pad ready. "So do you know what you want to order?"

Rylie scanned the menu and placed her order. Aaron did the same. The waitress left quickly.

"These yurts are so cool. I saw them the other day when I was here with Kinsley Logan. I was hoping to be able to eat in one someday," she said.

Aaron shook his head. "You sure do get around, Rylie."

"I've made lots of new friends here in St. Helena."

"You sure have." Aaron took a sip of his iced tea. "I stopped by to see you on Saturday, but you weren't home. So I stopped by again on Sunday to see if I could catch you, but you weren't home then either. I called Sophie and asked her if she knew where you were. She said you went to Lake Tahoe for the weekend with Alex Marchetti."

"Yes. I did."

"Are things getting serious with you two?" Aaron asked casually.

"You could say that. He asked me to move in with him. I moved all my stuff over to his house last night."

Aaron choked slightly on a sip of iced tea. "You what?"

They stopped talking while the waitress delivered their lunches and hurried off.

"But you just met him. You've only been in St. Helena for about a month now," Aaron said.

"I know. It's crazy. And I am so not an impulsive person. I don't like change in my life at all. But it feels right to me. He makes me happy," she said. "And it doesn't hurt that he can cook." She ventured a small smile.

Aaron looked completely undone. She saw him struggling to regain his composure.

"Wow," he said finally. "I don't know what to say. I hope you're happy."

He started in on his lunch. They ate in silence for a few long, awkward moments.

"That doesn't mean we can't be friends, Aaron. We can still hang out at the dog park with our dogs and stuff like that," she said.

"Ugh. The Friend Zone. That's not where I thought this was headed," Aaron said.

"I'm sorry, Aaron."

"Listen. I like you. Just because you decided to move in with Alex, that's not going to change things for me any time soon." He reached across the table and held her hand. "I'll always be here for you, Rylie."

A slew of emotions coursed through her that she couldn't define.

"Thank you, Aaron. That means a lot to me. And thank you for this nice lunch in a really cool yurt," she said.

Aaron smiled warmly at her. They finished their lunches shortly thereafter, and Rylie headed back to work.

Chapter 21

Rylie finished typing up her medical records and headed home to Alex's house. Two very happy dogs greeted her when she opened the front door.

"Hi Bella! Hi Amando, Mr. Fuzzy Face."

Alex was close behind the dogs. He wrapped her in a huge hug. Then he stepped back and kissed her briefly on the lips.

"Hello beautiful. Did you have a good day at work today?"

"It was okay. But I'm glad it's over. I feel like my stress level is pretty high right now," she said.

Alex put his arm around her and steered her towards the kitchen. He handed her a glass of red wine.

"Just what I need. Thank you, sweetie. I'm going to put my stuff away and get changed into something more comfortable."

Alex waggled his eyebrows at her. "Sounds good."

"Not THAT comfortable." Rylie laughed. Her stress level went down a few notches. This guy was good for her. How did she get so lucky?

She came back to the kitchen a few minutes later.

"I brought home a couple of pizzas from work for dinner," Alex said. "Does that sound good?"

"Sounds great. But I'd like to just relax and unwind a little before we eat, if that's okay with you."

"Sure. Come on. We can sit on the sofa with our wine. I'll turn on the gas fireplace."

"That sounds wonderful. I love watching a fire in the fireplace. It's so relaxing," she said.

They snuggled up on the sofa together. Alex gently took her wine from her and put both of their wine glasses on the coffee table. Then he wrapped his arms around her and kissed her thoroughly.

"So what are you stressed out about?" he asked.

"I can't remember."

Alex grinned at her. "Awesome!"

He pulled her in for another long kiss. Then he reached for their wine glasses and handed hers to her.

"I went over to my father's house this afternoon after work to walk around and see what I have to do over there. I haven't felt up to doing that until now. I've got to go through all his things and decide what I want to keep. And eventually I'll have to decide if I want to sell his house or use it as a rental. It felt awful walking through there today with the house so cold and quiet," he said.

"Oh, Alex! I'm so sorry. I'd be happy to go with you the next time you go over there if you want. I'm not sure what I could do to help, but at least I'd be there for moral support."

"That would be great. How about Saturday morning?"

"That works for me."

"Perfect. Thanks. Are you getting hungry yet?"

"Yes. I think pizza sounds good."

Alex put the pizzas in the oven and filled up their wine glasses.

"The pizzas will be done soon. Would you like a small green salad with your pizza? I can whip up a couple of salads pretty quickly."

"Sure. I'll help."

Bella and Amando laid down on the floor next to them as they ate their dinner at the kitchen dining table.

"Sorry, Bella. I don't think that spicy meat would be good for you," Rylie said. "But I'll get you something special after I'm done eating, okay?"

Bella thumped her tail on the floor several times. Amando looked at Rylie eagerly.

"You too, Amando."

Amando bounced up and ran to Rylie wagging his tail. Bella joined him and tried to push him out of the way.

"Go lay down. Both of you. You'll get your treats after I'm done eating."

The dogs obediently lay down close by.

"Do you always talk to Bella like she's a person?" Alex asked.

"Of course. She understands a lot. And what she doesn't understand, she fills in the blanks."

Alex chuckled.

When she finished eating, Rylie got two pieces of cheese from the refrigerator and gave a piece to each of the dogs. They both inhaled their piece of cheese and continued to look at her hopefully.

"One piece for each of you. That's it," she said firmly.

They cleaned up the kitchen together and then went to sit on the sofa in the living room.

"Aaron Michelson texted me this morning and asked me if I could meet him for lunch at The Charter Oak restaurant. He said he needed to talk to me. I got one of the other veterinarians at Valley View to take my 1:00 appointment so I could go. It turns out that my friend Sophie told Aaron that you and I went to Tahoe together for the weekend. He wanted to know if you and I were serious. I told him that you asked me to move in with you and that I moved all my stuff over here last night," she said.

"That's kind of personal information, isn't it? Why is Detective Michelson interested in your personal life?" Alex asked.

"I think he had the idea that he and I might get together someday. He told me on Friday that he'd like to get to know me better. I told him then that could be a bit of a problem since he's investigating Lucien as a possible murder suspect and Sophie is my best friend."

"Hmmm."

"After I let him know that you and I are together over lunch today, I told him that he and I could still be friends. We've met at the dog park with our dogs a couple of times to throw the ball and frisbee for them. I told him we could still do things like that together. I definitely don't want to close the door on communication with him. I've been going to him with anything that I find that I think might be relevant to your father's murder investigation."

"What? Why?" Alex asked.

"Because my best friend's husband is under suspicion for murder, and I know he didn't do it. I want to help him. And Sophie. This has been very hard on her. It's tearing her up."

Alex looked thoughtful.

"You're a remarkable woman, *cara mia*," he said finally. "A true friend to those that you care about."

He pulled her into a long, slow kiss. "Ready for bed?" He smiled sexily at her.

When Rylie went into the doctors' office at work around lunchtime the next day, there was a beautiful bouquet of blue and white flowers in a vase on her desk. There was also a big box from the local bakery. She lifted the lid of the box and took a deep whiff of the sweet aromas of the assorted cookies in the box.

Curious, she looked through the flowers in the bouquet to see if there was a card from a florist. There was a tiny envelope attached to a plastic card holder in the middle of the flowers. She opened the envelope and took out the note inside.

Thank you for everything you did for Oreo. She's finally back to her old self.

Oliver Davison

She took a couple of cookies out of the box and then asked Cassandra and Addison if they would like some.

"Oh, yum. These look great. Did one of your clients drop these off?" Cassandra asked.

"Yes. Oliver Davison. He brought in his cat Oreo about three weeks ago for anorexia and weight loss. I did some bloodwork and a urinalysis and found out she was in renal failure. I had him take her to a 24-hour facility to be hospitalized on IV fluids and meds. He came back for a follow-up appointment with me a week later. Then I had him start giving Oreo sub-Q fluids at home three times a week. I'm glad she's doing well."

"We have awesome clients," Addison said. "I love that they bring us so many treats. A little sugar rush helps me get through the day."

Rylie took the box of cookies to the break room and set them in the middle of the table.

She stuck her head in the treatment room and hollered, "There's cookies in the break room!"

She went up front and told Katie and the other receptionist about the cookies, too.

When she got back to her desk, she looked at the bouquet of flowers thoughtfully. I wonder if there's a message in these flowers. She looked for the name of the florist on the card. La Boutique des Fleurs in St. Helena. She looked up their address online, then grabbed the vase of flowers and her lunch.

"I'm going home for lunch today," she said to Cassandra and Addison. "I'll be back in time for my 1:00."

"No problem. Have a good lunch."

She took the vase of flowers into La Boutique des Fleurs and went in search of the checkout counter. As she approached the counter, a woman set aside what she was working on and looked up at her.

"Carolyn! I didn't know you worked here," Rylie said. "I thought you were an artist and that you have your paintings for sale at an art gallery in Napa."

"Rylie! So good to see you. I am an artist. But my paintings don't always provide me with a steady income. So my sister and I started this flower shop. Do you like the bouquet I made for you?" Carolyn nodded at the bouquet in Rylie's hands.

"Yes, I love it!" Rylie said. "I brought it in because I wanted to find out what these pretty blue star-shaped flowers are. I don't think I've ever seen them before."

"They're called Bellflowers. Oliver told me that he wanted to thank you for what you did for his cat, so I chose Bellflowers because they mean "gratitude." And the Lily of the Valleys mean "return of happiness.""

"Oh, how nice," Rylie said. "I was going to get the name of the blue flowers and then look up their meaning in the flower dictionary that I've got at home on my e-reader. That's awesome that you create bouquets based on the language of flowers."

"That's why our customers come here. They want flowers that are beautiful but also meaningful. They tell us the reason they want to give someone flowers, and then we create bouquets that express what they want to say with flowers. We've got several old Victorian flower dictionaries that we use."

On a hunch, Rylie said, "Oliver got a Black-eyed Susan for one of my friends about a week and a half ago. Do you remember that?"

"Oh, yes. He said that one of his friends had finally gotten something that he deserved. He said his friend was a man, so he didn't want a whole bouquet. Just one flower. So I sold him a Black-eyed Susan. Black-eyed Susans mean "justice.""

"Thanks, Carolyn. I'm on my lunch break so I've got to run now. But I'll definitely come here if I need flowers for anyone. See you tomorrow for lunch at Long Meadow Ranch."

"I'm looking forward to it. See you then."

Rylie drove home and put the vase of flowers on a table in the living room. She let Bella and Amando outside to do their business. Then she called Detective Michelson.

"Rylie! How are you?"

"I'm fine, Aaron. How are you?"

"Great. Nice to hear from you. What's up?"

"I know who's been vandalizing Vinterre and leaving weird things on the doorstep," she said. "Oliver Davison."

"How do you know that?"

"Did Lucien tell you that he almost caught the guy the other day when he went in to work early? The guy had just left a Black-eyed Susan on the doorstep. The flower was a coded message. I read a book recently about the language of flowers. In the UK in the 1800s, people couldn't talk freely about their emotions so they developed a system of communication using flowers. They created flower dictionaries with a different meaning assigned to each flower. So they could say "I love you," or whatever, just by handing someone a specific flower. Black-eyed Susans mean "justice.""

"So how does that equate with Oliver Davison being the perp?"

"Oliver Davison dropped off a bouquet of flowers for me at work today to thank me for helping his cat. It had some blue flowers in it that I didn't recognize and some Lilies of the Valley. I wondered if the flowers were a coded message, but I didn't know what the blue ones were. So I took the bouquet back to the florist who made it, La Boutique des Fleurs. I found out that my friend Carolyn Beaumont co-owns the shop with her sister."

"I asked Carolyn what the blue flowers were. She told me they're called Bellflowers and that they mean "gratitude." The Lilies of the Valley mean "return of happiness." Carolyn told me that they create bouquets for their customers based on the reasons their customers have for giving flowers. That's why their customers go to them instead of other florists. Their customers want to give flowers that are meaningful. Carolyn and her sister use old Victorian flower dictionaries to find out the meaning of each flower and create bouquets specific to each occasion."

"On a hunch, I told her that Oliver Davison gave a Black-eyed Susan to one of my friends about a week and a half ago and asked her if she remembered it. She did. She said that Oliver told her that one of his friends had finally gotten something that he deserved and that he wanted to congratulate him with a single flower. So she sold him a Black-eyed Susan. The Black-eyed Susan was left on Vinterre's doorstep the day after you went to Vinterre and told Lucien that all of his employees had to get fingerprinted."

"Interesting. Well, that's strong evidence that he left the Black-eyed Susan on Vinterre's doorstep, but it doesn't prove that he unscrewed the magnetic knife holder on the wall in Vinterre's kitchen or that he opened Vinterre's walk-in refrigerator door after hours so it would be open all night. But I'll talk to him. At least if he knows that we're onto him, that should be a deterrent to any further vandalism at Vinterre."

"Thank you, Aaron. I've got to run. I only have a few minutes left to get something to eat. Then I have to get back to work. Talk to you later."

She let the dogs back in and slammed down her lunch. Then she drove quickly back to work. When she had a few moments in between appointments, she texted Sophie and Lucien about what she had discovered. Lucien texted her back right away.

I called three different security companies after the last incident to come in and give me quotes on a security system for Vinterre including security cameras inside and out. I have two bids already. A guy from the third company came out yesterday and walked the property with me. He's supposed to get me a bid by the end of this week. Once I have everyone's bids, I'll pick one of them and get a security system installed as soon as possible. I should have done this years ago.

Chapter 22

Alex, Bella, and Amando greeted her at the door when she got home from work. Alex wrapped her in a warm hug, then took a small step back.

"You look hot. Why are you all dressed up?" Rylie asked.

"Because tonight, *cara mia*, I'm taking you out on our first official date. I've made reservations for dinner at a nice restaurant. We'll leave as soon as you're ready."

"A date? How weird is that. We're living together and we haven't even been on a real date yet. Where are we going?"

"Vinterre."

"Vinterre? Are you sure you're comfortable with that?" she asked.

"Absolutely. Vinterre is warm and romantic. And they have great food. It's the perfect place for our first date. So go get ready!"

Rylie took a quick shower and then looked through what she had available in her closet. She chose a black stretch knit mini with geometric patterned lace long sleeves. She paired it with slouchy black suede high-heeled boots. She found her small black purse and transferred a few things into it.

Alex gave a low whistle when she walked into the living room.

"You look amazing, honey," he said. He walked over and took her face in his hands. Then he leaned in and gave her a long, passionate kiss.

"We'd better get going before I get too distracted," he said in a husky voice. Rylie giggled.

They took Alex's Alfa Romeo to Vinterre and parked in the parking lot. Rylie felt like a princess as Alex escorted her through the grapevine arbor entryway twinkling with tiny white fairy lights. The hostess seated them at a table that afforded them a little bit of privacy and took their drink orders.

They scanned their menus.

"Everything looks delicious. But I think I'm going to have the salmon, grilled asparagus with hollandaise, and the potato and Gruyère gratin," Rylie said.

"I'm going to have the ribeye steak, sautéed wild mushrooms in a red wine reduction, and mashed potatoes," Alex said.

Rylie looked up at Alex and smiled happily. Her heart flooded with warmth as she looked at his handsome face, his eyes intense with love for her. *How did I get so lucky?*

When their waitress came to deliver their wine and take their food orders, Alex asked her to take their photo.

"I'd like to get a photo of us under the grapevine arbor with the fairy lights before we go," Rylie said.

"That's a good idea. We need to get some nice photos of us that we can have enlarged and framed for our house," Alex said. "We definitely need to commemorate our first official date."

After enjoying their meal together, they headed for Alex's Alfa Romeo. They took a selfie of themselves under the grapevine arbor entryway with the sparkling white fairy lights. As they were walking across the parking lot, they heard a noise.

Alex shouted, "Hey, what are you doing?" and took off at a sprint toward the shrubs around the parking lot.

He came back tightly grasping the hand of an impish-looking little boy with curly, reddish-brown hair and freckles who looked about ten years old. The boy held a cell phone in his free hand.

"Hi," Rylie said. "What's your name?"

"Carter. Carter MacAuley."

"I'm Rylie Sunderland. And this is my boyfriend, Alex Marchetti."

"Were you taking photos of us, Carter?" Alex asked.

"Yes."

"Why?" Rylie asked.

"I didn't mean anything by it. I like to play spy. I want to be a spy when I grow up. I can delete the photos I took of you if you want," Carter said.

"Do your parents know you're here?" Rylie asked.

"No." Carter looked down at the ground and shuffled uncomfortably.

"How did you get here?" Rylie asked.

"My house is just a couple of doors down from here. I sneak out at night when my parents think I'm sleeping," Carter said.

"Do you have any cool spy photos?" Rylie asked. Alex shot her a look.

Carter's face brightened. "Yeah. I have lots of cool photos. And I got a video the other day, too. Do you want to see them?"

"We'd love to see them, Carter," she said.

Carter played the video he had taken. Alex and Rylie watched as a guy in a dark hoodie with the hood pulled low

around his face walked through the parking lot at Vinterre checking out license plates. He stopped abruptly and
walked over to the driver's side of one of the parked cars.
The video cut off just as the guy lifted up the driver's side
windshield wiper.

"I had to duck behind a car when that guy turned my
way," Carter explained. "But after he left, I went over to
the car and took photos. He put an envelope under the
windshield wiper."

Carter showed them the photos he took of the envelope
under the windshield wiper and the car's license plate.

"Wow, you did some great spy work, Carter," Rylie said.
"But I don't think it's safe for you to be out at night
playing spy without your parents knowing where you are."

"I know," Carter said. "But I stay out of trouble. No one
has ever caught me before."

"Carter, would you mind if I took your cell phone to my
house for a little while to upload your video and photos to
my laptop so Alex and I could look at them some more? I
promise I'll return it as soon as I'm done," Rylie said.

Carter shrugged. "Sure. You can just leave it in the mailbox in front of my house when you're done. I'll come
down and get it later."

"Alright. It won't take me long," Rylie said. "And I'll put
Alex's and my cell phone numbers in your contacts list so
you can call us or text us if you ever see something that you
think looks suspicious. Okay?"

"Okay."

"We're going to walk you home now, Carter, so we make
sure you get home safely," Alex said.

"Could you please just walk me as far as the next-door neighbor's house?" Carter asked. "Then I can sneak back inside through the back door."

Alex and Rylie exchanged a look.

"Do you promise you'll go back inside?" Alex asked.

"Yes. I promise."

"Okay. But just this one time," Alex said. "It's not safe for you to be out alone at night. Something bad could happen to you."

Carter swallowed hard.

When they got back home, Rylie uploaded the photos and video that Carter had taken at Vinterre to the cloud storage on her laptop. Alex drove back to town to put Carter's cell phone in his mailbox.

When Alex got back home, they looked through Carter's photos and watched the video again.

"We're going to have to tell Carter's parents about what he's been up to," Alex said.

"I know," Rylie said. "We will. I've got to give copies of this video and these photos to Aaron. I'll take my laptop over to the police department in the morning before my lunch with Patricia Davenport's group. And I'll give some thought as to how we can best go about talking to Carter's parents about him sneaking out at night."

She called Detective Michelson early the next morning and told him she had a video and some photos to show him that could be important to Lorenzo Marchetti's case. When she walked into the police department with her laptop a little while later, the woman at the reception desk motioned her toward Detective Michelson's office. "He's expecting you," she said.

"Good morning, Rylie," Detective Michelson said. "Nice to see you. Playing detective again, are we?"

"This literally just fell into my lap, Aaron. I swear I didn't go looking for it."

"Okay. I believe you." Aaron smiled at her. "So what have you got for me?"

Rylie opened her laptop on Aaron's desk and pulled up the video of the guy in the hoodie in the parking lot at Vinterre.

"Alex and I went out to dinner at Vinterre last night," Rylie began. Aaron winced almost imperceptibly.

"Alex caught a little boy taking photos of us when we were walking back to his car after dinner. This video and photos were taken by that little boy. His name is Carter MacAuley. He lives a couple of doors down from Vinterre. He's been sneaking out of his house at night when his parents think he's sleeping to go to Vinterre to play spy. He wants to be a spy when he grows up."

"I think this is the guy that put the envelope on Hector Briseno's car offering to pay him for helping him "pull a little prank" on Lorenzo Marchetti, Aaron. Carter had to duck behind a car when the guy turned his way to put the envelope under the windshield wiper, but after the guy left, Carter went over and took photos of the envelope and the license plate. Do you have any way to check to see if this license plate belongs to Hector's car?" Rylie asked.

Aaron leafed through a file on his desk and compared the license plate numbers. "Yep. This is Hector's car. I'll have my team go through this video and the photos to see if there's anything that can help us identify the guy in the hoodie. Can you send them to me?"

"Sure."

"Thanks, Rylie. This might prove to be helpful to my investigation."

"I'm happy to help, Aaron. Now I have a favor to ask."

Aaron looked at her with raised eyebrows. He was kind of cute when he wasn't playing tough detective guy.

"Carter seems like a sweet kid, Aaron. I think he'd get a kick out of meeting a real police detective and seeing the police department. Would you be willing to give him a tour? With his parents' permission, of course."

"Sure. Just let me know after you talk to his parents. I assume that you're going to tell his parents that he's been sneaking out at night to play spy?"

"Of course. Alex and I told Carter that it's not safe and that he shouldn't be sneaking out like that. I'm going to ask Carter if he'd like to meet you and get a tour of the police department. Then I'll tell him that I have to ask his parents for permission for him to get the tour. I'll break it to him then that I also have to tell his parents that he's been sneaking out at night."

"Sounds good. I hate to run but I have a meeting I have to get to," Aaron said.

"No problem. Talk to you later."

She went home to get changed for her lunch with Patricia Davenport's group. Bella greeted her at the door wagging her tail enthusiastically with a happy golden grin on her face. Amando's whole body wiggled in happiness.

"Bella! Amando! You guys are the happiest dogs I've ever seen."

She bent over to pet the excited dogs.

"Do you guys want to go outside?"

Both dogs wagged their tails even faster. Rylie giggled and let them out the front door. She went to her bedroom to look through her closet for something to wear to lunch. She chose a dark teal turtleneck sweater and gray pants that she had purchased at Casual Chic so that Maggie could see that she was wearing the outfits that she had helped her put together. She headed to Long Meadow Ranch a little before noon.

The restaurant felt light and airy inside with its tall, vaulted wood ceiling and large windows letting in lots of natural light. Rylie spotted her friends at a table on the other side of the restaurant and made her way over to them.

"Hi, Rylie!" The women smiled and greeted her as she walked up.

"Hi. This place looks really nice," Rylie said. She sat down in the empty seat at the table.

"This place is the epitome of farm to table eating," Liza said. "You're in for a treat, Rylie. They have 650 acres here. They have other properties, too. I think they've got a couple of thousand acres between all of their properties. They raise their own cattle, sheep, and chickens and grow their own organic fruits and vegetables. They also have vineyards and olive groves. They serve their own farm-raised beef, lamb, and produce here in the restaurant."

"That's awesome," Rylie said. "Have you tried any of their wines?"

"I have," Patricia said. "They're good. Especially their cabernet sauvignons."

"I think I'll try one of their cabernets then," Rylie said.

A waitress came by and got their drink orders. Rylie scanned the lunch menu. "Everything sounds so good. I'm hungry. I think I'm going to try their grass-fed cheeseburger."

Maggie looked up from her menu. "Oh Rylie, you're wearing one of the sweaters you got at my boutique the other day. That color looks really pretty with your blond hair."

"It does," Kinsley agreed.

"Thank you," Rylie said.

The waitress delivered their drinks and got their food orders.

"My sister and I had dinner at Vinterre last night," Carolyn said. "I saw you there with Alex Marchetti."

"You did?" Rylie asked. "I didn't see you there last night."

"I think you were too busy making goo-goo eyes at Alex." Carolyn grinned. "So what's the deal, Rylie? Are you dating Alex Marchetti?"

All eyes were on her. Rylie tried to assess the group's reaction to Carolyn's announcement. Everyone just looked curious.

"Um, yes. You could say that. We've actually been doing things together as friends for a while now. Then he invited me to spend the weekend with him at his family's house in Lake Tahoe this past weekend. He said he needed to get away from here and from all the stress surrounding his father's death so he could have some time to process everything. We really bonded this past weekend. It took our relationship to a whole new level. On Monday night, he came to my house and asked me to move in with him. He said otherwise we'd be driving to each other's house every night so we could see each other. It made sense to me. So I'm actually living with him now."

Maggie choked on her wine and had a coughing fit.

"Are you okay?" Rylie asked.

Maggie waved her hand in front of her beet-red face. "I'm fine. I'm fine."

"Half the single women in St. Helena have had their eye on Alex Marchetti," Kinsley said. "Now you come in and take him off the market after you've only been here a few weeks? Wow. That's impressive." Kinsley smiled.

"He's a great catch, Rylie," Patricia said. "Not only is he handsome, but he's a good man. I can see you two together. I think you're a great match."

"Thank you, Patricia," Rylie said. "I'm not a person that likes change. I never do things spontaneously like this. But it just feels right. He makes me very happy."

"Cheers to that!" Kinsley said.

"Cheers to Rylie and Alex. May their relationship continue to grow and bloom," Carolyn said.

Rylie raised her glass to Carolyn. "Spoken like a true florist." Carolyn grinned.

"Alex and I are going over to his father's house on Saturday. Alex needs to go through his father's things to decide what he wants to keep. I'm going for moral support, but I'm also curious as to whether there might be some clue in Lorenzo's things as to who might have wanted to hurt him."

"You never know what might turn up," Patricia said. "That could prove very interesting."

After lunch with her friends, Rylie went home to change and wait for Carter to get out of school so she could call him. Carter answered on the first ring.

"Hi Carter. This is Rylie Sunderland."

"Hi Rylie."

"I wanted to let you know that I gave your photos and video to a detective at the police department because I thought they might help him on a case he's working on," Rylie said.

"You mean about Lorenzo Marchetti?" Carter asked.

"How did you hear about that, Carter?"

"I heard my parents talking about it. Some kids at school were talking about it, too," Carter said.

"Well, you're right. The guy you saw in Vinterre's parking lot might have something to do with Lorenzo Marchetti's case," Rylie said. "Detective Michelson is having his team review the photos and video you took to see if they can get any information that might help them in their case. Detective Michelson was very appreciative of your help. He said he would give you a tour of the police department if you're interested."

"Oh, yeah!" Carter exclaimed.

"I'll have to ask your mother for her permission for you to go. I also have to tell her about how Alex and I met you and how sometimes you go to Vinterre at night when you're supposed to be sleeping so you can play spy."

"Oh, man. That's going to get me in trouble."

"If I was your mother, Carter, I would be scared if I thought you were sneaking out at night and going to a restaurant to take photos of people. Something bad could happen to you. So if your parents tell you they don't want you sneaking out to go to Vinterre at night, it's only because they want to protect you and keep you safe."

"I know," Carter said grudgingly.

"Are you home now?"

"Yes."

"Is your mom home with you?"

"Yes."

"Do you think this would be a good time for me and Alex to come over to talk to your mom and see if she'll let you go on a tour of the police department?" Rylie asked.

"I guess so," Carter said.

"Alex should be home from work soon. As soon as he gets home, we'll head over to your house to talk with you and your mother."

"Okay."

She hung up and waited for Alex to get home from work. When he walked in the door, she went to greet him and gave him a quick hug and kiss.

"Well hello to you, too." Alex held her by her shoulders and looked in her eyes. "What's up?"

"Are you ready to go talk to Carter's mother and tell her what Carter's been up to?" Rylie asked.

"Did you talk to Carter and tell him we're coming?"

"Yes, he's expecting us. I don't know if he's told his mother we're coming, though," Rylie said.

"Well, we have to do this. It's for Carter's own good. So let's get it over with," Alex said.

"Right."

They took Alex's Alfa Romeo over to Carter's house. Alex looked over at Rylie as he knocked on the door.

Carter's mother opened the door. "Yes? Alex? What a surprise! What are you doing here? How did you know where I lived?"

"Eileen?" Alex said. "How are you? I haven't seen you in Il Capriccio for your morning cappuccino and cornetto in a long time. I had no idea you lived here. My girlfriend Rylie and I met Carter last night, and we came here to talk to his parents."

"What's going on with Carter?" Eileen asked.

"We met Carter when we were coming out of Vinterre after dinner last night. He told us that he's been sneaking out at night to take photos of people in the Vinterre parking lot," Alex said.

Eileen's eyes widened. "What? Carter! Carter, come here!"

Carter eyes were glued to the ground as he shuffled over to his mother.

"What have you been doing sneaking out at night to take photos of people in the Vinterre parking lot when you're supposed to be in bed sleeping?" Eileen demanded.

"I don't know," Carter said in a barely audible voice.

"Carter told us that he likes to play spy. He wants to be a spy when he grows up. Right, Carter?" Rylie said.

Carter looked up at Rylie and nodded mutely.

"Apparently Carter has been doing this for a while," Alex said. "He showed us a video and some photos that he took of a guy in the Vinterre parking lot that may be involved in my father's murder. Carter let us make copies of them, and Rylie took them to Detective Michelson at the police department this morning. Detective Michelson is having his team review the video and photos for any information that might help in my father's murder investigation."

"Detective Michelson really appreciated getting the video and photos," Rylie said. "I told him that Carter wants to be a spy when he grows up. I asked him if he would mind giving Carter a tour of the St. Helena police department. He said he'd be happy to give Carter a tour, but that Carter would have to get your permission first."

"Hmmm," Eileen said. She looked sternly at Carter. "I don't know about that. Carter may be grounded for some time after this. I'll talk to his father when he gets home. For now, Carter, please go do your homework."

Carter hurried off.

"Thank you for letting me know about this," Eileen said. "I'm so glad that nothing bad happened to Carter when he was out taking photos in the middle of the night. The thought of him doing that terrifies me."

"No problem, Eileen," Alex said. "I can definitely understand how you feel. I'm glad nothing bad happened to him, too. I hope I see you at Il Capriccio soon."

Alex turned to go.

"Bye, Eileen," Rylie said.

They got in the Alfa Romeo. Alex looked over at her.

"I need to get some wine and housemade salumi for Il Capriccio from V. Sattui Winery. Would you like to come?"

"Sure."

Chapter 23

A lex turned on the Alfa Romeo and headed towards V. Sattui Winery.

"They make the best Soppressata. It's Italian salami made with zinfandel and red chilies," Alex said. "We can get a nice bottle of wine to take to Sophie and Lucien's house tonight while we're there. And I can take you down to the Members Cellar Club wine tasting cellar for a glass of wine, if you'd like."

"Yes, I'd like that. So you're a member?"

"Yes, I'm a Silver Club member. You have to purchase $5 00.00 worth of wine in one transaction to become a member. All I have to do is purchase a few cases of wine for Il Capriccio once a year, and it keeps my membership current. Members get complimentary tastings and barrel samplings for two, complimentary vineyard and winery tours for two, discounted tickets to winery events, entry into the Cellar Club, and great discounts on cases of wine."

"Sounds like a good deal."

"Have you ever been to V. Sattui Winery?" Alex asked.

"I think so. Maybe once many years ago. I don't really remember it, though. Maybe I'll remember it once we get there."

Alex drove in the driveway to V. Sattui and parked. They held hands as they walked over to the stone winery building with its ivy-covered walls. Alex took her to the deli first so he could get his salumi. Rylie browsed items for sale while she waited for him. After he paid for his Soppressata, Alex took her to the Cellar Club.

There was a lively group of people at the bar in the Cellar Club. They found an open spot at the bar and browsed the wine list.

"I'd like to try their 2018 Ramazzotti Vineyard Zinfandel," Rylie said. "The description says it has aromas of black raspberry, sweet spice, and chocolate. Yum! And it's won lots of awards."

"That sounds good. I'll have the same," Alex said. The tasting room server poured some zinfandel in each of their glasses.

Rylie took a sip of her wine and smiled. "This is fantastic. Let's get a bottle of this to take to Sophie and Lucien's house tonight."

"It is nice, isn't it? I'll get a case of it. Then we'll have some for ourselves, too," Alex said.

When they finished their wine, Alex purchased two cases of wine for Il Capriccio as well as a case of the 2018 Zinfandel they had enjoyed at the bar. One of the staff helped Alex take the cases of wine to his Alfa Romeo.

"Maybe I should have brought my SUV?" Alex said wryly. Rylie smiled.

They dropped off the cases of wine and some salumi at Il Capriccio and headed home to get changed for dinner at Sophie and Lucien's house. The dogs greeted them ecstatically at the front door.

Rylie bent down and hugged Bella. "Hi, Bella! Hi, Amando!"

She left the front door open for the dogs. They raced outside to do their business and then quickly ran back inside so they wouldn't miss anything. Rylie stood in the open doorway until they came back inside.

Alex went to put the wine and salumi away. He came back into the kitchen with the bottle of wine they planned to take to Sophie and Lucien's house. He set the bottle down on the counter and reached for her. He pulled her close and gave her a long, deep kiss.

Rylie's insides warmed with pleasure. How did she get so lucky?

"We'd better get changed and get ready to go," she said finally.

"Yes, we'd better," Alex said huskily.

She went through the clothes in her closet and chose a V-neck burgundy cardigan sweater with gold buttons. She put on a pretty black lace camisole and buttoned up the cardigan over it. The top of the black lace camisole was just visible at the lower edge of the V-neck sweater. She paired the cardigan with some charcoal-colored pants.

Alex looked very handsome in a black turtleneck sweater with dark gray pants. Rylie threw her arms around his neck and kissed him lightly.

"You look so handsome." She smiled.

"You look beautiful," Alex replied. "Are you ready to go?"

"Yes. Let's go."

As they walked up to Sophie and Lucien's house, Sophie opened the door with a smile. "Rylie! And you must be Alex. So nice to meet you, Alex. Please come in!"

"Oh my goodness! It smells so good in here!" Rylie took a deep breath of the rich red wine sauce that perfumed the air.

"Yes. It smells amazing," Alex agreed.

"Lucien is making Coq au Vin for dinner. It's one of his favorite meals to make at home," Sophie said.

"This is for you," Alex said. He handed Sophie the bottle of wine they got at V. Sattui.

"Oh! V. Sattui Zinfandel! I love their wines. Thank you," Sophie said. "Please come say hi to Lucien. He's in the kitchen."

They followed Sophie to the kitchen.

"Lucien! Rylie and Alex are here."

Lucien turned around from where he was stirring the Coq au Vin on the stovetop.

"Alex! Good to see you, man. I haven't seen you for a while. I'm so sorry about what happened to your dad," Lucien said. He walked over and grasped Alex's hand.

"Thank you, Lucien," Alex said. He put his free hand over Lucien's and looked him in the eye. After a few seconds, Lucien walked back over to the stove.

"Your Coq au Vin smells amazing, Lucien," Rylie said.

"Thanks, Rylie." Lucien grinned at her. "I'm going to serve it with a side of haricots verts sautéed in butter with sliced shallots. And warm, crusty French bread. Sophie made a green salad with butter lettuce, chopped red Swiss chard, cucumbers, red bell pepper, red onion, and kalamata olives with a balsamic vinaigrette."

"Yum!" Rylie said.

Rylie and Alex helped bring everything out to the table.

"Alex, would you like to pour some wine for everyone?" Sophie asked. "I have a nice bottle of pinot noir that I opened for us on the kitchen counter."

"No problem," Alex said.

They sat down at the table and started serving themselves Coq au Vin, haricots verts, and crusty French bread. Sophie had already put small plates of her salad at each place setting.

"It tastes as wonderful as it smells, Lucien," Rylie said.

"Yes, it's *deliziosa*," Alex said.

"Thanks." Lucien smiled.

Lucien served them individual peach soufflés in small ramekins with vanilla bean ice cream for dessert.

Lucien set a souffle in front of Rylie. "Oh, how pretty!" she exclaimed.

"You're a fantastic chef, Lucien," Alex said. "This has been an incredible meal."

"The salad was really good, too, Sophie," Rylie said. "I've never had chopped red Swiss chard in a salad before. I don't know that I ever would have thought to add Swiss chard to a salad. But it was really good. I'm going to add Swiss chard to my salads at home now."

Sophie smiled. "Thanks, Rylie. It was kind of an accident that I ended up putting Swiss chard in a salad. One time when I didn't have any other greens to use for a salad, I decided to try using the Swiss chard I had in the refrigerator. I was surprised by how much I liked it. I'm glad you liked it, too."

Sophie, Rylie, and Alex worked together to clear the table, put the leftovers away, and do the dishes. They told Lucien to go relax in the living room since he had prepared the meal. When they were finished, they joined Lucien in the living room.

Lucien stood up when they came in. "Can I get a digestif for everyone? I have a very nice Mirabelle plum *eau de vie*. It's brandy made with plums from France."

"Sure," Rylie said.

"Sounds good," Alex said.

Lucien poured a small amount of the plum brandy into small brandy snifters for each of them.

Rylie swirled the brandy in her glass, smelled it, then took a small sip. Alex did the same. Lucien looked at them expectantly.

"It's nice," Rylie said. "Fruity. I can taste the plums."

"I like it," Alex said.

Lucien looked at Alex. "Alex, I want to address the elephant in the room. I'm sure you know that Detective Michelson considers me a suspect in your father's murder. I want to assure you that I had nothing to do with your father's death. Your father was a good friend to me. I would never hurt him."

"I know that, Lucien."

"Detective Michelson has brought up some things that he thinks could have given me motive to kill your father. I think the biggest thing that he found out is that your father loaned me money for the renovation work required to open Vinterre. Your father took a second mortgage on Vinterre to secure his loan. I got behind on my payments to him after PGE shut off the power to our area for four days in August. Your father's attorney sent a letter to my attorney threatening foreclosure on Vinterre after I got three months' behind in my payments. That letter was dated the week before the Chamber awards dinner at Vinterre," Lucien said.

Alex slowly took a sip of his *eau de vie*. "I agree that doesn't look good. But I just can't see you killing anyone, Lucien. Ever. Especially not my father. You were friends."

"Thanks for believing in me, Alex. I didn't tell anyone that I was having financial problems at Vinterre. Not even Sophie. I wanted to take care of everything myself. But after Detective Michelson took me in for questioning about the money I owed your father, I finally told Sophie about the financial problems I've been having. Sophie took it upon herself to pay off all of the back payments that I owed your father. She said she knew I'd do the same for her. So I'm all caught up now, and I plan to keep it that way."

"You may have also heard that I had an argument with your father at Auberge du Soleil on the day before the Chamber awards dinner," Lucien continued.

"Actually, my father was the one that told me about that," Alex said. "He was hoping that you would host my cousin's wedding reception dinner at Vinterre. He was pretty upset that you wouldn't do it. He said that you said that you weren't set up for that type of thing. But I hardly think that argument could be construed as a motive for murder. I think Detective Michelson will agree when he finds out what that argument was about."

"Has Detective Michelson talked to you about it?" Lucien asked.

"No. He hasn't been very good about keeping me in the loop about my father's murder investigation," Alex said. "Honestly, that's probably been for the best. I've had a hard time dealing with my father's death. I've had to juggle the added responsibilities of taking over Il Capriccio and planning my father's funeral. I still haven't gone through his things or decided what to do with his house. I didn't even have the time to grieve or work through my feelings until Rylie and I spent the weekend up at Lake Tahoe. If Detective Michelson was constantly calling me with updates on the investigation, it would probably have put me over the edge."

Rylie reached for Alex's hand and held it in her own. He squeezed her hand in return.

"There's one more thing that you should know if you don't already," Lucien said. "Then everything will be out in the open and we can move on. The latest thing that Detective Michelson has discovered that he thinks is suspicious is that I went wild mushroom hunting with Kinsley Logan the week before the Chamber awards dinner. Kinsley was looking for Death Cap mushrooms to photograph. I was looking for Chanterelle mushrooms to serve at Vinterre."

"How do you know Kinsley?" Rylie asked.

"I went to one of her presentations about poisons at the St. Helena library earlier this year. I heard it was really inter-esting, and I wanted to check it out," Lucien said. "I went up to introduce myself to her after her presentation. I asked her if she ever sees any edible wild mushrooms when she goes looking for poisonous plants to photograph. I thought it might be fun to have some fresh wild mushrooms to work with at Vinterre. She told me that she does see them from time to time. She said she'd let me know the next time she planned to go wild mushroom hunting. Then she called me about a month and a half ago and said it was the time of year that Chanterelle mushrooms fruit. She thought I might like some to use at Vinterre. I jumped at the chance."

"And in case you're wondering," Lucien continued. "Chanterelles don't look anything like Death Cap mush-rooms. Chanterelles are bright golden yellow with wavy caps. They're very distinctive looking. And they can get really large. Death Cap mushroom have a more typical dome-shaped cap."

"I don't think Detective Michelson can build a case against you for hunting wild mushrooms," Alex said. "That's just circumstantial evidence. So is having an argument with my father. Missing three mortgage payments and running the risk of losing Vinterre seems like a more likely motive for murder, but not in your case. My father would never have loaned you the money unless he really liked you and believed in you and your character."

Lucien breathed a sigh of relief. His shoulders visibly relaxed. He sat back in his chair.

"So now that we've cleared the air, we can talk about other things. Alex took me out for our first real date last night at Vinterre," Rylie said.

"You were at Vinterre last night?" Lucien asked. "You should have had the hostess tell me. I would have done something special for you."

"I know, Lucien. Thank you," Rylie said. "But we were just happy to have a wonderful meal in a warm and romantic spot. Our meals were excellent, by the way."

Lucien smiled. "Good to know."

"Something interesting happened when we were leaving Vinterre last night. We heard a noise when we were walking to the parking lot. Alex caught a little boy taking our photos. His name is Carter MacAuley. He looks like he's probably about ten years old. He lives a couple of houses down the street from Vinterre. He's been sneaking out at night so he can play spy. He got a video of the guy who put the note on Hector Briseno's windshield that told Hector to mix the brown powder in Lorenzo's dinner as a prank. Carter also took photos of the note and Hector's license plate," Rylie said.

"You're kidding!" Lucien said. "Did you see the video and the photos?"

"Yes. I have copies on my cell phone and my PC. I gave Aaron Michelson copies this morning. He's having his team go through them to see if they can find anything to help in their investigation."

"Can we see them?" Sophie asked.

"Absolutely. I'll just squeeze in here between you and Lucien on the sofa so you can watch the video on my cell phone," Rylie said.

She played the video for them and then showed them the photos.

"Wow. That's crazy," Lucien said. "But what about the little boy? Carter? He can't be out photographing people at Vinterre late at night like that. It's not safe."

"Alex and I went to talk to Carter's mother this afternoon and told her what's been going on."

"Good," Sophie said.

"I watched the video very carefully," Alex said. "I can tell that the guy in the hoodie is not you, Lucien. You're taller and thinner. The other people that are on Rylie's and my suspect list are Sean Kavanaugh - he's the guy my father threw out of Il Capriccio for making unwanted advances on a woman sitting at the bar - and the guy that Rylie met on the Napa Valley Wine Train whose wife suffered a miscarriage after she slipped and fell in a puddle on the floor in the bathroom at Il Capriccio The guy in the video doesn't look like Sean Kavanaugh to me. I've never seen the guy that Rylie met on the Napa Valley Wine Train, so I have no idea if it's him."

"You mean Derek Firth," Rylie said. "I can't tell if it's him either."

They heard a knock at the door.

"I'll get it." Lucien strode away to answer the door.

After a few minutes, Sophie said she was going to see who it was. Rylie and Alex followed her. Hector Briseno was standing by the door talking to Lucien.

Alex reached him in two strides, grabbed him by his shirt collar, and slammed him up again the wall.

"What the hell?" Hector said. He struggled to free himself from Alex's grasp.

"I know who you are," Alex said. "You're the guy who poisoned my father."

Hector spluttered and tried to hit Alex's arms away.

Lucien put his hand on Alex's shoulder. "Alex, man, he's not worth it. Let him go."

"Alex!" Rylie said. Alex turned to look at Rylie without letting go of Hector.

"Alex, let him go. He was just a pawn for the real killer. He did something stupid, but he didn't intend to kill your father," Rylie said.

"I have proof," Hector said.

Alex released his hold on Hector. Hector got out his cell phone.

"I took a photo of the note that someone left on my windshield. Whoever wrote it said it was just a prank. I didn't know it would kill him. Here. look at this." Hector handed Alex his cell phone with the photo of the note from the person who wanted Lorenzo dead. Alex read the note out loud:

I want to play a little prank on a friend of mine, Lorenzo Marchetti. He'll be attending the St. Helena Chamber of Commerce awards dinner on October 8th. Make sure that you're the waiter for his table during the awards dinner. Depending on what he orders, carefully mix the contents of this packet in the brown sauce for the steak if he gets the steak, the cream sauce for the salmon if he gets the salmon, or the risotto if he gets the risotto before you serve it to him. Make sure there's no powder

*visible that hasn't been mixed in. Be careful that no one sees
you.*

*Don't speak to anyone about this including your friends
or family. If you pull this off and do a good job, there'll be
another $3,000 in it for you. I'll be watching.*

*Here's a photo of Lorenzo. He's an old, overweight Italian
guy.*

Alex handed the phone back to Hector. He pushed past
Hector and went out the front door. Rylie exchanged a
look with Sophie, then ran outside after Alex. She caught
up with him in the driveway. She saw his shoulders heav-
ing. She put her arm around his waist.

"Alex, honey, why don't we go home? I'll drive."

Alex didn't respond.

"I'll go get our coats and my purse. Where are your car
keys?" Rylie asked.

"In my jacket pocket."

"Okay. I'll be right back."

Rylie went inside. "Alex and I are going to call it a night.
Thank you for a wonderful meal. I'm just going to get our
coats and my purse."

When she went back outside, she found Alex in the same
place she'd left him. She unlocked the Alfa Romeo's doors
and got in on the driver's side. Alex got in on the passenger
side. She looked over at him and took his hand.

"I'm sorry this happened, Alex."

He didn't respond. She started the car and drove to
Alex's house. Alex was silent the entire ride home. When
she parked the car at his house, he got out and walked to
the front door. Rylie unlocked the front door and let him
in.

"I'm going to get a glass of wine. Do you want one?" Alex asked.

"Sure."

"Hi, Bella! Hi, Amando! Let's go outside," Rylie said.

She went out with the dogs while they did their business. It was cold and quiet outside. She pulled her coat tighter around herself while she waited for the dogs. A few minutes later, Bella came bounding up to her with Amando close behind. Rylie wrapped her arms around Bella's neck and buried her face in her warm fur.

"You're nice and warm, Bella." Bella wagged her tail.

Rylie felt Amando's cold nose on her neck. "You're a good boy, Amando."

Amando tried to squeeze in closer. Rylie petted him a little. Then she stood up and headed inside.

Alex was sitting on the sofa in the living room with a glass of red wine in his hand. His eyes were unfocused. He looked a million miles away. She turned on some soft music and the gas fireplace before she sat down next to him on the sofa. After she took a sip of wine, she snuggled close to him and sat quietly watching the flames flickering in the fireplace while she gave him time to work through his feelings.

Chapter 24

The next morning after Alex left for work, Rylie sat down at the dining table and took a sip her coffee. She was feeling guilty that she hadn't spoken to her mother in some time. Her mother didn't even know anything about her relationship with Alex.

"I guess I should call mom, huh, Bella?"

Bella thumped her tail up and down on the floor in reply. Amando rushed over to Rylie and put his head in her lap. He looked up at her expectantly.

"Are you a jealous boy, Amando?" She pet Amando's head. Bella came over to get a piece of the action. Rylie stroked Bella's soft golden fur.

"First, I need to call Sophie and find out what Hector Briseno was doing there last night." She figured Sophie was probably still at home eating her breakfast before leaving for work. She called Sophie on her cell phone.

"Hi, Sophie."

"Hi, Rylie. I knew you'd call this morning."

"I just called to find out what Hector Briseno was doing there last night," Rylie replied.

"He came to ask Lucien for his job back. Lucien told him that he wouldn't be able to have him work at Vinterre again after everything that's happened."

"I think Hector is going to have a hard time finding anyone that will hire him after what he did," Rylie said.

"I know."

"I don't want to keep you. I know you have to get ready for work. But I wanted to let you know that I think I'm going to call my mother this morning and tell her about Alex."

"You haven't told her yet?" Sophie asked.

"No. Everything's happened so fast," Rylie replied. "And I didn't feel confident enough in the relationship to get her involved until now. I didn't want to tell her about Alex if it just turned out to be a brief fling. But I really believe Alex and I have something special. Something real. So it's time to let Mom and Dad know."

"Good luck with that. Let me know how it goes."

"I will. Talk to you later."

Rylie hung up and sat staring into space for a few minutes. Then she dialed her mother's cell phone number.

"Hello? Rylie?"

"Hi, Mom."

"How are you, honey? How's everything going with your locum veterinarian job in St. Helena?"

"The job is going great, Mom. I've also gotten involved with a local women's group that gets together to do fun things every Thursday, so I've made a lot of new friends."

"That's great, honey. That will make your time there a lot more fun. I heard on the news about that man getting poisoned at a restaurant in St. Helena. That's so horrible. Do you know anything about it?"

"Yes. It happened at Lucien Marchand's restaurant," Rylie said.

"Your friend Sophie's husband?"

"Yes."

"Is Lucien a suspect?"

"Yes, unfortunately. But he didn't do it, Mom. The police have other suspects that they're also investigating. I actually called to talk to you about something else, Mom."

"I'm sorry. I didn't mean to interrupt you. What did you want to talk about?"

"I'm seeing someone, Mom. It's pretty serious. I've moved in with him at his home in St. Helena. His name is Alex Marchetti. He's the son of the man who was poisoned."

"What? When did this happen? Why am I just hearing about this now?"

"I didn't want to bother you with it if it just turned out to be a brief fling. Now that I'm sure it's serious, I wanted to call you to let you know about it," Rylie said.

"Oh my goodness, Rylie! I can't believe that you moved in with a man without your father and I even knowing that you were seeing someone!"

"I know. I'm sorry, Mom."

"Are you sure it's a good idea to move in with someone that you've only known for a short time?"

"Alex made a good point when he asked me to move in with him. He said that if I didn't, that we'd be spending all our time traveling to each other's houses every night. It made sense to me. But I still have the house that Dr. Corbyn rented for me until the end of November. So if things don't work out, I can easily move back out. I don't see that happening, though."

"I'm just a little shocked that everything has progressed so quickly in your relationship."

"It's nothing that I ever expected either, Mom. But Alex is so perfect for me. You'll see when you finally meet him."

"So when do we get to meet him?"

"I'm not sure. There's a lot going on right now. Alex is having a hard time coping with his father's death and the additional responsibilities that he's had to take on. His father owned a bar on Main Street in St. Helena called Il Capriccio. Alex has had to take over the management of the bar. He had to plan his father's funeral. Now he feels like he's finally ready to go to his father's house to go through his father's things and decide what he wants to keep and what he's going to get rid of. We're going to his father's house to do that tomorrow."

"That's a lot for anyone to deal with. That poor man. He's lucky that he has you to support him through all this. Please let us know when you think the time is right to bring Alex to meet us. I'll make a nice dinner."

"I will, Mom. I've got to go now. I'll talk to you later."

"Bye, honey."

The next morning, Rylie and Alex ate an early breakfast and got ready to go to Lorenzo's house.

"Should we bring the dogs with us or leave them here?" Rylie asked.

"They can come. There's no reason to leave them here. They can keep us company at dad's house."

"Want to go bye-bye in the car?" Rylie asked Bella and Amando. Both dogs leaped at the suggestion and ran to the front door. Rylie and Alex smiled.

Rylie got the dogs' leashes and water bowls. They all piled into Alex's SUV. Rylie snapped Bella into her seatbelt in the back seat while Alex put Amando's seatbelt on.

Lorenzo's house was not far from Alex's house. Rylie was instantly charmed by the renovated white farmhouse. The front porch was flanked on one side by a grapevine arbor that shaded the brick walkway to the front door. They walked into the great room. Rylie took in the massive white wood beams that ran horizontally overhead below the whitewashed vaulted ceiling. Skylights flooded the room with natural light. Through large French doors on the other side of the dining area, Rylie could see mountains in shades of soft blue in the distance.

"Alex, this is beautiful!"

Alex smiled. He caught her up in a hug and kissed her. "Thank you, *cara mia*. I've always loved this house. It's an old 1890's farmhouse that my father had renovated when we first moved here from Italy. It feels like home to me even now."

"Maybe you should consider keeping it in the family rather than selling it," Rylie said. "I love this place."

"But what would we do with it?" Alex asked.

"I'm not sure. But I don't think you should be in any rush to sell it," Rylie said. "I assume that the mortgage on it is paid off?"

"Yes."

"Then it's not a burden financially. Maybe we could use it as a place for your family from Italy to stay in when they come to visit us," Rylie said.

"That's an idea. Come on. I'll show you around."

The quaint farmhouse kitchen had all the modern conveniences and a large picture window that looked out over the pool. Alex led the way out to the backyard. There was a gleaming white bathtub on the deck near a hot tub.

"I don't think I've ever seen an outdoor bathtub before. I guess it's private enough here that you could use it," she said.

"I don't think I'd feel comfortable using it," Alex said. "But I know my father used it from time to time."

Alex took her to see the bocce court in the backyard.

"A bocce court!" Rylie said. "I've never played, but I'd like to learn."

"I'll teach you," Alex said. "It's not hard, and it's a lot of fun."

They walked back into the house.

"I want to start by going through my father's office and all his paperwork. I might be able to find something that could provide us with a clue as to who might have wanted to kill my father," Alex said. "There might be other things in the house that could help Detective Michelson in his investigation. He and his team already went through everything here, but it never hurts to go through everything again. Maybe we'll find something they missed. You're welcome to go through anything you want." He walked away in the direction of his father's office.

Rylie looked around, not sure where to start. She decided to start with Lorenzo's bedroom closet. Lorenzo's bedroom was beautifully designed. It had a sunny bay window with a window seat. Butter-colored pillows and large cream-colored accent pillows were arranged along the back of the window seat. It looked like a wonderful place to curl up with a good book. There was a built-in bookcase filled with books and art pieces next to the bay window.

She slowly walked around the large walk-in closet taking everything in. She lifted the lid of a clothes hamper and looked inside. There were some dirty clothes in there. She dumped them out on the floor and started going through pockets. In the back pocket of a pair of Lorenzo's pants, she found a photo of a beautiful young woman with long black hair and large dark brown eyes. She went to Lorenzo's office to show Alex the photo.

"I found this photo in a pair of your father's pants that were in his hamper," Rylie said.

"Hmmm. She looks familiar. I think I've seen her in Il Capriccio. Wait. I remember. Her name is Eva. I don't know her last name. I'll take this photo with me when I go to work on Monday and show it around. Someone will probably know her last name. Then we can find out where she lives and go talk to her and find out why my father had her photo in his pocket."

"Okay. I'm going back to see what else I can find in your father's closet," Rylie said.

"I found a lawsuit from Derek and Stefanie Firth in my father's files. They were suing my father because of her fall in the bathroom at Il Capriccio that resulted in her having a miscarriage. But the lawsuit was dropped with no explanation," Alex said. "At least none that I can find."

"That's weird," Rylie said. "Do you think they settled out of court or something?"

"I don't know. I'll call my father's attorney on Monday to find out more."

Rylie went back to look through Lorenzo's closet some more. She saw some boxes on top of the wood-framed glass cabinets that enclosed the clothing racks and shelves lining the walls. She pulled the rolling library ladder over and climbed up to bring the boxes down.

She found a very old wooden recipe box with an ornate metal clasp in one of the boxes. She opened it up to find it full of recipes handwritten in a foreign language that she assumed was Italian. She rushed into Lorenzo's office with her find.

"Look what I found, Alex! An old recipe box full of hand-written recipes! I think they're in Italian."

She handed the box to Alex.

"Wow. I can't believe you found this. This was my mother's recipe box. I remember her using it all the time when I was growing up. This is fantastic! I'll translate the recipes so you can use them if you want."

Alex put the recipe box down on his father's desk.

"I found paperwork showing that there are a number of people in addition to Lucien that owe my father money. I've seen payments coming in from all of them except one. The guy who hasn't been making any payments lately is named Todd Saunders. I found a letter from my father's attorney to Todd's attorney about Todd being late on his payments. Todd's attorney lives in New York, so I assume he does, too," Alex said.

"It looks like Todd borrowed money from my father to start a men's clothing store in St. Helena called Je Ne Sais Quoi. I vaguely remember it. I think it went out of business after only being open for a couple of years. Todd must have moved to New York after his business went under. I'm going to have my father's attorney send another letter to Todd's attorney about this."

Rylie went back to look through the rest of the boxes she had pulled down off the shelves in Lorenzo's closet. She opened a file box and started looking through the papers in it.

"Oh my goodness." Her mouth fell open. She put the papers back in the file box and brought it to Lorenzo's office to show Alex.

"Alex, I think you should look at this."

"What did you find now?"

Alex came over, opened the file box, and pulled out some of the papers. His jaw clenched tightly as he read.

"Why didn't my father ever tell me about this? How could Leo do this to my father? After my father took him on as a business partner and treated him like family. I can't believe this."

Alex's eyes were hard and dark.

"This is proof that Leo embezzled hundreds of thousands of dollars from Il Capriccio over the course of five years. My father dissolved the business partnership when he found out. No wonder Leo moved away. But why did my father keep this a secret all these years? It doesn't make sense."

Rylie put her hand on Alex's arm. "I didn't know your father, but from what I know about him, he was a good man. Maybe he didn't want to destroy Leo's reputation. Maybe he thought that throwing Leo out of the business was enough of a punishment for his crime."

Alex shook his head. He pounded his fist down on his father's desk. Rylie jumped.

"I've had enough for today. Let's get out of here. I'll take this file box home and look at it more later after I've had a chance to calm down," Alex said.

"Okay. I'll bring your mother's recipe box, too."

Alex didn't talk on the drive home. Rylie left him to his thoughts while her mind raced. She thought about everything they had found and all the questions their finds had raised. Did Lorenzo have a young girlfriend? Where was she now? What was Todd Saunders' relationship with Lorenzo? Could he be a suspect in Lorenzo's murder investigation? Why did Derek and Stefanie Firth drop their lawsuit? Did Lorenzo pay them off? Where did Leo Bernardi go after Lorenzo dissolved their business partnership? Did he hate Lorenzo for throwing him out of the business? Enough to want him dead?

Chapter 25

When they got back home, Alex took the file box from his father's closet into the living room to continue going through the contents. Rylie went into the kitchen to make them some lunch. Bella and Amando followed her into the kitchen and laid down nearby in case any treats happened to come their way.

She made them sandwiches for lunch with some of the Soppressata Italian salami with zinfandel and red chilies that Alex had gotten at V. Sattui Winery's deli. She spread mayonnaise and champagne mustard on organic mixed seeds bread and then layered jack cheese, sliced Campari tomatoes, and green leaf lettuce on top of slices of Soppressata.

She brought Alex his sandwich and a Pellegrino mineral water and set them down on the coffee table. He looked up briefly from the papers in his hands.

"Thank you, *cara mia*."

"You're welcome."

She went back to the kitchen to give him some space and sat down at the kitchen dining table to eat. Bella and Amando laid down nearby. She lifted the top piece of bread from her sandwich and pulled out a small piece of jack cheese for each of them.

Bella and Amando were instantly by her side panting happily. She gave them each a small piece of jack cheese. They both swallowed their cheese so quickly she was sure they didn't even taste it.

She heard Alex talking to someone in the other room.

"Luisa? Hi! It's Alex Marchetti. How are you?"

Alex was silent for a minute as he listened to Luisa.

"Thank you, Luisa. My father's death came as such a shock. It has been very hard for me to deal with losing him."

Pause.

"So where are you living now?"

Pause.

"Oh, San Ramon? That's not far away. I was wondering if you would mind if I came to visit you and Leo sometime and brought my girlfriend, Rylie?"

Pause.

"Great! Rylie and I are both off work tomorrow. I know it's short notice, but would tomorrow work for you?"

Pause.

"Okay. How about 10:00 tomorrow morning? What's your address?"

Pause.

"Great. Thanks, Luisa. We'll see you tomorrow. Bye."

Alex came into the kitchen with an empty plate.

"That sandwich was delicious, honey. Thank you," he said. He rinsed off his plate in the sink and put it in the dishwasher.

"I just spoke with Luisa Bernardi, Leo Bernardi's wife. I asked her if she would mind if we came to visit her and Leo and their son Silvano tomorrow. They're living in San Ramon, so it's only about an hour and a half from here. I made arrangements for us to visit them at their house tomorrow morning at 10:00. I need to talk to Leo and find out more about what happened with the embezzlement and the dissolution of his partnership with my father. I hope you don't mind that I made plans without asking you first. I'm just so upset by this whole thing that I didn't think to talk to you first and ask you if you would like to go with me when I visit them. Do you want to come?" Alex asked.

"Of course," Rylie said. "I definitely want to learn more about what happened between Leo and your father. I came across some information a little while ago that made me think that there might have been some bad blood between your father and Leo, so I talked to Aaron Michelson about it. But he said that he thought that if Leo wanted to do something to hurt your father that he would have done it a long time ago."

"What information did you get that made you think that there may have been some bad feelings between Leo and my father?"

"I sat across from Viktor Bergman at Gott's Roadside when I went there for dinner after work one night. Viktor told me that he had just found out that he must have accidentally pressed the record button on the voice recorder app on his cell phone during the Chamber of Commerce awards dinner. He was sitting at the table with your father that night. He sent me the recording, and I sent it to Aaron. I think it was the same night that you asked me to move in with you. I'm sorry. I should have told you about it then, but it slipped my mind after you asked me to move in with you and we were racing around packing everything up that night," Rylie said. "I have the recording on my cell phone. Do you want to hear it?"

"Yes. Definitely."

Rylie played the recording for Alex.

"My wife and I wanted our son, Alessandro, to have more opportunities for colleges to attend and jobs after he graduated from college. My family in Italy had a bar. I grew up in that bar. I felt like running a bar was in my blood. So I started my own bar here in the U.S."

Garbled noises.

"Whatever happened to your business partner, Leo?"

"We had some disagreements."

Garbled noises.

"We dissolved our business partnership and he and his family moved away."

"I heard that Leo had a stroke after he left St. Helena."

"I don't know. I haven't spoken with him since he left."

"Leo had a stroke?" Alex said. "I can't believe I never heard about this. It's like Leo and his family disappeared off the face of the earth after they left."

"How old is Leo's son Silvano?" Rylie asked.

"He's about five years older than me so that would make him forty now."

"Were you close with him?"

"No. We never really hung out with each other except at Il Capriccio when our fathers were working. He had his own group of friends, and I had mine," Alex said.

"I feel like I need to get out of here and get some fresh air," Rylie said. "I'm going to take Bella and Amando to the dog park. Do you want to come?"

"No. I still have some more papers to go through about the embezzlement."

"Okay. We won't be gone long," Rylie said.

"Want to go bye-bye in the car and go to the dog park?" Rylie asked the dogs.

Bella and Amando jumped up and wagged their tails furiously as they ran to the front door. Rylie grabbed their leashes and packed some bottled water and portable dog water dishes in her backpack.

"See you later!"

She buckled the dogs into their seatbelts in the back of her SUV and headed to the dog park. It was a bit more challenging trying to handle two dogs at a time than it was to handle just one dog, but she finally managed to untangle the dogs and their leashes and get them through the gate to the dog park. She unclipped their leashes after she got inside. They both took off like they had been shot from a cannon.

Bella and Amando both ran straight for a large black dog with pointed ears. Rylie recognized Max, Detective Michelson's Belgian sheepdog. She looked for Aaron and saw him a little way away from Max and the two other dogs. He looked her way and waved at her. She headed over to him.

"Hi, Aaron. How are you?"

"I'm doing great. How about you?"

"Not so good. Alex and I went to his father's house this morning so he could start going through his father's things and decide what he wants to keep and what he wants to get rid of. I found a file box in Lorenzo's closet with information about why his business partnership with Leo Bernardi was dissolved. Apparently, Leo embezzled hundreds of thousands of dollars from Il Capriccio over the course of five years. Alex is furious. He didn't know anything about it. He called Luisa Bernardi when we got home and made arrangements for us to go visit her, her husband Leo, and their son Silvano tomorrow morning at their home in San Ramon. I'm kind of nervous about it. I've never seen Alex so angry before. I'm afraid things might get ugly," Rylie said.

"And I'm worried about how Leo Bernardi might feel about all this. He might have held a grudge against Lorenzo all these years for throwing him out of the business. What if he's a violent person? I'm afraid about how Leo might react when Alex asks him about the embezzlement," she continued.

"The Chief of Police at the San Ramon police department is a friend of mine," Aaron said. "I'll call Jeff this afternoon and tell him what's going on. I'll ask him to keep his cell phone close tomorrow in case he needs to send some officers to the Bernardi's house. I'll make sure to have my cell phone close, too. Text me if things start getting out of hand, and I'll have some police officers at the Bernardi's house in no time. What time are you supposed to meet them? Do you have their address?"

"We're supposed to meet them at 10:00 tomorrow morning. Hang on. I'll text Alex for their address."

She texted Alex and told him that she had run into Aaron Michelson at the dog park and that she had let Aaron know about their meeting with the Bernardi's. She told Alex that Aaron was going to have his friend, the Chief of Police in San Ramon, on standby in case things got ugly.

"Here's their address." Rylie held up her cell phone for Aaron to see. "Wait. I'll text it to you. It makes me feel much better knowing that you're going to be on standby while we're at the Bernardi's tomorrow."

"No problem, Rylie. I don't want you or Alex or anyone else to get hurt. I hope that things can be discussed amicably between Alex and Leo tomorrow."

"Me, too."

Max, Bella, and Amando were milling around sniffing things. Aaron held up a tennis ball.

"Ready to get the ball?" He threw it hard, and all three dogs tore after it.

Max got there first and snapped up the ball. Delighted with his prize, he pranced around in a celebratory dance for a minute before heading back to Aaron with the ball. Bella and Amando hopped up and down on either side of Max trying to get him to relinquish his prize as he made his way back.

Aaron threw the ball a few more times for the dogs before they started to get tired. When the dogs came back panting heavily with their tongues lolling out the sides of their mouths, he decided the dogs had had enough.

Rylie set out some water for all three dogs and they lapped thirstily. On impulse, she hugged Aaron.

"Thanks, Aaron. I'm so glad I ran into you today."

Aaron's face turned slightly pink. "I'll always look out for you, Rylie."

He looked intently at her for a minute and then turned his face away.

"Come on, Max. Let's go." Aaron started walking toward the gate with Max.

"Bye, Rylie. Bye Bella and Amando."

"Let's go home, Bella. Come, Amando." Rylie snapped leashes on both dogs and followed Aaron and Max to the gate.

Chapter 26

It was still dark outside when Rylie woke up the next morning. She rolled over to look at the alarm clock. 4:30 a.m. Her thoughts immediately went to their meeting with Leo Bernardi and his family later that morning. She snuggled up closer to Alex and tried to get back to sleep. The 6:00 alarm went off shortly after she had finally gotten back to sleep.

Alex stirred next to her in bed.

"Morning, sweetie," Rylie said.

"Morning."

"We have to get up and get going. We've got to be at the Bernardi's house by 10:00," Rylie said.

"Right."

Alex gave her a quick kiss and got out of bed. Rylie pried herself out of bed and headed to the kitchen to make coffee. Bella and Amando followed her to the kitchen.

"Want to go outside?" She let the dogs out.

She put coffee beans in the grinder in the top of the coffeemaker, filled the reservoir with filtered water, and turned it on. She went to take a shower while the coffee was brewing.

When she got back to the kitchen, Alex had already showered and dressed and was pouring their coffee. She went over to him and put her arms around his waist. She tilted her head up to him.

"I love you," she said simply.

"I love you, too, *cara mia*."

Alex wrapped her up in his arms and gave her a deep kiss that made her toes tingle.

She let Bella and Amando back inside and got them each their breakfast. The dogs made quick work of their food and then laid down on the kitchen floor.

"Alex and I are going on a little trip today, Bella, Amando. You guys are going to watch the house for us while we're gone. Okay?"

Bella thumped her tail up and down on the floor. Amando followed suit.

They decided to take Alex's Alfa Romeo to San Ramon. Rylie tried to keep her hands from clenching in her lap. She took some deep breaths to try to calm herself. Alex was mostly quiet during the drive. He got off the freeway in San Ramon and followed the GPS directions to the Bernardi's home.

"I think this is it," he said finally.

The Bernardi's house was an older home with cream-colored vertical wood siding and olive-green trim. They walked up to the door. Alex knocked.

An older woman with wavy, shoulder length, dark gray hair answered the door. Rylie recognized her from the photo in Alex's house.

"Alex! *Che piacere rivederti!*" the woman said. She looked at Rylie. "I am Luisa. And you must be Rylie. *Benvenuta*, Rylie. Come in! Come in!"

Luisa stepped back from the doorway to let them in.

"Please, come sit in the dining room. Would you like some coffee?" Luisa asked. She ushered them into the dining room.

A guy that looked a little older than Alex with dark hair and eyes came into the room.

"*Ciao*, Silvano," Alex said.

"*Ciao*, Alex," Silvano said.

An older gentleman walked slowly in. His right leg appeared to be a little stiff.

"*Ciao*, Alex," he said.

"*Ciao*, Leo," Alex said. "This is my girlfriend, Rylie."

Luisa bustled into the dining room with a tray of coffee cups filled with steaming coffee. She handed a cup of coffee to each of them and put cream and sugar on the table.

"Please, sit down. It's been so long since we've seen you, Alex," Luisa said.

Everyone sat down at the table. Despite Luisa's attempts at hospitality, Rylie sensed a brittle tension in the air.

"I had no idea where you went when you left three years ago," Alex said. "My father never told me what happened between you and him, Leo. When I asked him about it, he would always find a way to avoid talking about it."

"Your father... was a good man," Leo said haltingly. "I'm sorry... about... what happened to him."

Alex's jaw clenched. Rylie could feel his whole body tensing up next to hers. A shiver of apprehension sliced through her.

"Yes. He was a good man," Alex said. He took a long sip of his coffee, and then carefully placed the coffee cup on the table.

"Rylie and I started going through my father's things yesterday. Rylie found a file box in his closet with papers about the dissolution of your business partnership with him. You stole from my father, Leo. Hundreds of thousands of dollars over a five-year period. My father treated you like family. And this was how you repaid him?"

"Uhhh...." Leo stammered.

Silvano leaped up from his chair. "My father made a mistake! And your father made him pay dearly for his mistake. Your father knew that my father had high blood pressure and couldn't handle a lot of stress. When your father found out about my father's mistake, he threw him out of Il Capriccio - out of his livelihood. Your father said he never wanted to lay eyes on my father again. He said that if he ever saw my father or any of our family again, that he would press charges against my father and have him sent to jail."

Alex jumped up from his chair and sent it flying backwards. The chair banged loudly on the wood floor. Rylie jumped.

Alex was face to face with Silvano in a couple of strides.

"Your father should have gone to jail for what he did!" Alex yelled.

"Your f-f-father... Your father caused my father to have a stroke!"

Silvano backed up as he spoke until his back was up against the wall. "His right arm and leg were paralyzed. Even now he has to walk with an ankle support brace. He has trouble talking. He can't remember words."

"My father did not cause your father to have a stroke. Your father brought that on himself," Alex said through gritted teeth.

"Yes, he did! It's all his fault! And look at my poor mamma! She's just a shell of the person she used to be. She used to be happy. Now she's quiet all the time. She never smiles. She never leaves the house. We have no friends. This is what your father has done to my family," Silvano said.

Alex grabbed Silvano by the throat with one hand. "Did you kill my father?"

Silvano's face turned bright red. "Let go of me!"

"Not until you tell me if you're the animal who murdered my father," Alex growled. He tightened his grip on Silvano's throat.

"Okay, okay! I did have that waiter put poison mushrooms in your father's food. But I wasn't trying to kill him. I thought he'd go see a doctor when he got sick. I had no idea that he wouldn't go to the doctor. I wasn't trying to kill him. I just wanted him to suffer like he's made my family suffer."

"*Figlio di un cane!*" Alex screamed.

Rylie frantically texted Detective Michelson.

Get the police here quick. Silvano Bernardi just confessed to killing Lorenzo. It's getting ugly.

She got a text back a minute later.

The police are on their way. Open the front door. I'm right outside.

Rylie ran to the front door and opened it. Detective Michelson rushed inside.

"Where are they?" he asked.

"In here!"

Rylie ran into the dining room with Detective Michelson close behind.

"Alex!" Detective Michelson shouted.

Alex turned around. His face was twisted in rage.

"Let him go, Alex! The San Ramon police will be here any minute," Detective Michelson said.

"Not on your life, Detective. This slime will make a run for it if I let him go," Alex said. He let go of Silvano's throat and roughly twisted one of Silvano's arms behind his back. Silvano winced. "I'll just hang onto him until the police get here."

A couple of minutes later, two police officers ran into the room with the Chief of Police close behind.

"Detective Michelson! ! I didn't expect you to be here," the Chief said.

"I'm only here as a concerned citizen, Chief," Detective Michelson said. "Not in any official capacity."

"Is this Silvano Bernardi?" the Chief asked Alex.

"Yes, sir. He just confessed to murdering my father, Lorenzo Marchetti," Alex said tersely.

One of the police officers handcuffed Silvano and took him out to the police car parked out front.

"You're welcome to come down to the police station with us and sit in while we question Silvano, Detective," the Chief said.

"Thanks, Chief. I'll do that," Detective Michelson said.

Rylie let out the breath that she wasn't aware she'd been holding. Luisa and Leo stared after their son with their mouths slightly open.

Alex still looked enraged. She went over to stand beside him and touched his arm to get his attention. He looked down at her. The tension in his body relaxed slightly. He took her hand and grasped it tightly.

"We're going to need all of you to come down to the station and give your statements," the Chief said.

"Okay," Alex said. "I'll take everyone in my car."

Chapter 27

R ylie was glad when Thursday finally came around. With everything that had happened on Sunday with Silvano Bernardi confessing to the murder of Lorenzo Marchetti, she had had a hard time focusing on work. After Alex left for work, she sat at the dining table nursing her coffee. Bella and Amando had already gone outside to do their business, wolfed down their breakfasts, and were now sleeping on the floor nearby.

"I'm going to another new restaurant today with my friends, Bella and Amando."

Bella lifted her head part-way off the floor, looked at Rylie, and gave half a wag of her tail before going back to sleep. Amando partially opened his eyes, saw that Bella wasn't moving, and closed his eyes again.

"Guess you two aren't that excited about it. That's okay. I am. I'm going to go pick out something to wear."

She looked through her closet and decided on what she would wear for lunch at Brasswood Bar and Kitchen. Then she showered and got dressed in some jeans and a light sweater. It was too early to get ready for her lunch with Patricia Davenport's group. She called Sophie.

"Hi, Sophie. How are you? Sorry to bother you at work."

"That's okay. What's up?" Sophie said.

"You said that Lucien has Thursdays off now, right? I was thinking it might be fun for Alex, me, you, and Lucien to have dinner at Pizzeria Tra Vigne tonight. What do you think?" Rylie asked.

"Sounds good to me. I'll text Lucien and see what he says and text you right back."

"Okay."

Rylie texted Alex at work.

I just called Sophie to see if she and Lucien would like to join us for dinner at Pizzeria Tra Vigne tonight. I thought it would be fun for the four of us to go out. I've never been there, and I want to check it out. What do you think?

Alex texted her back.

Let's do it. Their made to order fresh mozzarella is amazing.

Sophie texted her back a couple minutes later.

Lucien's excited. We love to eat there. We'll meet you there at 6:00. Okay?

Okay. See you then.

Later that morning, Rylie got changed and drove to Brasswood Bar and Kitchen in St. Helena to meet her friends for lunch. The hostess seated them at a large booth with tufted, dark brown leather banquettes. The massive, vaulted ceiling had large skylights. On the other side of the restaurant, large bell-shaped polished brass light fixtures hung from the dark wood beams that ran overhead. The hostess got their drink orders and then hurried off.

"I read in the St. Helena Star this morning that Silvano Bernardi confessed to murdering Lorenzo Marchetti," Patricia said.

All the women looked at Rylie expectantly.

"Yes, that's true," Rylie said. "Alex and I went to see the Bernardi's at their home in San Ramon on Sunday. Silvano told us that he blamed Lorenzo for his father having a stroke. Leo was paralyzed on his right side after his stroke. He's not paralyzed anymore, but he has to use an ankle support brace when he walks. He has trouble remembering words, and when he talks, sometimes his words come out haltingly."

"I'd heard that Leo had a stroke after they moved away," Liza said. "That's a shame. They moved away so quickly, and we never heard from them again. Do you know what happened?"

"Apparently no one knew what happened except for Lorenzo and the Bernardi's. Not even Alex knew why they moved away. Now everything has come out in the open. Leo embezzled a lot of money from Il Capriccio during the last five years of their partnership. When Lorenzo found out, he dissolved the partnership and told Leo that he never wanted to see him or his family again. He said if he ever saw them again, that he would press charges against Leo, and Leo would go to jail."

"Oh my goodness!" Patricia exclaimed.

"No wonder they moved away so quickly," Kinsley said.

"So why did Silvano kill Lorenzo?" Carolyn asked.

"Silvano told us that he blamed Lorenzo for his father's stroke and all the medical issues his father has had since then," Rylie said. "He said Lorenzo knew that his father had high blood pressure and couldn't handle a lot of stress. He thinks that Lorenzo dissolving the partnership and making their family move away was too much stress for his father and caused him to have a stroke. He was also upset because his mother isn't the happy person that she used to be. He said she's quiet all the time now. Silvano said he wasn't trying to kill Lorenzo. He just wanted Lorenzo to suffer like he'd caused his family to suffer. Silvano said he thought that Lorenzo would go see a doctor when he got sick. It never occurred to him that Lorenzo wouldn't."

"Wow," Maggie said. "This is a small town. I can't believe that no one in town ever knew the details about why the Bernardi's moved away so quickly."

"How's Alex doing, Rylie?" Patricia said. "I'm sure this has been very hard on him."

"It has been very hard on him. But I think he's relieved to finally find out who killed his father and why. He just needs some time to process everything. And time to heal," Rylie said.

"I'm glad he has you to support him while he's going through all this," Patricia said. "He's very lucky to have you."

Rylie felt her face get warm. "Thanks, Patricia. I'm lucky to have him, too."

After lunch, Rylie took Bella and Amando to the dog park to get some fresh air and clear her head. The dogs had a great time sniffing everything and running around. She threw the ball for them several times. She got home a few minutes after Alex got home from work.

"*Ciao, bella,*" Alex said as he swept her up in a hug and kiss. "Did you have a nice lunch with your friends today?"

"Yes, it was great. I guess there was an article in the St. Helena Star this morning about Silvano confessing to the murder of your father. They wanted to know more about what happened, so I explained everything to them," Rylie said.

"Including about Leo embezzling from Il Capriccio?"

"Yes."

"It will probably be common knowledge by the end of the day then. Gossip spreads like wildfire in this town," Alex said. "I think my father kept it a secret out of respect for the friendship that he had with Leo all those years. But I think he should have pressed charges and made Leo pay for what he did."

"Leo might not have gone to jail, but he did suffer some consequences as a result of his actions," Rylie said. "He had a stroke which still affects him to this day, he lost his business, he lost his home, and he lost his friendship with your father."

"True," Alex said. "And according to the paperwork I read, Leo wasn't paid back for his original investment in Il Capriccio when the business partnership was dissolved. The amount of money that Leo embezzled was more than his original investment, but at least my father had something to help offset all the money that Leo stole."

Rylie put her arms around Alex's neck. "I'm glad everything is out in the open now so you can get some closure."

Alex wrapped his arms around her waist and stared thoughtfully into space.

"I'm glad I finally know what happened to my father. But I'd give anything to be able to undo it all. I feel so lucky to have finally found the woman of my dreams. But it makes me sad that my father will never get to meet you. He won't be here to see me get married. He'll never get to meet my children or see them grow up."

"I'm so sorry, Alex. It makes me sad, too. But I'm sure all of your family in Italy will be there for you," Rylie said.

Alex gave her a half smile. He bent down and kissed her lightly.

"Want to go for a walk with the dogs? I haven't ever really explored all the land around the house. We have some time before we have to get ready to go out for pizza with Sophie and Lucien," Rylie said.

"Sure."

Rylie's cell phone rang. She looked at the caller ID.

"Oh, it's Dr. Corbyn. I have to take this. I'll be right back."

Rylie went in the other room to speak to Dr. Corbyn for a few minutes, then went back to where Alex stood waiting for her. She grinned broadly.

"I have some good news," she said.

Chapter 28

Rylie and Alex spotted Sophie and Lucien sitting at a table when they walked inside Pizzeria Tra Vigne. They went over to their table.

"Hi Sophie. Hi Lucien," Rylie said. She and Alex sat down at the table.

"I love the food here," Alex said. "Especially their fresh mozzarella on grilled crostini. Mozzarella al Minuto."

"We love that, too," Sophie said. "Rylie, you have to try it."

"It sounds really good. But I don't want to fill up on appetizers. Can I have a bite of yours?" Rylie asked Alex.

"Sure."

"Their arancini is really good, too," Lucien said.

"What's that?" Rylie asked.

"Breaded risotto balls filled with mozzarella and then fried," Lucien replied.

"I'll have to try them sometime. But I came here to check out their pizza, so I think I'll just stick with that this time," Rylie said.

A waitress came and took their drink orders.

"I'll give you guys a minute to look at the menus. I'll be right back," she said. She hurried off.

"How does it feel to have Thursdays off now, Lucien?" Rylie asked.

"I feel a little at loose ends. I'm not used to having so much time on my hands," Lucien said.

"But you've been catching up on a lot of things that you needed to get done," Sophie said.

"That's true," Lucien said. "And I've always been interested in learning more about winemaking, but I've never had time to do anything about it until now. So once I get through my To Do list, I'm going to figure out how to pursue that interest."

"I'm interested in that, too," Alex said. "Maybe we can learn together. Take a course somewhere or something."

"That'd be great," Lucien said. "Maybe we could both do some searching online and ask around to see what we can find out."

"I can do that. I'll let you know what I find out," Alex said.

The waitress came and delivered their drinks and took their food orders.

"So Alex and I have some good news." Rylie beamed at Sophie and Lucien.

"I could tell something was up," Sophie said. "Spill."

"Dr. Corbyn offered me a permanent part-time associate veterinarian position at Valley View Veterinary Hospital. He's said he's getting older, and he wants to slow down a little. I'll keep working there Monday through Wednesday each week. So I won't be going back to Brentwood at the end of November. Alex wants me to move in with him permanently."

"Oh, Rylie, that's great!" Sophie smiled warmly.

"Yeah, that's fantastic, Rylie. Congratulations, you two," Lucien said. "I think you make a great couple."

"Thanks," Rylie said. She smiled at Alex and took his hand.

"Yes, thanks," Alex said. "I'm thrilled that Rylie doesn't have to leave at the end of November. Now we can work on making a life together." He leaned over and kissed Rylie lightly.

"I'm so happy, Rylie," Sophie said. "I've missed you when you've been living so far away. Talking on the phone and texting just isn't the same as being able to hang out with each other and do things together. Now that Lucien's name has been cleared and you're done with being an amateur sleuth, everything can finally get back to normal. Right?"

***

If you enjoyed this book and would like to support me in my author journey as I write and publish more books in this series and others, please take a few minutes to post a nice review on Amazon (and Goodreads and BookBub, if you're on those sites). Just a couple of sentences saying what you liked about the story will do.

If you don't have time to post a review, if you could please take a minute to post a nice star rating on my book's page on Amazon (and Goodreads and BookBub, if you're on those sites) that would also be very helpful to me and would be greatly appreciated.

People read reviews and look at a book's ratings when they're deciding whether to read a book. Wonderful reviews and lots of four and five-star ratings (and a high average rating) encourage readers to take a chance on a new author and are vital to an author's success. Thanks for your support and for taking the time to do this. It means a lot to me.

For information about my books, photos from my adventures, news for book lovers, and the opportunity to participate in fun contests and giveaways, please sign up to receive my Cozy Chat monthly e-newsletter using the link at the top of my website (rachelebaker.com).

If you'd like to receive alerts when I have new releases, please Follow me on Amazon. You can also connect with me on Facebook, Instagram, X, Goodreads, and BookBub.

About the Author

Rachele Baker is a veterinarian and mystery author. She lives in northern California close to Lake Tahoe and the Napa Valley wine country where the Rylie Sunderland Mysteries take place. She drew on her many years of experience as a practicing veterinarian to develop the main character for this series, Rylie, who is also a veterinarian. Rachele's golden retriever Savanna was the inspiration for Rylie's golden retriever Bella.

In her free time, Rachele enjoys exploring northern California wine country, Lake Tahoe, and areas along the California coast like Mendocino, Monterey, and Big Sur. Some of her favorite things include freshly brewed coffee in the morning, walks in nature, and, of course, golden retrievers.

Made in United States
North Haven, CT
13 January 2025

64367060R00188